HIGH PRAISE FOR NA[...]

"Stephen King's influence i[...] er...an impressive panoramic sweep that shows the horrors manifesting subtly and insidiously through the experiences of a large cast of characters."

—*Publishers Weekly*

"Crisp prose and straightforward storytelling make *Bloodstone* a must-read!"

—Brian Keene, Bram Stoker award–winning author of *Dark Hollow*

"A dark, disturbing, white-knuckler of a page-turner!"

—Douglas Clegg, Bram Stoker and Horror Guild award–winning author of *The Priest of Blood*

"[*Bloodstone*] delivers...there are chills and suspense and gripping action with characters you come to know and care about. A fully satisfying read that will hook you from page one."

—Rick Hautala, bestselling author of *The White Room*

"*Bloodstone* is a stunning debut. The writing is smooth and refined, the imagery striking and vivid, and Kenyon proves adept at involving the reader and dragging him or her along for a very dark, very disturbing ride."

—Tim Lebbon, Bram Stoker and British Fantasy award–winning author of *Face*

"Reminiscent of *Salem's Lot*, *Bloodstone* is a terrifying horror novel that is action oriented yet doesn't neglect the development of the characters that come across as believable to the audience....This is the kind of horror novel that will make readers want to sleep with all the lights...shining brightly."

—*Midwest Book Review*

"Tense and entertaining, this is one of the strongest debut novels to come along in years. Highly recommended."

—*Cemetery Dance*

MORE PRAISE FOR *BLOODSTONE*!

"*Bloodstone* by Nate Kenyon gives the state of Maine another reason to fear the dark. Atmospheric, creepy and fun, *Bloodstone* delivers the spooky goods!"

—Jonathan Maberry, award–winning
author of *Ghost Road Blues*

"Kenyon's debut evokes an atmosphere of small-town claustrophobia…[a] tale of classic horror."

—*Library Journal*

"An enviable first novel….Vivid references to guilt, penance, and redemption, duty, and familial obligations, all grant the narrative an additional moral layer of meaning….Just perfect for those who prefer their horror cerebral rather than graphic."

—*Chizine*

"[The] writing style is so clean, his confidence in his story so strong, and his overall narrative arc so compelling….Your time will most definitely not be wasted with [his] excellent debut!"

—Gary A. Braunbeck, Bram Stoker
Award–winning author of *Mr. Hands*

"While it certainly reads as a horror novel, complete with a satisfyingly unexpected plot twist, *Bloodstone* is ultimately a story of love and redemption, giving the reader more to chew on than the average exercise in fright."

—*Fangoria*

"The characters are strange in this dark and disturbing book, and the voices guiding them are even stranger, but it fits together into a horrific tale…"

—*RT BOOKreviews*

"*Bloodstone* is a very impressive first novel. [It] is a very well written, detailed story that will really keep you thinking all the way to the end. It's a book for horror fans who like to get really deep in the history of characters and the mystery that surrounds them."

—The Horror Review

PLAYING WITH FIRE

"Sarah, can I ask you something? Why do you think they give you the pills and the shots?"

"It's a game, see, a big mean game, they're trying to get something from me and I won't let them have it. And they don't really want it anyway because they're scared."

"Do you know what this thing is?"

"I can't tell you. It's a secret."

"Hmmm. I like secrets. Maybe you'll share yours with me sometime."

"You wouldn't like this secret. And anyway, maybe you're on their side and it's all a big trick."

"No, Sarah, I would never do that. I would never make you do something you don't want to do, or put you someplace you don't want to be. We're friends, remember?"

But Sarah wasn't listening. "They want to get rid of me. They're trying to kill me." She walked to the table and picked up her bear, clutching it to her chest. Then she went back to the window.

"I'm going to break out of here soon," she said, looking into the sunshine. She was trembling. "Then they all better watch out. Oh, boy, they better…"

Other *Leisure* books by Nate Kenyon:

BLOODSTONE

THE REACH

NATE KENYON

LEISURE BOOKS NEW YORK CITY

For my parents, Pamela and David Kenyon.

A LEISURE BOOK®

December 2008

Published by

Dorchester Publishing Co., Inc.
200 Madison Avenue
New York, NY 10016

If you purchased this book without a cover you should be aware that this book is stolen property. It was reported as "unsold and destroyed" to the publisher and neither the author nor the publisher has received any payment for this "stripped book."

Copyright © 2008 by Nathaniel Kenyon

All rights reserved. No part of this book may be reproduced or transmitted in any form or by any electronic or mechanical means, including photocopying, recording or by any information storage and retrieval system, without the written permission of the publisher, except where permitted by law.

ISBN 10: 0-8439-6021-3
ISBN 13: 978-0-8439-6021-1

The name "Leisure Books" and the stylized "L" with design are trademarks of Dorchester Publishing Co., Inc.

Printed in the United States of America.

10 9 8 7 6 5 4 3 2 1

Visit us on the web at www.dorchesterpub.com.

ACKNOWLEDGMENTS

As with everything I do, this one couldn't have happened without the support of my family. I love them more than I can say, and I'm very glad they continue to put up with me. Thanks to my late grandfather Morris "Papa" Brown, who showed me what flying is all about, and answered my questions about small-engine planes and flying clubs. To Don D'Auria and the crew at Dorchester Books, many thanks for all your hard work on this book and your faith in me.

Finally, thanks to the "real" Cristina Voorsanger, who won an earlier contest and received the dubious distinction of appearing in this book. For the record, she is nothing like the character in *The Reach*, but she let me borrow her name anyway, and then waited patiently for longer than I would have to see her name in print. Here's to you, Cristina.

THE REACH

PROLOGUE

Ten years ago

Beyond the frosted panes of double glass, the wind screamed its displeasure. Day had slipped into night with the coming storm. The WKOB weatherman was predicting three feet of snow today, another six inches tomorrow; the worst storm to hit in thirty years, he said. *Do not leave your homes unless it's absolutely necessary.*

The young doctor was listening intently to the radio at the second-floor station when her pager beeped. She checked the code, slipped quickly across the wine-red carpet to the nearest window, and peered out on a desolate winter scene. The little hospital parking lot wore a sheet of inch-thick ice pinned by mountains of plowed snow. It was mostly empty, the hospital all but shut down in preparation for the storm. Only three patients today, and two of them had come in on the same call, a couple of skiers who got disoriented in the woods and had frostbite. One of them, a pretty young thing, lost the little toe on her left foot. The doctor found it necessary to amputate.

Blood. The doctor saw it again as she closed her eyes, bright red blood coating her gloved hands.

The radio buzzed now and then as the wind made the

signal come and go. She opened her eyes. The parking lot lights barely cut through the snow as it started to fall faster. Nothing that looked like an emergency; but she could hardly see anything at all. She shivered as the scene below her faded into a writhing white blanket of dim and mysterious shapes.

Down at the front entrance the admitting desk was empty. Above the little waiting area with its row of plastic-molded chairs, a nineteen-inch television set flickered from a bracket on the wall. The rug here felt damp and the color had faded in a trail from the waiting area to the front desk. It smelled like cleaning solution.

The doctor spotted movement through the sliding glass doors. Two emergency techs were unloading a woman from her car. One of them slipped to his knees and cursed, a black man in a green hospital coat and slacks, bare hands and head, tight, coal-black hair frosted with snow. James or something. No, Jack, that was it. *Likely to lose his earlobes to the cold if he isn't careful, and maybe the tips of his fingers too.* It could happen in five minutes in this weather. The other one had a scarf wrapped around his neck and wore knitted pink mittens that had been sitting in the lost and found, and he looked warmer, but not much. A country boy, thick and heavy like he might play linebacker on the local college football team. Stewart was his name, or Stan. Young kid. She had only been working there a week and couldn't remember everybody yet.

The sliding glass doors opened and they wheeled the woman inside on a stretcher. A gust of wind hit the doctor like a gut punch. For a moment the lobby was transformed into a blizzard; the doors closed and the snow settled in the silence like one of those Christmas globes that had been shaken and then put to rest.

She stepped forward to break the spell. The woman was sitting up on the stretcher, wrapped in a white horsehair blanket and curiously calm. She appeared to be suffering from shock. It took the doctor only a moment to discover that her new patient was naked under the blanket, and in labor.

The woman's heart beat slow and steady in spite of the pain she must be in. How was it possible? *The contractions are coming almost on top of each other.* She would deliver soon. And yet her breathing hardly changed.

The empty car sat sideways just outside the entrance, lights shining away from them, motor still running. The doctor leaned forward, close to the pregnant woman's face. "What's your name?" she asked. The woman smiled vacantly. "Your *name,*" the doctor said again, sharply this time. No response. She pinched the fleshy part of the woman's upper arm, watched it flush pink. Her skin was creamy and perfectly smooth, almost poreless. She had the look of a backwoods girl, but there was something more to her, some special kind of glow or aura.

Pregnant women can be like that, the doctor thought. She'd witnessed it before, but this sort of glow seemed unnatural under the harsh glare of the hospital lights. She stared at the woman's naked legs beneath the blanket, felt herself enter a slow dream free fall, and shook her head to clear it. Something seemed to be buzzing far away, like a fluorescent bulb about to blink into life.

"Creeps me out," the black tech said. "She was doing that in the car when we went to get her. Just sitting there smiling like that."

"Is there anyone with her?"

"Car's empty," he said. "Lights are on but nobody's home, know what I mean? How in Sam Hell she drove here all by herself—"

"Get the delivery room ready," the young doctor said. Her hands felt clammy and she wiped them across her white coat, then raked her fingers through her hair. She looked at the pregnant woman again. What was wrong with her? Drugs? The situation was maddening. She had come to this little town to get away from the pressure of the big city hospitals and their twenty-hour shifts, and now here she was in the middle of something her very first week. Should have gone into psychiatry like the rest of her friends back at UDA.

They were wheeling the woman toward the delivery room when the power went out.

First there was a great cracking sound, like a tree limb snapping under tremendous pressure. Then a back-surge of air, as if something huge and warm had taken a deep breath.

And then they were plunged into darkness.

"Don't move," the doctor said. Dim red lights blinked on down the hall. She waited a moment for the main generators to kick in and give them something more, but nothing happened. It was no good; without lights the delivery room was useless.

They stood bathed in red.

The wind howled. The doctor put her hand on the woman's belly and found the swelling had moved lower and turned. This baby was coming now.

They set her up right there, lying on her back on the stretcher with her legs spread under the blanket. The two techs held flashlights, one on either side; a nurse appeared with boiling water from the gas stove in the staff kitchen, and towels, along with a few instruments on a stainless steel tray from the delivery room. The doctor crouched between the woman's legs, going through a checklist in her head. She could see something now, wet and bloody at the woman's opening, bright and strange in the flashlight beams.

Sweat stung her eyes. She blinked it away, glanced up and over the blanket.

Something was wrong. "Push," the doctor said, getting a grip on the baby's slippery head. "We've got to get it out *now*. Do you understand me?" The woman did not respond, but the doctor felt her muscles working. How could she be so calm? She hadn't even been given a painkiller; it was too dangerous without knowing what else she was on.

The doctor raised her hands. Blood, dripping from her fingers, her palms. She hadn't put on any gloves.

Blood.

She felt the room spinning. The hairs rose on the back of her neck. That great dark something around them took another sweeping breath.

They were engulfed in a huge, smothering silence. The lights blinked on, stuttered, and went off again. She found herself staring at the woman's face over the blanket as shadows danced in the beam of the flashlight. So beautiful, the doctor wondered through the buzzing that filled her head. She had to be the most beautiful woman in the world. She felt herself falling again, that sweet dizzy rush, and this time she let it pull her down to her knees.

A rattling sound filled the room like the beating of a hundred tiny drums.

"Oh, Jesus Lord," one of the techs said in a hoarse whisper. "Look at that. Would you the Christ *look* at it?"

The doctor glanced over through the fog that had begun to claim her, and saw the glittering steel instruments marching across the tray like tiny soldiers across a silver field. A hollow, deep-throated booming began. The floor shook under her. A great light poured out from somewhere now, and the young doctor squeezed her eyes tightly shut, her head seeming to split wide open. She heard a howling noise like a creature coming at her down a long tunnel, and then she opened her eyes and looked down at what she held in her hands.

Somebody screamed.

It took the doctor several seconds to realize it was her own voice she heard.

All things are preceded by the mind, led by the mind, created by the mind.

From the *Dhammapada* (Quotations from the Buddha)

"I could stop all these cars. I could make them all wreck just by raising my hand."

Excerpt from a July 6, 2003, interview with a twelve-year-old psychiatric patient, recorded by Dr. Susan Watts, M.D., Ph.D.

STAGE ONE

—1—

Present day

The Thomas Ward School of Psychology is located on Boston's Beacon Street, within a connected row of converted private homes that seem to ask nothing more than to blend in and keep out of sight. It is a small school, modestly funded, but well known within certain circles as one of the best of its kind in the country.

Jess Chambers climbed the front steps to the porch and paused by the door to the administrative offices, looking absently at the small bronze sign and readying herself for whatever waited for her within. She had been here many times before, but this time was different and she knew it. Professor Shelley's voice on the phone had contained a conspiratorial edge, something she had never heard before. Shelley was not the sort to fraternize with students outside of class. The call had piqued Jess's curiosity, as it had obviously been meant to do.

She checked the fall of her black cotton slacks and adjusted the collar of her blouse before stepping through the heavy wooden doors and into the reception area, a small, cramped room guarding the administrative and faculty offices.

The room smelled of stale coffee. Several Styrofoam cups sat discarded on the horseshoe countertop facing the door, and Jess resisted the nearly compulsive urge to straighten them up. Computer printouts were tacked to the walls, listing current events relating to the field and lecture times, along with an upcoming conference poster. A table to her left contained stacks of papers and magazines in an organized clutter, below a window that looked out onto the street and the T-tracks, where the trains rattled and shook on their way into the city. A bit of gray light filtered inside, but did not do much for the decor.

Though she could hear muffled voices somewhere, the outer rooms were empty. In Professor Shelley's office she sat down in the slick vinyl chair facing the desk and crossed her hands in her lap.

The room was filled with odds and ends, files and folders, curling news photographs of various unsmiling people tacked to the walls. A few of them she recognized as researchers or faculty members; most she did not.

Though Shelley was known for throwing an occasional pop quiz, she was well respected among her students. It was the mystery that surrounded her which gave them pause; some claimed to have seen her sitting in the butterfly position for hours, her eyes closed. A few had even insisted they'd seen her levitating. These stories were told in the thirdhand way of urban legend, often around a bar table, and Jess did not believe them for a second.

But Shelley's private life remained a mystery. What was it about psychiatrists and psychologists anyway? Complex minds unraveling each other. And yet such a need for secrecy. Jess found herself staring in mild amusement at a chart that supposedly revealed the details of the human aura. One thing was certain, no one had ever accused Shelley of being dull.

The professor was at the door; Jess hadn't heard her come in. "There you are," Shelley said. "Hope I didn't pull you away from something important?"

"I've caught up on my reading."

"You always did seem to be ahead of the game. Maybe I should give a bit more, just to keep you busy."

Jess risked a smile. Students complained that Shelley gave more reading than the rest of their classes combined. Slightly more to it than good-natured grumbling, she thought, to be fair. She took Shelley's classes for the challenge, and she welcomed it, but there were others who did not feel they should be spending every spare moment in the library.

Shelley moved rather carefully now around a mountain of old exam papers to her desk, a tall woman in her early forties who bore a striking resemblance to the actress Diane Keaton. She wore a chocolate long-sleeve mock-ribbed cardigan that looked expensive. Her hair was cut in a fashionable, shoulder-length style, and she was blessed with aristocratic bone structure and very long fingers. Slight calluses on the tips, Jess noticed. A piano player, perhaps, or strings.

Normally she carried herself with elegance and style, but she seemed worn down today, too pale, and the circles under her eyes were darker than usual. Something was clearly going on with the professor, though what exactly that might be, Jess could not guess.

"Let's see how much of that reading made an impression, then," Shelley said, sitting down in her chair. "You're familiar with Jacob's reconstructive study on depression?"

Jess recited from memory. "A five-step model, beginning with a long-standing history of early childhood problems, which leads to an acceleration of problems in adolescence, an isolation from peer groups, and a dissolution of social relationships, which finally ends in a justification of the suicidal act or attempt."

"And earlier than that?"

"Extreme separation anxiety or isolation in early childhood, regressive behavior. Complaints of stomach pains."

Shelley nodded, her graceful fingers steepled before her nose. "But I'm referring to instances of total withdrawal.

Come on now. No more book definitions. Give me your thoughts."

Jess felt slightly off balance and didn't like it. *Come on, girl, get a grip*, as her friend Charlie would say. "Let's see. The child is dependent on a caregiver to an unusual degree. Any unfamiliar event or surrounding sends her into a fugue state, caused mainly by the child's inability to accurately express what is wrong. Undue stress would come from *feeling* depressed, without actually understanding the concept. In the most severe cases, lack of response can be a sign of a serious mental disease—brain damage, autism, even schizophrenia."

"Interesting." Shelley was not one given to praise easily. Jess could not tell if she was satisfied or not. The professor shuffled some papers on her desk. "Now you're wondering why you're here."

The thought had crossed her mind. She had taken a class with Shelley once before and received an A, one of two that had been given that semester, she'd heard. Now she had her for neurobiological disorders, which she was finding very interesting. Male teachers had approached her in a less professional manner before; she was well aware of the effect she had on men. But Shelley was a woman. And this was certainly not a private tutoring session.

"I took the liberty of examining your records," Shelley said. "You're interested in child psychology, severe developmental disorders in particular. Any reason?"

"My younger brother was autistic."

"I see. So there's a personal element in your interest. But it has to stay out of your professional conduct. I say this because what I'm going to talk to you about requires it."

"Professor, with all due respect, if I didn't think I was capable of remaining professional, under any circumstance, I wouldn't be enrolled here."

It came out a little more forcefully than she'd intended. But Shelley simply nodded and smiled. "You've done well in my courses. Don't think I haven't noticed. That's one of the reasons you're here today. And the reports from your internship at the DSU clinic are stellar. You haven't chosen a topic for your dissertation?"

"Not yet."

"There's a girl whose case I've been keeping an eye on for a long time," Shelley said. "Right now she's in the Wasserman facility downtown. She's severely medicated, completely withdrawn for the past several weeks, though she has shown the ability to communicate. The director of the clinic has asked for my help in the past, and we've had some success. We haven't been able to reach her this time."

"Is there a diagnosis?"

"Dr. Wasserman believes she has a schizophreniform disorder."

Jess felt the familiar early buzz of excitement that came with an opportunity. "How old is she?"

"Ten."

"Awfully young for that sort of illness to manifest, isn't it?"

"It is. Here's the nuts and bolts of it, Jess. I'm not sure the diagnosis fits, but Dr. Wasserman disagrees. We do agree, however, that she may be more responsive to someone younger, less polished, if you forgive the description. To be honest, we could have given this to a counselor on staff, but I wanted to give the experience to one of my own."

"I'm glad to have it."

"Good. You have a rare mix of intellect and empathy. I think you might appeal to her. I want you to test her—Stanford-Binet, Weschler, Peabody, Rorschach. Let's hear any hypotheses you might have, suggestions for treatment. Then, if I like what you've done and Sarah shows progress, I'll allow you to present the case to the board of trustees."

"It would be an honor, Professor."

"You'll do just fine, I'm counting on it. But I want you to understand something. This is not some case study from a textbook. It is not a hypothetical situation. This is a very disturbed child we're talking about. She can be unpredictable, even violent. She's had an unusual history from the moment she was born. I know because I delivered her. I've been keeping tabs on her ever since."

Jess tried to picture a younger Professor Shelley in hospital scrubs. She had heard that the professor had been a practicing physician, but had thought it nothing more than a rumor. Shelley was a very good teacher. It seemed to Jess that she had been born to it.

"This girl is . . . unusual. She's been in foster care and institutions since she was little more than a year old. I don't know if she's seen the outside world more than a handful of times in her life. Don't misunderstand me. Most of the time she is simply catatonic, and that may be all she'll be for you. But I want you to be on your guard."

Shelley rose, signaling an end to their chat. A thread on her cardigan dangled down and trailed through the papers on her desk, at odds with the rest of her. She didn't seem to notice.

—2—

The Wasserman Children's Psychiatric Facility is located in the Boston neighborhood of Mattapan, in a section of town that has not enjoyed the improvements new money can bring. It sits on the edge of a 250-acre parcel of land that formerly housed the Boston State Hospital for the mentally ill, until that campus was shut down in 1979.

The location is an odd mix of desolate, abandoned wildlands in the middle of urban sprawl. In this particular neighborhood and its cousins, Roxbury and Dorchester, it is not unusual to hear gunshots on a sunny Wednesday afternoon. Still, the facility is as pleasant as it can be considering the circumstances, a large brick building resembling an elementary school, set well back from the road and against a backdrop of wild grasses and shrubbery, with a wide lawn and a playground in the rear. The only details that set it apart from other buildings of its type are the wire mesh and bars on the windows, and the chain-link fence and guardhouse, where the man or woman on duty has a police baton and pepper spray within easy reach. There are many disturbed young patients here, some in their late teens, not all of them easily controlled.

Dr. Wasserman stood when Jess Chambers entered his office, and extended his hand. He was a bit younger than she had expected, mid to late forties, balding in front and mildly

effeminate, wearing a forest-green turtleneck and cor-
duroys, and delicate glasses with thin wire frames balanced
upon a hawkish nose. His grip was moist and limp, and he
had a slight eye tic that made it seem as if he were trying to
wink at her.

"So glad you could come. Jean has told me all about you.
You're quite a student, isn't that so? *Lovely* to know of the
talented young people joining the profession."

"Thank you."

"Please, sit."

Dr. Wasserman's office was in marked contrast to Professor Shelley's organized clutter. Everything was neatly in its
place here, from the framed diplomas and awards on the
walls, to the neatly labeled file cabinets. A polished-wood
coatrack stood in the corner. The huge oak desk was bare
except for an intercom, pen and pencil, notepad, file folder,
a lamp, and a notebook computer. Too neat; to Jess, it
hinted at a compulsive personality.

Wasserman sat down behind the desk and leaned forward
on folded hands, as if imparting a secret. "Jean has told me
the course and fieldwork you've completed so far, and has
assured me you are competent. So I'll skip by that and assume that you'll handle Sarah extremely gently."

"Of course."

"Now, there are some things you should know before we
proceed further. One, Sarah has no relatives and no visitors.
She rarely leaves the grounds. If you'd like to take her anywhere during your visits, and I mean *anywhere*, even inside
this building, you must contact me first. Agreed?"

"Fine."

"Secondly, she is on a strict schedule of medication. This
schedule must be kept *to the minute*. We'll try to plan your
visits at alternate times, but that will not always be possible."

"What is she on?"

"Hmmm." Wasserman pushed at his glasses with a finger, opened the file folder on his desk. He punctuated each

word by tapping on the file. "*Let. Us. See.* Neuroleptics, mostly. And sedatives. Sarah is extremely sensitive and can be devilishly clever. We had a new orderly here once who felt such a number of pills weren't necessary. Sarah managed to get out of her room. It took us hours to find her. She'd holed up in a ventilation shaft. Lucky she didn't make it out to the street."

Lucky for who, Jess could not help thinking. "I understood from Professor Shelley that you would tell me a little about Sarah's psychiatric background. It would help to know the case history. Perhaps if I could look at your file—"

"We'd prefer you to open your own file. Start fresh, so to speak. We're really looking for a new perspective from someone who has no preconceived notions of the case. I can tell you all you need to know for the moment. Feel free to ask me what you like." Wasserman stood up abruptly and took a white lab coat from the rack near the window. "Shall we take a quick tour?"

The Wasserman Facility was indeed a converted school building. "We're a modest enterprise, privately endowed, but we do receive the occasional grant for research purposes. We have three psychiatrists on call, not including myself of course, four full-time counselors, and a number of support staff. Classrooms and evening quarters on the second floor, private rooms and conference areas on the third. This first floor is mostly staff offices, along with a small exercise facility and playroom. And then there's the basement, where the more difficult patients are given quiet time."

It was like most facilities Jess had seen. White tile floors, prints of colorful paintings hung on cream-colored walls, along with the occasional cluttered bulletin board and posters of children's television characters. They passed a small room that contained the sad remains of someone's birthday party: sagging balloons tied to the door handle, trash bags spilling over with paper plates and napkins. The corridors were cool, clean if a little tired. Everything had the look of having been scrubbed too many times.

Jess was reminded of her mother's struggle to keep her brother out of places just like this. Her youngest memories of Michael were filled with a sense of nostalgia mixed with regret. The Chamberses did not have enough money for proper treatment, and after her parents' divorce an even larger burden was assumed by Jess's mother. Eventually they had moved from the little saltbox in Edgecomb to a trailer park on Indian Road in White Falls. During their years living there Jess was constantly confronted with reminders of a life that could be hard and cruel. Drunks, wife beaters, and abused animals were her constant neighbors.

They walked back down the hall, their footsteps echoing through the empty corridor. An open doorway revealed a black man in blue janitor's overalls pushing a mop across a bare floor; he smiled as he glanced at them and then away, his mop moving with more purpose.

"That's Jeffrey," Wasserman said, after they'd passed. "He's sort of a jack-of-all-trades around here, I've had him for years. He cleans up the place, acts as a general handyman, even helps with the patients. They love him."

The raised voices of children grew louder as they turned a corner and passed by the empty cafeteria. "Forgive me," she said, "but you seem young to be running a place like this."

"My grandfather started a clinic many years ago in Westwood, and moved to this location when I was just a boy. He was a great man. I'm simply following in his footsteps." Wasserman stopped in front of a set of wide double doors. "This is one of my favorite places."

Inside the carpeted room were different kinds of play sets, tunnels and rings, blocks, tables, and chalkboards. Eight or nine children crawled and tumbled over themselves and played with several white-shirted adults, and for a moment Jess was fooled into thinking she was in a playroom like any other, before the details bled through. Wire mesh over the windows. A child of perhaps six in the corner rocking slowly back and forth in repeated, rhythmic motion, another muttering to himself and patting his head roughly with his palm. A third rubbing her chapped hands together again and again over a plastic toy sink.

She had done group casework before, assisted in community outreach programs, visited hospitals and sat in on counseling sessions. But this would be different.

Face it, head-on. This is what you want, what you need.

Her brother's death had given Jess a deep resolve to make the health care environment easier and more accessible for mental health patients, especially children. It had been a long road, but now here she was and it was time to put up or shut up.

"We try to keep the numbers down," Wasserman was saying. "They're easily distracted."

"Is she here?"

"Sarah? Oh no. These children are minimally supervised and generally nonviolent. We've had to keep her separated for some time now."

A young man spotted them from across the room. He moved in a sidestep, shuffling motion, skirting the younger children and coming to their side like a nervous bird looking to be fed. "Twenty-three. Twenty-three steps."

"Hello, Dennis." Wasserman smiled. "Dennis helps out with the younger children."

"Do I go to bed early tonight?" Dennis said. He had a plump, boyish face; he was dressed like a boy of six or seven, red baseball cap, blue striped pullover shirt and blue shorts, Velcro shoes with long, white socks pulled up almost to his knees. The stubble on his cheeks stood out in awkward contrast to the rest of him. "Is it Thuuuurrrs-day? Thursdays are early nights. Friday I go outside. Not Wednesday."

"This is Miss Chambers, Dennis. She'll be visiting us for a while. You might see her, and if you do I don't want you to be afraid. She's our friend."

"Do you love me? Then say it. Sa-aaay it."

"I love you, Dennis."

"I make her spirit glow." Dennis smiled brightly and shuffled away, muttering to himself and pulling at the brim of his cap.

"One of our roles here is to place various psychopathologies in a developmental context. Most of Dennis's mannerisms would not seem all that out of place in a four-year-old. However, in a boy of almost eighteen, they are extreme. At the core is our belief that most adolescent pathologies stem from normal childhood development."

"Sigmund Freud."

"He pioneered the concept, yes."

"But you don't adhere to his theory of psychosexual development."

"Not as a general rule. Piaget's cognitive theory is more appropriate."

They watched the group of children for a moment. "There are things to learn about each of them," Wasserman said. "For example, Dennis doesn't like to be touched. Most of the time he's harmless and quiet, but if you touch him he'll become extremely agitated. That is a simple rule. For Sarah, you'll have to learn more."

"And what about biological causes of mental disorder?"

Wasserman looked at her like a parent at a misbehaving child. She was suddenly aware that he was lecturing to her. "This is a progressive facility, Miss Chambers. Our staff is well educated. We treat chemical imbalance with medications, and provide support with play therapy and modeling."

Wasserman turned and proceeded out the door. After a moment, and a deep breath to calm her singing nerves, Jess followed, her briefcase tucked tightly under her arm.

"Sarah's in the basement level at the moment, in one of our quiet rooms," Wasserman said, as they walked to a set of elevators next to the fire stairs. "You might be a bit shocked at first by her appearance. Let me assure you that everything has been done to make her life here as comfortable as possible. However, she's been very difficult recently. There are precautions that must be taken in regards to her safety and that of those who work around her. She's deceptively strong, and as I said before, she can be very clever."

"I'm curious, Doctor. Why did you introduce me to Dennis?"

"To show you that not all of our guests are so severely restricted. And to see how you reacted to him."

"I hope I didn't disappoint you."

"It's important that they not sense your discomfort. If you're unsure of how to proceed in a given situation, and all of us are at some point, it is best to refer to your superior."

The elevator doors opened onto another world. Heavy cinder block walls and bare concrete floors met them as they stepped from the elevator into a narrow rectangular room. The overhead lighting was bright and unwavering, but it was the shadows Jess noticed. Clinging like cobwebs to the corners, they disappeared when she turned her gaze on them, but then returned to lurk at the edges of her sight. Perhaps it was her mood.

A heavy woman wearing a white coat stepped out from behind a desk as they approached. She was large through the shoulders and hips and very dark-skinned, and moved with a quiet shuffle so that she seemed to avoid the light, slipping through it like one of the shadows.

"This is Maria. She'll be here whenever you need anything. Maria is well trained in handling our difficult patients. And her English is getting much better. Isn't that so?"

"*Sí*," Maria said. Pockmarked skin stretched across darkly plump cheeks. Her expression was inscrutable, but her eyes darted nervously back and forth. "*Gracias*, thank you."

They entered a corridor lined with solid metal doors on either side, each of them with an eye-high, centered window. The air smelled damp with the slightest hint of lemon cleanser.

Jess could hear noises from behind the walls, thumps and muffled shouting. She concentrated on Wasserman's back as he spoke over his shoulder.

"Most of our patients are assigned a counselor and a team that works together to ensure that things are progressing. I've taken a personal interest in Sarah, and in this instance you'll be working directly with Maria and myself. Often you'll be alone. Sarah tends to react badly to crowds." Nearly at the end of the corridor, he stopped at a door and turned to her. "Are there any more questions before you have a look?"

About a million of them. Jess squared her own shoulders and faced him. "I have to admit here, Dr. Wasserman, I don't feel comfortable with what you've given me. Really it would be better if I could study the file. I need to know what tests she's been given, what sort of diagnoses have been made—"

"Sarah has a schizophreniform psychotic disorder. She was diagnosed at age six. As I'm sure you're aware, diagnoses of this sort prior to six years of age are *extremely* rare. Sarah was always difficult, but by her sixth birthday she was showing signs of marked withdrawal, looseness of association, and a breakdown of reality testing. There were hallucinations—"

"I understood that those didn't start until early adolescence."

"Not in this case." Wasserman paused and seemed to choose his words carefully. "Sarah began to believe . . . still believes . . . that she could influence people. That she could bend things to her will. Fantasies of omnipotence are not uncommon—again, this stems from early childhood—but in Sarah these fantasies extended far beyond the normal stages. And then the phobias and the suicide attempts began. Recently she has grown so uncontrollable that we've had no choice but to confine her to the basement for good portions of the day. She fought us by withdrawing in her therapy sessions and refusing her medication. She hasn't spoken a word in over three months now."

Wasserman's gaze kept slipping from the tiny window in

the door, to Jess's face, to some point in the corridor beyond her head.

"What about her parents?"

"Sarah has no surviving relatives, as I believe I told you. That's the case with so many of the children here, unfortunately. They've been either orphaned or abandoned, and the foster care system is simply not well equipped to handle those with more severe mental disorders." Wasserman glanced at his watch and then dug a set of keys out of the pocket of his white lab coat. "Now, Jean and I agreed that your first contact with her should be alone. Our intent here is to shake things up, draw her out, expose her to someone she might eventually be more comfortable with and who is not associated with me or my staff."

"I'd still like to see her file."

Wasserman blinked at her from behind his glasses. "You're persistent, I'll give you that. I've made my decision. If you need assistance there's a button on the wall. Maria will let you out." Wasserman fumbled the key into the lock as if he couldn't get a handle on it. Then the key turned and the metal door swung open.

—3—

The girl crouched in the middle of a padded room. The restraint jacket that pinned her arms over her chest seemed to swallow her slender, boyish frame. Her black hair hung down far enough that Jess could not get a good look at her features.

If Sarah heard the door open, she gave no sign. Her breathing came slow and deep. A thin line of spittle hung trembling from a strand of hair to the floor.

Jess stopped just inside the door and listened as it swung shut behind her. The noise was enough to make her jump, but she caught hold of herself inside like the clenching of teeth.

"Hello, Sarah," she said firmly. "My name is Jess Chambers. I'd like to visit with you for a while, if that's all right."

There were two ways to go about this: pretend to be occupied with something fascinating, and see if she became curious, or try to engage immediately. Either way it could take days, weeks, to break through. Both options assumed that Sarah was even reachable at all.

The girl had not reacted to her presence, and Jess found herself staring. Were the restraints really necessary? How violent could a ten-year-old possibly be? Perhaps she had tried to harm herself; Shelley had mentioned that she was suicidal. Jess had heard of psychiatric patients tearing at their faces, pulling out their own eyes, digging out their throats. It was difficult to kill yourself with your bare hands, but that didn't stop some of them from the attempt.

She did not want to appear threatening and so she sat down on the floor against the wall, keeping a good distance, but getting into the girl's line of sight. She had worn loose clothes specifically for this, a soft suit in neutral colors that covered her wrists and left only her hands and part of her neck bare. She wore contact lenses, her hair held up by a plain, white-cotton Scrunchie.

Remember what you have learned. Finding the real world too much to bear, Sarah had formed her own. It was up to Jess to interpret it. She would be a translator of sorts. To do this she would have to form a bond, allow herself to let the girl in and hope that Sarah would trust her enough, be lucid enough, to let her in too.

She opened her briefcase and removed a lined notebook and pencil. At the top of the first page, she wrote *interpersonal contexts*, and then, under it: *Interaction with peers? Foster homes? Teachers?* As she did this she spoke quietly, repeating her name, and why she was there.

It was like talking to herself. When she was a small girl her grandmother Cheryl had a stroke, and the family visited her at the Maine Medical Center in Portland. It was a place she was already well familiar with from various visits with Michael. They had gathered around Grandma Cheryl's bed, and everyone spoke as if she could hear them, as if at any moment she would sit up and answer their questions. Her grandmother died three days later, having never uttered another word.

But this is different. Obviously Sarah was in a catatonic state, but that did not mean she had always been that way, or that she would not come out of it again. Studies indicated that catatonics were often aware of their surroundings and simply unable to respond. Jess had to believe the girl was listening, that whatever barrier she had erected in her mind did not entirely cut her off from the world.

After a few minutes of note-taking on her observations of the surroundings and Sarah's condition, she risked a glance, saw that the girl had not moved. *The buckles must be hurting her.* She thought about loosening the jacket, decided against it. She did not know exactly what Sarah was on. Tranquilizers, Wasserman had said. Neuroleptics.

"I wonder if you could help me come up with some fun things to do," she said, scribbling on the notepad. "We could try painting. I used to paint a lot when I was your age. I still do, like sometimes when I'm feeling sad or lonely. It's like I'm putting those feelings down on paper where they can't hurt me."

Had the girl moved her head? This was silly. *Damn you, Wasserman, for leaving me in here alone.* She continued, feeling like a fraud, forcing the anxiety from her voice. This was a familiar, unsettling discomfort. *Sarah is not Michael.* She was much older than her brother when he died. The two were nothing like each other. *Just keep going.*

"There are other things I like to do when I'm lonely. I like to watch old movies and eat popcorn. I'm a sucker for a classic romance—Bogart, Grant, Bacall." She talked some more about the world outside the walls, keeping her voice slow and steady. She held up the notepad to show off a few sketches. After a while she tried a different approach: "Dr. Wasserman told me you've been here a long time, Sarah. How do you feel about this place? Do you like it?"

This time she was sure she saw movement, a slight trembling. It could be nothing more than muscle fatigue. Keeping her voice calm and smooth, she said, "I've seen places like this before. Most people don't want to be here. Most people need a friend. I can be your friend. I'll come visit you whenever you'd like. We can talk about anything you want."

She shifted, up onto the balls of her feet so that she was mirroring the girl's crouch. "A place like this would make me upset. All those kids upstairs having fun while you're stuck down here alone. I wonder if you've ever been to the zoo, or a ball game. We could go to those places, if Dr. Wasserman says it's okay."

She was concentrating so hard that when the rattling came at the door she jumped. Gaining her feet, she went over and peered out the little window, but could see nothing except the opposite wall of the corridor. The noise did not come again. The button that would bring Maria was at eye level, housed in a small plastic casing, but she did not press it.

When she turned around again, Sarah began to shake. The shaking started in her lower body and spread upward. The buckles on the straitjacket made a slight tinkling sound.

The line of spittle attached to her hair danced and curved, but did not break.

"I know you can hear me. I know you're in there. I'm not going to hurt you." Jess approached the girl and crouched, showed her open hands. "What are you afraid of, Sarah?"

When the ringing began, she at first thought it was a distant noise of the clinic, or the lights humming over her head. But then the ringing grew louder, and with it came a buzzing as if the air itself were electrified. Jess felt a familiar disorientation, her mind growing heavy and sluggish, and thought of alcoholic haze, those dim nightclub dreams of her undergraduate days rushing back like a distant train coming at her through a tunnel. And something else, a memory so old and fragmented it was like a part of her she had forgotten was there.

Dimly she felt herself falling, felt the impact from the floor run up her spine.

Then Sarah raised her head. Instantly Jess knew that everything she had assumed about the girl was wrong. Her eyes were like flecks of white lightning surrounded by darkness, gathering themselves for a storm. Jess lay half on her back and could not move, watched as the girl stared back at her and continued to shake, as the ringing grew louder and Sarah's lips moved in a silent, pleading prayer.

Help me.

Somehow Jess gained her feet and stumbled to the door, laying her hand against the button and her forehead against the glass of the window. She felt a cool looseness deep in her belly.

In the distance she could hear the buzzer and the sound of running feet.

—4—

The student lounge (or "The Cave," as it is somewhat affectionately called) is underneath the Thomas Ward main buildings, reached by a wide set of stairs from the street, which end at a triple set of glass doors. A converted basement, it holds a big-screen television and a small eatery with snacks and sandwiches available at outrageous prices, along with huge quantities of very bad coffee.

The two women had chosen a booth out of the way of general traffic.

"So you've seen her," Professor Shelley said. "What do you think?"

"She's heavily sedated, restrained, isolated in a padded cell. And she's immobile. I think she's buried inside herself somewhere. I just don't know how deep."

"Do you feel that you're in over your head?"

Jess glanced at her murky coffee. She was afraid of what she might see when she tipped the cup. A rumor continued to circulate about someone finding a dead roach once among the grinds. Right now the whole thing seemed quite possible. "I had a little run-in with Dr. Wasserman. He refused to show me Sarah's file. And I disagreed with his methods and I think he took offense to it."

"What exactly did you say?"

"I told him Sarah's treatment was abusive and that I was going to report him."

"And how did he react to that?"

"He basically said that I didn't know what the hell I was talking about."

When Jess had burst into his office, Dr. Wasserman had looked up but did not seem surprised to see her. She did not slow down until she was at his desk, and a small juvenile part of her had wanted to go at him with her nails like a cat. Wasserman had seemed to regard the whole thing with amusement, sitting and watching her with an earpiece of his glasses tucked in one corner of his mouth, a half smile on his face.

She'd wanted to hit him. Only now had she calmed down enough to talk about it. It was a stupid, childish move, threatening to report him. She would be working with him for the foreseeable future, and this wasn't going to help their relationship.

But if she were truthful to herself, the part that really burned her was that he was right. She knew nothing about Sarah's violent side, or the kind of drug therapy the girl needed. There was only her intuition, and trusting in that was naive at best. And yet the image of that room stayed with her, and the look on the girl's face.

What more do you need to see?

Shelley's keen gray eyes seemed to appraise her carefully. "You don't back down from anything, do you?"

"I was angry. I felt I had been put into a situation without being properly prepared for it."

"What exactly bothered you the most?"

"She's just a little girl, and she's scared. She's all alone. There's nothing in that room that's remotely human."

"So you feel that Sarah would be better served in a more friendly environment."

"A child in this situation needs more intense therapy, interaction with peers. Schooling, if it's at all practical."

"Yes," Shelley said. "That's true. But let me play devil's advocate for a moment. You can't know what she has available to her or how she's been treated. She's been Evan's patient for eight years, most of her life. There's no one else who knows her better."

"Which is exactly why I asked to see her file."

"Evan wanted to minimize any prejudices that might enter into your thinking."

"If that were true, he wouldn't have told me anything about her condition."

"Did it ever cross your mind that he might be testing you?" Shelley sipped at her coffee. "You know that I chose you for a reason. There are plenty of talented students in my classes, but none of them have the gift that you do. I've read your essays, your case studies, and they're all first-rate."

High praise indeed. Jess did not know how to respond. How could she talk about her secret doubts now, the strange disorientation, the helplessness she had felt when Sarah looked at her and mouthed those words? *Had* she mouthed them? Or was it just a figment of Jess's imagination, something she had wanted to see and created from nothing more than random muscle spasms?

"Quiet rooms are used in a lot of facilities like this," Shelly said. "As for the sedatives, those are very carefully monitored. There's nothing terribly unusual that you wouldn't see in another violent case, especially when the patient's violence is self-directed." She reached out to touch Jess's wrist. "I don't mean to confuse you. I have to admit, Evan's tendencies are a bit more extreme than my own, and you know how I feel about the diagnosis. I've been concerned lately with her treatment, which is another reason I decided to bring you into it. So I'm glad to have your thoughts. I'll ask you again. Do you feel like you're in over your head?"

Jess tipped her coffee cup once more, saw something swirling like oil across the surface, and set it down. She examined her level of confidence and found it sound. She could continue, but not with the odds stacked against her the way they were. "I have to be honest with you. Without a proper understanding of her background I don't see how I could do Sarah any good."

Shelley nodded. Wrinkles bunched around her mouth and eyes and she looked ten years older. "All right. Stop by my office tomorrow afternoon. I don't care what Evan says. I'll do what I can to get you that file."

—5—

Jess could not get herself to slow down. Her mind raced at warp speed, pulling up bits of fact and memory, expressing theories and then discounting them. These were things she had filed and then put away in her mind, where they had been gathering dust for years.

Always at the top of the class, even in elementary school, Jess had often been given special projects and work to complete on her own. The school was small, fifteen to twenty to a grade, a little brick building with a playground in back and temporary trailers to hold the overflow of younger students. Gradually she came to realize that the other children resented her special treatment, and it instilled in her a need to hide most of herself from the world.

Then there was Michael. Her brother's autism had been so severe he could not possibly relate to anyone. Cases like these tore people and families apart; she had seen it first-hand. Michael's condition had put a terrible strain on them all. It had caused her parents' divorce, her mother's slow and painful free fall from their comfortable farmhouse to the trailer in the poor part of town. Then came Michael's accident, and her mother's drinking binges, taking her to a deeper and blacker place than Jess could reach.

But that was ancient history. What she could not discount now was the feeling that the look in Sarah's eyes was nothing like her brother's disconnected gaze, that no matter how deeply sedated she was, Sarah's eyes were *alive*.

Back at the desk under the eaves in her cluttered little top-floor apartment, with the windows open to the breeze and her cat curled at her feet, she jotted down everything she remembered about the girl. The file was in her briefcase, but she did not touch it, not yet. She wanted to formulate her thoughts first. Traffic moved sluggishly on the street below, the train clacking by on its way downtown, filled with freshly scrubbed college students looking for some kind of nightlife. For a moment she wished she were with them. But she knew she would not be fit company for anyone. Once she had something in her teeth she had to worry at it until it was gone.

She flipped through her developmental psychopathology book, looking for anything on schizophrenia. Most of what she could find dealt with the adolescent transition; there was a frustrating lack of information about younger schizophrenics. She got up and went around the narrow counter to the stove. The real estate agent had sold her on the charm of the place, a long, narrow studio added into the attic of a three-family home; after living in it for a week, she'd come to understand that "charm" meant hopelessly run-down and open to drafts. The best part of the apartment was the seat under the eaves near the west window. It overlooked a line of trees and grassy lawn, and it was where she kept her easel and paints. She painted to calm herself when life became too stressful. Bits and pieces of artwork, some freshly done, decorated the walls.

The rest of the apartment was like everything else in Boston. The kitchen counter was scratched Formica, the floors dull and battered hardwood and linoleum. Wind moaned around the closed windows at night, and the radiators banged and rattled at all hours.

But Otto loved it. There were mice.

She put a pot of water on the stove for tea. Otto came clicking over and curled himself around her bare legs. "You're the first male to do that since I can't remember when," Jess said. She sighed. Men had always found her attractive, but there was something about her that put them off, some sense of distance. Or maybe she pushed them away intentionally. More than one man had described her as chilly, stuck-up, or spoiled.

But she was none of these things, far from it.

Several times when she was younger she had had unnerving experiences with first dates who would not stop pawing at her as soon as they were alone. By the time she was in high school her mother was a full-blown drunk, in and out of AA meetings, unable to stay sober, going through boyfriend after boyfriend. One of these had taken a special interest in Jess, cornered her in an empty room, and tried to kiss and touch her. She never told anyone about it, not even her mother. Especially not her mother. She took a few self-defense classes after that, bought pepper spray for her purse. Loss of control was something she could not tolerate, in herself or in others.

She studied herself briefly in the faux-antique pub mirror to the right of the door. *Not so bad, old chum.* Her body had always been slim and athletic, stomach flat and tight without much effort on her part. Her face looked a bit worn down and puffy from lack of sleep, and her hair could use a brushing. But overall, the effect softened her features and made her look as if she'd just rolled out of bed.

Soft and full lips, her best attribute. Her nose held the slightest bump on its ridge, the result of a childhood injury and the one thing about her face she'd always wanted to fix.

"Gives you character, girl," her friend Charlie would say.

She scooped the cat up in her arms and breathed in his fine, soft hair. He purred, stretched, and jumped down. "So much for cuddling," she said. "You just want me for my can opener anyway."

Otto meowed accusingly at her. She had come home late;

how dare she? Jess fixed a can of food for him and waited for her water to boil.

Her mind drifted back to Sarah. Something was not making sense. What she was supposedly dealing with here was a fragmentation of the thought process, where so many unrelated topics intruded on directed attention that the patient became overwhelmed and simply withdrew. Delusions of grandeur and auditory hallucinations were common.

But was that really what she had seen today? Sarah was immobile, seemingly unresponsive, but in the end she *had* moved, she *had* responded.

Jess crossed the room and removed Sarah's file from her briefcase. She set it next to her cup on the little kitchen table, poured steaming water over her tea bag, added milk and sugar. Then she opened to the first photocopied page.

Height and weight had remained within normal range, if closer to the small end of the scale. No distinguishing marks except for a slight scar, approximately three centimeters, near the temple.

She was being examined on the recommendation of Dr. Jean Shelley. The specific reasons for the recommendation were not given. Jess was surprised to see Shelley also listed as court-appointed guardian.

This was followed by a battery of tests, many of them medical and focusing on brain function and brain wave activity. Each opinion was backed by a second and sometimes a third. But the physicians' notes were lacking any real insight, and the entire section seemed fragmented. She flipped further, into psychological testing. They had tested Sarah at various age levels for motor skills and language and found her ahead of developmental stages. Detachment and marked withdrawal were noted, which indicated an absence of a familiar caregiver. Sarah showed unusual cognitive abilities for her age. The phrase "unusual cognitive abilities" was not defined.

What little schooling she had received was largely on a one-on-one basis. Still, Sarah had learned her alphabet quickly and read at a third grade level by the time she was seven. But almost from the beginning she had shown a lack of contact with reality, delusions of grandeur. These went beyond normal developmental stages. When she was just four years old she became convinced she could force open locked doors, simply by thinking about it. It was noted that, in fact, she did become quite proficient at breaking and entering. Several times they found her wandering around areas of the facility when she should have been confined to her room.

A year or two later she got suddenly worse. She believed she could read people's thoughts. Sarah became violent with those who tried to restrain her during these fugues.

Bender, Children's Depression Inventory, CMMS, Goodenough-Harris, all were given as the girl grew older. Apparently she had cooperated well enough for the tests. Wasserman's notes (at least she assumed they were his) were scribbled in a hand so slanted and confused they were all but illegible. *At least his handwriting is a mess.* Perhaps his impeccably neat office was an attempt to hide a cluttered psyche. Jess felt as if she had just caught him with his pants down, and she smiled a secret smile.

And that was about all of it. She went back and looked for anything physically abnormal. Blood pressure was high, especially during morning and evening hours. Sarah's CAT scan had shown some accelerated activity in the parietal lobe, but this did not seem to be substantiated on further trials.

Studying the file further, Jess was convinced there were missing sections. Where were the initial indications, problems, developmental abnormalities? Where were the extensive physical follow-ups, blood work, chemical screens? Where was the family history, the events of early infancy? Months were missing, whole blocks of time. Had nothing of interest happened, or had someone removed the record?

Feeling energized, Jess picked up the phone and dialed information. But when she obtained the number for the

Wasserman Facility and finally got through, she was told Dr. Wasserman was not available.

She dialed information again. There were no listings for a Dr. Evan Wasserman in the immediate area.

Her tea was cold. Frustrated, she went to the window, and found herself beginning to drift. Outside, it had begun to drizzle, the streets stained dark, water reflecting the ripple of passing headlights.

She had been left hanging. She did not like to wait for anything. When she was little she was always grabbing things off the supermarket shelves, running off alone, driving her mother crazy. But then had come Michael, to draw the attention off her. When her brother was born they all knew something was wrong right away. He did not respond to them properly, did not play, did not cry, did not sleep at night. She became free to do what she wanted; Michael required constant supervision. Like her, he could and would do anything. But for him it was not a matter of choice.

Jess fought against the images from the past, and finally succumbed to them, images of pain and fear, and most of all, guilt. She listened to the soft patter on the roof and let them wash over her like rain.

Later Otto wandered over from his hiding place under the bed and curled up in her lap. She sat with him by the window and watched the trains go by.

—6—

At the Wasserman Facility, all of the rooms were dark, except one.

Evan Wasserman sat at his desk, listening to the sounds of his charges settling in for the night. These were familiar to him now. He often worked late, and sometimes stayed over on the army cot he kept in his closet. On these nights he left strict instructions for the overnight nurses that he was not to be disturbed unless it was an emergency.

His apartment was all the way in Newton and the traffic was murder. If it weren't for the rumors among the staff, he might sleep here more often. It was easier that way; he didn't have to make the drive in the morning, and there was no one to keep him at home.

Night sounds. Someone shuffling somewhere, an occasional shout, an incoherent cry. He swung around in his chair and looked out the window. Darkness outside, swarming at the glass. Beyond a certain length of manicured backyard stretched acres of wild, abandoned land. A series of crumbling brick buildings, part of the old Boston State Hospital, sat about half a mile away through the brush. All this unused acreage in the middle of the city, some would say it was a shame. But right now it gave him space to breathe. That space was under attack. There were two development proposals currently with the city, and if he wasn't careful they would mean the end of his business.

He could not think clearly tonight. The uneasy feeling threatened to explode within him, and it kept him from his usual lists. Dr. Wasserman was a list man, everything neatly in its place, he would cross his tasks off with a freshly sharpened pencil when he had completed them, one by one. If something was not done on time he became very agitated. His grandfather had been like that too; during his early years he had often come across fragments of Grandfather's paper that had been scratched and rewritten and worn clean through.

After his grandfather had passed away, his father had taken over the family business, but he was hopeless at it. Wasserman had spent many nights slipping through these very floors as a child, his father locked away in an office downstairs, diddling one of the nurses. When the sounds of their union grew to be too much to bear Evan would ride up the creaking elevator to these vast and then empty rooms, crumbling paint and chipped linoleum, footsteps echoing like the whispers of a ghostly companion. There were always interesting games to play, closets and more hidden spaces to explore. Every once in a while he would discover one of his grandfather's lists, tucked away in the back of a drawer or cabinet like some sort of treasure map in code.

How he had loved this place, even then. How he had hated his father for letting it fall to pieces. His father was not fit for the job; his grandfather's death had forced the issue.

He wondered what his grandfather would think of all this now. The children's welfare had been the most important thing to him. *He was a much better man than me*, Wasserman thought. *I am putting them all at risk.*

He wondered why he was so restless tonight. Perhaps it was the girl Jean had sent him. She was attractive, certainly, more attractive than most with her high cheekbones, raven-black hair, and determined mouth; a glow about her, a focused strength. She seemed very bright and capable. All this worried him very much. He picked up the phone and hit a number on his speed dial.

The phone was picked up on the fifth ring. There was a long moment of silence. "I'm sorry to bother you," Wasserman said. "You weren't sleeping? I didn't wake you?"

"As a matter of fact, you did."

"That girl, Jess Chambers. I don't know that she's right for this."

"We've talked it to death, Evan. We've gone over it a thousand times. You know the odds, they're worse than winning the lottery."

"She's headstrong, very pushy. She has a problem with authority. I don't like her."

"You don't have to like her. It's Sarah we're concerned with. The bond will form, take my word for it. I think the first session went well."

"She was agitated afterward. We had to sedate her again."

"That's a good sign. Look, you've been with this from the beginning. But if you want to throw in the towel, by all means, let me know. We can pull the plug right now. Just never mind what it would mean for your funding. I hate to be selfish, but you know what that will mean for *me*. It's a death sentence, Evan."

Wasserman clenched the phone. He fought his instant panic at the thought, and hated the way his voice sounded afterward. "Don't say that. We'll go on, of course we will. We'll get things up and running again. I'm just concerned about introducing a new element into all this. I don't want Chambers . . . testing me. And she'd better not talk to anyone."

"It doesn't matter. Nobody's going to believe her."

That was right, of course. He was a respected member of the APA, and no matter how unconventional his treatment, there would be nobody who would get through security to see it.

But there were countless other things to consider. The late-night hours invited so many insecurities. He worried about money-hungry developers trying to yank the land out from under him, or worse, putting a strip mall in his backyard. He worried about what he might have to do if their plans backfired. They were sitting on a time bomb, for God's sake.

But most of all, he worried about losing the only person other than his grandfather who had ever meant anything to him.

He sighed. "I don't have to tell you what could happen here if she loses control again."

"We don't have a choice. That's a risk we have to take. Now stop worrying and get some sleep, please. You need to be fresh when Helix comes in for the next site visit. Impress them, or we're both in trouble. You know what I mean, Evan."

There was a long pause on both ends. *I need you*, he thought, but didn't say anything. Damn it, he was never able to say it.

Don't even think about dying on me.

"Good night," he said softly.

He hung up the phone and stared out at the murky night sky.

It was all true, of course; he needed to get his head together and prepare, or things would get bad very fast. He had worked very hard to regain the upper hand in this case, and he did not want to lose it now. The possibilities were far too frightening.

He thought about the Room upstairs, and his mind seemed to stretch and threaten to get away from him.

He set about making a list of the things they wanted to accomplish. The list was long. He scratched things out and started again, working silently in his office until it was far too late to go home. Began to imagine the girl housed somewhere below his feet. Just below his feet. Then he unfolded his bed from the closet and went to sleep with the lights still burning as a talisman against a deeper darkness.

—7—

In classes Jess felt as if she had been set adrift, awash in the steady drone of flat voices, the words in her textbooks failing to hold her interest. She was anxious to be doing something. The gaps in Sarah's file bothered her terribly. Through all the reports there had been precious little psychiatric opinion. She had to have some more information before she met with Wasserman. She was determined never to allow him to have the same advantage over her again.

In her class on personality disorders, Professor Thomas singled her out to be his latest target. The little auditorium was filled with the rustling of papers as everyone tried desperately to look busy. They were trying to avoid "the stick," a nickname students had for the wooden yardstick the professor used to point out offending members of his class. As far as anyone knew, he had yet to make physical contact with it; but nobody wanted to be the first.

Thomas was a very large black man in his sixties with a full head of gray hair, which most of his students assumed was a wig. He was also an expert on personality development, and he often traveled across the country to speak on the subject.

"Self-control," Thomas said. "Is acting-out behavior 'outgrown'?" He tapped the stick lightly on the back of an empty seat. "Miss Chambers? Do you feel that aggression is an inherent trait, or something that can be unlearned?"

"Kohn shows us a definite link between defiant behavior in preschoolers and subsequent aggression during adolescence. But not all of his subjects remained aggressive throughout their lives."

"What is your personal opinion?"

"It's a matter of degree. If we looked at the severity of the aggressive behavior, I think the data would hold up. The behavior has to fit into the parameters of the subject's stage of development."

"Example."

"If a three-year-old is throwing temper tantrums, that's normal for his age. If the tantrums involve beating another child senseless with a yardstick, that's cause for concern."

Snickers from several people in class. "All of you should stop laughing long enough to clear your ears," Thomas said, pointing. The yardstick quivered in the air as if it were eager to strike. "Miss Chambers's logic may seem obvious to you all, but she has just given us an excellent example of using what we have learned to form an opinion. A diagnosis and eventual treatment follows the same line of thought. Now, what would you do to diagnose the disorder in such a hypothetical?"

"It's difficult to say without more information. Is the problem chemical? Biological? Environmental? I'd investigate a number of factors: abuse in the home, previous patterns of behavior, any relatives with overaggressive tendencies. Is he learning by example? Or are there other indicators of a chemical imbalance, previous head trauma, even possible brain damage?"

Thomas nodded. "Each case is unique," he said. He let the yardstick touch to the floor, and it thumped. "It's vital not to have any biases when you begin. You must weigh the evidence and eliminate possibilities, one by one."

After class they stood below the semicircle of seats as students slowly filed out, a few of them staring curiously back like drivers past the scene of an accident.

"I want you to know that the yardstick comment did not go unnoticed," Thomas said. "By the way, I never beat my students unless they truly deserve it."

Jess hoped her small smile was properly apologetic. "Of course not, Professor. I did wonder if you could help me, though. I'm writing a paper on the symptoms and treatments of schizophrenia—mainly younger patients, preadolescents."

"Then you won't have much data. The adolescent transition tends to trigger a schizophrenic type."

"But there are cases as young as, say, six years old?"

"Extremely rare. Where before a child might be hyperactive, or moody, or even aggressive, the hormonal changes during puberty wreak havoc in the brain and you see personality fragmentation, psychosis. I'd be surprised to see a confirmed diagnosis as young as six."

"If a diagnosis were in doubt—say a child has been labeled as schizophrenic by an expert, but others had reason to question it—what would you look for?"

"Organization of any kind, Miss Chambers. In schizophrenics the thinking process has been interrupted, scrambled, if you will. Without medication a patient is often unable to focus on a particular line of thought and carry it through. Autism is often mistaken for schizophrenia, and vice versa."

"Would a child in this situation be sedated, restrained? Would neuroleptics be an effective treatment?"

Thomas frowned. "I would emphasize family therapy and behavioral modification techniques. You want to reward a patient's good behavior while controlling his environment to the utmost degree."

"So you would not isolate a child in these circumstances?"

"Absolutely not. Now if you'll excuse me, I've got another class to teach. Unless you'd like me to write your paper for you?"

When Jess arrived back at her apartment, there was a message on the machine from Professor Shelley.

"Have you had time to take a look at her file?" Shelley asked, when Jess had reached her at home.

"I read through it, yes."

"Any questions?"

"Something struck me. It said that you were the one who recommended her admittance. It also said that you're her court-appointed guardian."

There was a long pause on the other end. Jess imagined Shelley sitting in a wing chair by the light of a lamp. Did she have an apartment or a house? Did the professor live alone? She realized how little she knew about Shelley's personal life. At the same time she wondered why it mattered.

"I did recommend her, yes," Shelley said. "I kept close track of Sarah after she was born. She had family who raised her for a year or so. Sarah's mother was not entirely stable, her parents were taking care of both of them. It was difficult. Sarah's grandparents had my number, and when she got to be too much to handle, they called me. I agreed to watch over her treatment."

"None of this is in the file. Do you know why?"

"That you'd have to ask Dr. Wasserman." A sudden sharp intake of breath; then the professor moved on. "I think it's important to capitalize on any progress you made during your first meeting. You should get down there as many times as you can this week." Then, quietly, a bit more gently, she said, "I know you feel that we sprang this on you without proper warning. I can only say that if it were completely up to me I might have handled things differently."

"I appreciate that."

"Take another look," Shelley said. "You've read the file, you're better prepared. Now's your chance to get through to her. Write down everything you see, everything you feel is important. We'll meet in my office on Monday."

—8—

The next few days passed uneventfully. But when Jess Chambers reached the hospital for what would be her fourth session with Sarah, she was informed by the admitting secretary that Dr. Wasserman had gone to attend a psychiatric conference in New York. He had left instructions for her.

> I am allowing you to continue with your sessions while I am gone on one condition: that you hold them only in Sarah's room and only after she has received her medication. She remains in restraints for the time being at my request. If you are alone with her, be alert and do not allow her to touch you.
>
> The staff has my instructions and will follow them to the letter. I do not want Sarah moved while I am gone for any reason. Maria is perfectly capable of handling any request. She is aware of the situation and will decide what is reasonable.
>
> Please record in your notes everything that occurs. If you have any questions I may be reached through my secretary.

Jess did not know whether to feel angry or relieved that Wasserman was gone. He had hovered over her for much of the week, and pushed her a bit after her last visit, asking her in detail about her observations and theories. She hadn't had much to say; each of the hour-long sessions since the first had been spent in silence. Sarah had not moved or made a sound, and after long periods of note-taking, sketching, and the occasional unanswered question or thought, Jess had left to go home again, her frustration levels growing.

She knew it would take time for Sarah to get used to her presence. And there was always the chance she'd never respond to anyone or anything again. But still, it was a depressing experience. She had begun to wonder if Sarah mouthing those words during that first visit had been her imagination playing tricks on her. Muscle spasms could sometimes look like attempts at speech.

Maybe I'm crazy. Maybe I just saw what I wanted to see.

She made her way down to the basement, feeling the chill of the place settle into her bones. Do not allow her to touch you. A strange warning indeed. She wondered whether it was simply Wasserman's way of lending a greater importance to the proceedings. His instructions made her feel like a child left home alone for the first time, and of course that was exactly the way he wanted it. *Goddamn it if I'm going to play his games.*

Maria was out from behind the desk before the elevator doors fully opened. Her voice was tense and her face and neck rigid, and sweat stood out on her forehead.

"She is not still," the big woman said. "The way she looks, it is not right."

"Has she had her medication, Maria?"

Maria shook her head. "Soon. I do not like to go there. I let you in the hall, no further." The woman nodded again. "You go see what I tell you."

This time at Sarah's door was subtly different than the last. The hallway seemed darker than before. A bulb was out and the lights farther down the hall cast strange shadows. Jess stopped for a moment before swinging the door open.

Sarah was crouched against the far wall, rocking slowly back and forth, her long black hair sweeping across her face. She still wore the straitjacket. At the sound of the door closing she jumped, and then continued rocking from the heels to the balls of her feet.

Any change is a good sign, Jess told herself. *Something is better than nothing.* She examined her own state of mind, reaching deep down inside where cold things grew. On the way here she had been jumpy for some reason, nervous enough that she checked for sweat stains under her arms. But now that she was in the room with Sarah she felt her anxiousness subside. Wasserman's instructions had made her angry, and the anger helped her focus.

Establish trust, Jess told herself. The first goal. "I'm going to release your arms now, Sarah. Do you hear me? I'm going to release you." She reached over, slowly, slowly, undid the buckles. Slipped the girl's arms from the jacket and let it fall, and stepped back. Through it all Sarah remained limp, pliable as soft clay. The rocking had ceased abruptly as soon as Jess touched her.

Later she would admit to herself that releasing the girl had satisfied the small, petty part of her she had allowed Wasserman to reach. Now she only thought of it as an attempt at a connection.

The signs of schizophrenia. *Disorganized thinking, unstructured thoughts. Bizarre and illogical behavior.* What else had Professor Thomas said? Study the facts and make your own determination.

Crouching by the girl's side, she spoke once again of her reasons for coming, trying to be as honest and straightforward as possible. She told Sarah that they could be seeing each other a lot in the future, and that they could be friends if she wanted that. She reassured the girl that all she wanted to do was help.

Then she spoke of anything that came into her head: her classes, her cat Otto's unexpected arrival on her doorstep last fall, her family. Jess concentrated on keeping the words coming, keeping her voice calm and even, letting the sound soothe the girl who was rocking once again back and forth at her feet.

Eventually her thoughts began to go off onto new tangents, so that it was several moments before she realized something else had changed. She heard a single sound, slow, muttered, unintelligible. The rocking had slowed; Jess kept her voice close to the same pitch while she shifted gears.

"I know you've been treated badly by some people in the past. It's just you and me now."

Sarah did not look up, but her hair had fallen away from her face, and she had stopped moving. Silence lasted for what seemed like hours. Then, in a remarkably clear, quiet voice, she said, "They're *looking* at me. *Staring* at me. All the time."

Bingo. A thrill ran up Jess's limbs. "Who, Sarah? Are they with us right now?"

Sarah did not move or indicate that she had heard. Jess got the sudden idea the girl had been talking to herself. Still, she glanced around, more to satisfy Sarah than anything else. All she saw were the ash-gray walls and ceiling, and the padded metal door.

She took this opportunity to examine the girl's face more closely. A plain face, pale and broad, but her eyes were large and set widely apart above a long nose. She was the sort of girl who might have been pleasant-looking, under certain circumstances; but here under the blue-white lights she looked like a dog that had been kicked too many times.

Of course she was drugged. And judging from the way the skin stretched across her skull and limbs, Sarah had not been eating well.

Jess tried again: "Who's watching you, Sarah?"

Sarah looked up from beneath a black slash of hair. Jess was pinned by the sparks of light dancing in her eyes. Those eyes did not belong to that face. She felt like a burglar caught in a searchlight, exposed, naked, open to ridicule.

Don't be silly. She's just a child.

"I could kill you. Stop your heart if I wanted. If you're lying." Suddenly Sarah dropped her gaze from Jess's face and turned, muttering, "No. No. No. She isn't one of them. Not that one. No." Her voice had quickly become rhythmic, almost a muttered incantation. A method of coping with something that cannot be faced. A defensive tactic meant to soothe the mind. Meaning to distract her, Jess moved quickly to her briefcase for her notepad, but as she moved she felt the girl's eyes seize her again, and for a single, groping moment a hand tightened inside her chest.

And then it was gone. She froze with her fingers on the notepad inside the case, her heart fluttering.

She was imagining things. She was too keyed up, her adrenaline pumping. There were moments in time that coincidence lent a greater importance; this was simply one of them.

Jess took the notepad out very slowly, telling Sarah exactly what she was doing in an easy, quiet voice. "What I said before, everything I told you is true. I'm here to listen to you, when you're ready to talk. That's all. Do you understand?"

"No friends for me here."

"I see why you might feel that way. But I'm not from this place. I was asked by a friend of mine to come see you. They thought I might be able to cheer you up."

The girl regarded Jess with some curiosity. Jess was reminded once again of an animal that had been abused. Her heart ached for this girl.

"Do you remember when I came to visit you the very first time? You asked me to help you."

"My head. It's fuzzy."

"When you want to say something, it comes out different. All mixed up. Is that it?"

"*They* do it. They're *watching* me all the time."

Delusions of persecution was a common symptom of a schizophreniform disorder. And yet, so far Sarah had followed their conversation better than Jess could have hoped. She had showed a clear progression of thought, memory recall, cause-and-effect reasoning. These things didn't add up.

"Do you know where we are, Sarah?"

"Prison."

"Do you know why you're here?"

"I was bad."

"And what did you do when you were bad?"

"Hurt people."

"Who put you here?"

"Them."

"Am I one of them?"

"They're *white*."

"You mean they have white skin? What do they look like?" For a moment she was puzzled, and then, suddenly, "You mean they have white clothes. White coats. Is that it?"

Sarah just looked at her.

"They're doctors," Jess said, "and you're right. I'm not a doctor. You can tell that, can't you?"

"No doctors."

"Why don't you like them?"

"They hurt my head."

"Does your head hurt right now?"

"Yes. I know what they're thinking. They don't like me."

Where to go from here? She was running the risk of overwhelming the girl, of pressing too hard. "Sarah, would you like to play a game?" Jess dipped into her briefcase again and pulled out a series of test cards. "I'll ask you some questions, and show you some pictures, and you tell me what you think. Okay?"

She went through the deck, testing Sarah first on colors, then shapes, both concrete and abstract. She had to use tricks several times to make the girl focus. Then she moved on to a TAT test, giving Sarah scenes on cards and asking her what was happening in them. It was a simple way of determining mood, the idea being that the subject would describe a scene in a certain light depending on how he or she was feeling, giving the interpreter a glimpse of the deeper emotions underneath.

Sarah reacted mostly as Jess had expected, when she would react at all. Her answers indicated hostility and depression.

Jess tried Rorschach. "What do you see here, Sarah?"

"People. Big and mean people. Ugly."

"And here?"

"Fire. A roof on fire."

"It's a building? A house?"

She shook her head. "It's burning. They're gonna go away. They're gonna be gone." She wouldn't say anything more. Jess tried another inkblot, and another, but Sarah kept silent, withdrawn inside herself again.

Jess found herself at a loss. Sarah was exhibiting signs of mental distress, but nothing to the extent that had been described by Wasserman. Absent were the unusual postures or mannerisms, loose associations that were common to schizophrenics. Her observation about the "white" doctors was perceptive and her fear was understandable.

Something still did not add up. It was as if her file were written about someone else.

Suddenly the girl stiffened. Jess paused and put the inkblots down. Sarah had turned to face the door and was clearly growing agitated. Her eyes seemed to turn a deeper, violent color. And there was something else in her gaze, something Jess could not pin down. The feeling she got was of looking at a lake of dark water and seeing a huge, black shape rising to the surface.

Jess stood up and stumbled to the narrow window, aware of a new depth to the air, a sudden charge. She could hear muffled footsteps coming along the corridor. She craned her neck as Maria came into view, carrying a tray and another set of restraints. Maria stopped outside the door, fumbled in her pocket as if for her keys; then she looked up and made a gesture. The door was locked.

Jess tried the bolts, but they wouldn't budge. She fumbled in her own pocket. Maria's keys were here somewhere; she had let herself in with them. But they were not in her pocket. They were nowhere to be found. She rattled the handle.

When Sarah began to shout, the sound was so sudden and so loud in the tiny room that Jess flinched and whirled around.

"Leave me alone!" There was fear in the girl's eyes, and something else. "I don't want you to come here!"

Jess saw Maria freeze outside the door. She heard a popping sound and the tinkle of glass as several lights blew in the hallway. Maria's tray clattered to the concrete floor. Jess Chambers felt the hair on her head lift as if she were rubbing her feet across a carpet. The air temperature dropped. Something had entered this room; she felt the air ooze thick and heavy, filled with a presence that snapped and writhed like live electrical lines.

She tried the bolts again, but they would not budge. She scanned the room and struggled to keep herself calm. She had never been irrational; there was no reason to start now. There on the floor, nearly at her feet, were the keys.

She looked back at the girl through the liquid air.

Sarah's eyes had rolled up into her head. Droplets of sweat slid off her forehead and spattered to the floor. Her limbs were shaking. Jess immediately thought of an epileptic fit, but the indications were not quite right. It was more like a concentration so tense and desperate as to cause a seizure. She shouted Sarah's name, and the girl whipped her head back and forth, teeth chattering together, making one long unintelligible sound: "N-n-n-n-n-n-n-n—"

It built, swelled—

—then, all at once, ceased. It was as if a wave of water had broken over their heads, as if a light switch had been flicked off. In the sudden stillness Jess could hear Sarah's unconscious body slump to the floor, and her own breathing, rough and ragged, loud in her ears as a bellows. Quickly she went to the girl, felt her pulse, quick and light as a bird's wing, her breath fast and shallow. But the skin of her forehead had smoothed and she looked peaceful.

Jess went back to the door. This time the bolts slid back smoothly into place with a soft click, and the door swung open. Maria was on the floor on hands and knees, scrambling to sweep up the contents of the tray. A syringe and several vials, more pills . . .

Emergency lights had blinked on, throwing feeble orange light on the hallway. Slivers of glass from the broken bulb glinted orange on concrete. There were shouts from the other rooms, someone running above their heads.

"She's okay," Jess said into the silence, more for herself than the nurse. "She's out cold."

Maria seemed to flinch at her voice. Then the big woman climbed to her feet and took a new syringe out of her pocket. Wordlessly she entered the small room and knelt at Sarah's side; lifted the syringe to the light with trembling hands, tapped it, squirted a tiny fount of sparkling clear fluid, and bent again to the girl's arm.

Only then did Jess remember that she had forgotten to put Sarah's straitjacket back on. But Maria did not seem to notice.

—9—

"Evan Wasserman called this morning," Shelley said. She sat straight in her chair with her hands folded over the papers strewn across her desk. "He told me you went directly against his orders and removed Sarah's restraints."

"I felt that she had to trust me. I took a chance."

"A very dangerous one, according to Evan. Sarah has been aggressive with people before. You went in before she had her medication. He was extremely upset about that."

"What could she possibly have done? She's ten years old."

"That's not the point." Shelley paused. "Evidently there are problems between the two of you. I understand why. But the simple fact of the matter is that this is his hospital and his patient. You have to follow his rules."

Jess tried to keep down the sudden blood that rushed to her cheeks. She nodded, feeling like a scolded child. It was ridiculous, really. Shelley was right. And yet she felt betrayed.

"Tell me exactly what happened."

Jess related the previous day's visit, beginning with her arrival in Sarah's basement room. She tried to remember everything Sarah had said, each indication of her mental state, including her paranoia about the "white" people. Still, Jess had the frustrated feeling that she was unable to get across the thrust of events exactly the way they occurred. There were things that happened that would sound crazy if she repeated them now: the way the lights had blown out in the hall, the sudden jamming of the door locks, the way Sarah knew her medication was on its way long before there was any sign of Maria and the tray. Jess prided herself on her logical, orderly mind. Those things were not logical and she tried her best to dismiss them.

And yet she couldn't, damn it. They kept pushing themselves back in.

When she had finished, Shelley said, "She's all right, you know. Evan wanted it stressed, however, that she was in a very dangerous state and that it was touch-and-go for a while. Apparently she's had seizures before."

"Has she been tested for a lesion in the temporal lobe?"

"I'm sure they would have taken an EEG to rule that out."

"Her file had a lot in it about brain wave activity. Maybe they suspected some sort of damage, or tumor."

"I suggested it myself, actually, when Sarah was first assigned to state care. Though she was only a little over a year old, the symptoms indicated some physical trauma. We looked for swelling, collections of fluid, anything that might suggest an injury. We thought epilepsy, searched the readings very carefully. But there was nothing."

"She thinks she's in prison," Jess said. "They've got her scared to death."

Something must have shown in her eyes. Shelley leaned forward intently. "You've done more with her in your visits than that entire staff has in months. She had shut down entirely with me, saw me as some kind of enemy, which is one reason I haven't gone to see her the past few weeks. But she's connecting with you, you're building trust. That's good. That's one reason why we decided to bring you into this. Still, you have to be careful to view her as your patient and nothing more. Getting too attached can only be painful. There are bound to be setbacks."

Jess nodded. She had read about a case involving a young

girl and a home care specialist; the child had been ill with a lengthy terminal disease, the sort that led to many highs and lows and false hopes. The specialist and the child spent most of the day together, and slept near each other at night. By the time she died the specialist had formed such a strong attachment that she refused to return to work, and in fact reported many of the same false symptoms of the disease. She described the death as if her own child had died.

"I want to ask you something," Shelley said. "This may be painful too and if you don't want to talk about it I'll understand. Earlier you mentioned your younger brother was autistic."

The use of past tense did not escape Jess's notice. Either Shelley had remembered from their previous conversation, or she had taken a guess. "And now you're wondering whether that has something to do with it. Whether I have some hidden agenda."

"The thought crossed my mind."

Maybe Shelley was right. She would have been a fool not to realize that her brother's death had pushed her toward child psychology in the first place.

Just because I'm interested in Sarah's case doesn't mean I'm looking for some kind of payback.

A familiar memory slipped up on her. Michael, standing on the sidewalk, the sound of the children in the playground, the noise of passing cars. She reached out to him but he did not see her. He did not see anything or hear her screaming.

"I was supposed to be watching him. We were near the park. My mother was at a pay phone and Michael stepped out into traffic. He was hit and killed instantly."

After countless looks of pity and murmurs of sympathy through the years she had learned to keep the whole thing to herself. But Shelley's reaction was not the one she had expected. Shelley simply looked at her and said, "And you blamed yourself for this."

"My mother had put him in my care. I knew what he might do. I should have stopped him."

"You were how old?"

"Nine."

"You must see," Shelley said gently, "how ridiculous that is."

"I was old enough for it to matter."

"Of course. But not old enough to be blamed for it."

Shelley said this as if it were a common truth. And Jess supposed that under normal circumstance it was, but she was not a normal girl. She knew what she was capable of and what she wasn't, and that was what had made it so difficult. Anyone could say that she had been too young, that her mother should never have left her alone with him. But that didn't change anything. It only shifted responsibility.

"And what happened then?"

"My mother started drinking more heavily, staying out at night. She treated me as if I weren't there. I suppose she blamed me too, in her way."

"Or herself, for leaving you to watch him."

"Maybe so." But now they were getting too far off the subject. She did not want to dig into the past any longer. Suddenly she felt as if there weren't enough air in the room to breathe.

"I've thought this case over very carefully. I've studied the facts and the data at hand and I do not believe Sarah is schizophrenic. She has some obvious adjustment problems and hostility toward the staff, but I won't know what else she needs until she's given a better chance to be lucid. I don't believe she should be locked up alone and I don't think she's a danger to anyone."

Jess listed off her reasons; Sarah had followed their conversation, been receptive to questions, showed short-term memory recall, scored well on cognitive tests. Her paranoia about the people in white seemed valid given the circumstances. And there were other, less tangible reasons; Jess might have called them gut instincts.

"Perhaps the antipsychotics are finally having an effect?"

"I just don't see it happening all at once like that. According to Dr. Wasserman she's been having breaks with reality for several years now, and the medications haven't done a thing. She's been so withdrawn and then so violent they've been forced to confine her to what is basically a cell. But I've seen little evidence of any of that."

Wasserman's voice, inside her head: *she can be devilishly clever.* Sarah playing possum. Could she be doing that again now? But she couldn't be *this* clever, Jess thought. How could you be psychotically disturbed and still plan such an elaborate game?

Instead of dismissing her, Shelley looked troubled. "I feel like I let her down," she said. "I should have been more involved the past few months, checked in more frequently. When Evan called I was ashamed because I hadn't looked in on her recently." She paused and her long, elegant fingers plucked absently at her sleeve.

"I've been distracted," Shelley said. "But of course that's no excuse."

"You could come with me to see her. It might do her some good."

"Sarah may associate me with the people in white coats. She'd see you with me and then in her mind you'd be one of them too."

"Maybe that's a chance we should take."

"No." Shelley shook her head. "That would complicate things. Evan is a capable psychiatrist and the Wasserman Facility is well known. I know from our conversations that he is at the end of his rope. Bringing you into this was quite a gamble. If you don't get anywhere, he's still exposed an outsider to an extremely difficult and controversial case. He opens himself up to criticism. And if you do succeed in making a connection with Sarah, he'll be getting questioned left and right as to why a graduate student could come in and do in a couple of weeks what he's failed to do in eight years."

Because he's an unimaginative asshole, Jess thought, but resisted saying it in spite of the pleasure the idea gave her. "I have to ask you. You delivered this girl. Was there any indication from the start she wasn't normal?"

"The circumstances were unusual. It was a difficult time."

"How do you mean?"

Shelley looked away. For a long time Jess was not sure if she would speak at all. "Sarah was born in the middle of one of the most intense snowstorms I have ever seen. What made matters worse was that somehow the storm turned electrical. I don't know the physics of it, but when Sarah's mother went into labor we lost power. Everything happened very quickly. We were working under primitive conditions to say the least.

"She delivered very fast. One moment she was dilated and there was nothing, and then . . ."

Shelley became very still and her face grew tight. The professor did not even breathe. And then she seemed to ease, as if a sharp pain had come and gone.

"The hospital was hit by lightning. We weren't sure what had happened at the time. All we knew was that all hell was breaking loose. The world seemed to be caving in. The emergency lights were on but most of the equipment was useless. The noises . . . it sounded like the earth was splitting at the seams." Shelley smiled, but her face held no warmth. "We got out but it was close. The hospital burned to the ground."

My God. Jess tried to imagine the scene, the frantic cries of the hospital workers, the storm howling all around them as the flames reared up and licked across the building's innards. "I think Sarah has some sort of memory of it. Could that be possible? When I administered the Rorshach she described something about a building being on fire."

"As far as I know no one has ever mentioned it to her. It hasn't been proven that newborns are even aware of their surroundings, at least in the way you or I might be. Sarah wouldn't have had any idea what was happening. She wouldn't even have a working concept of life and death."

"Her mother, then. Maybe she picked up on her mother's feelings."

"Sarah's mother is mentally disturbed," Shelley said. "I never saw her react to anything."

Jess breathed in deeply. *Is?* She felt a spark of something and fumbled for it. Talking about this case with Shelley was like pulling teeth, and she couldn't understand why. Wasserman too, for that matter. What were they hiding and why would they feel the need to hide it from her, when they had been the ones responsible for bringing her into this in the first place?

"You're wondering why that isn't in her file," Shelley said. "Evan and I have been going back and forth on this from the start. The fact is that there are some ethical and legal issues involved. But we all know that one of the most important aspects of diagnosis and treatment of mental disease is a family history, and you've been denied that."

"What are you talking about?"

"Sarah's grandparents are alive," Shelley said. "Her mother too. They live in Gilbertsville, New York."

—10—

The Newton Fliers' Club meets every third Friday of the month in the Jacob's Field Lounge. Made up of people who don't have the money to own a plane privately, members contribute to the initial cost and maintenance by paying monthly dues and sign up for use of the aircrafts.

Jess Chambers had been a member since she moved to the area two years ago. "Before that I logged my hours at a private strip back home," she explained as she pulled through the gates of the tiny airport. "There was a man in my town who used to fly in air shows, doing tricks in an old single-engine Cessna he kept in his barn. They called him the Flying Frenchman. He ran a small farm with a dirt landing strip in a cornfield. To make more money he would crop-dust during the summers, and give flying lessons. He taught me to fly when I was twelve."

It was another thing she had learned to keep to herself. The truth was she had always loved planes and flying was something she had dreamed of doing since she was five years old.

Most people said something like it was the last thing in the world they expected. Boys grinned and punched her in the arm, as if she were putting them on. Jean Shelley just looked at her from the passenger seat. "Your mother let you go up in a plane with someone called the Flying Frenchman?"

"She had other things on her mind."

Shelley shook her head. "Interesting. And you're sure there's a plane available today?"

"They said there'd been a cancellation. You're not afraid to fly with me, are you?"

"Of course not. I'm sure you're very capable."

Jess stole a glance at her professor. She remembered Shelley's look of surprise when she suggested they fly to Binghamton that afternoon. They could be there and back by supper.

But this wasn't just an excuse to log some hours. She needed to meet Sarah's family. She needed some background on the case. And most importantly, she needed to know just what could be so horrible to make a mother give up her own child.

The family had been through too much and it was too painful for them. They agreed to sign a voluntary placement agreement, with me acting as guardian. There was a custody transfer. It was the only way they could deal with what they were doing.

"You mean they didn't want to give her up?"

"There's more to it than that. I'd rather just let you see and judge for yourself."

She stopped the car in front of the one-room lounge and office and turned off the ignition. The engine ticked in silence. "Could I ask you something? Why did you decide to tell me about Sarah's family now?"

"I felt it was essential to your diagnosis and the development of your and Sarah's relationship. I'd always felt that way, but Evan disagreed. The family had requested anonymity. And there are other reasons that you'll understand soon enough.

"I want you to know that ordinarily I wouldn't agree to something like this. But I think we do owe you this much."

Jess nodded. "You're sure you don't want to call the family and let them know we're coming?"

"I don't think they'd agree to see you. It will be more difficult for them to refuse when we're standing on their front step."

The plane, a class-four V-tail Beechcraft Bonanza in brown and white, was tethered outside the lone hangar. The Bonanza had a variable pitch propeller, an oil-operated device that rotated on its axis and worked like a gearshift in a car; in high pitch the angle of the blades took a bigger bite out of the air and allowed for a higher cruising speed.

It was her favorite plane. When she'd first joined the club she trained with a Cessna 150 High Wing. It took her three months to move up to the Bonanza, and that only because she had to find hours between her classes.

Jess filed a VFR flight plan and prepared herself as she always did, checking the plane by hand, a familiar thrill hastening her step and quickening her fingers. It would be an easy flight and the weather looked clear. Soon they were on the runway and the throb of the engines increased to a steady buzzing pitch as she tipped the throttle, the edges of the ground flashing and blurring and finally slipping away as the plane lumbered into the air.

Fifteen minutes later they were at a cruising speed of 150 knots. Jean Shelley sat silently by her side and watched out the window as the ground slid by far below their feet. Jess wondered again about her professor; what did she do on her off-hours? The legends continued to grow. When she'd mentioned to a fellow student that she was working with Shelley outside of class, the girl had looked at her as if she'd just sprouted an extra head.

Some said Shelley belonged to a cult. It was rumored that she had spent a month in the Himalayas, searching for spiritual peace on the back of a donkey. There were stories of strange-looking bag lunches and greenish liquid in thermoses. And yet none of these things seemed to damage her professional reputation. She remained as aloof and un-reachable as ever. It was as if her students were afraid to ask, for fear of what she might say.

They rented a car in Binghamton for the drive to Gilbertsville, passed through narrow, shadowed streets lined with two-story clapboards and Victorians with new plastic gutters and sagging front porches. Dogs napped in long grass. Swing sets moved gently in the afternoon breeze.

Jess stopped and asked directions at a gas station with two pumps and a sign that said PLEASE PUMP, THEN PAY. The girl behind the counter looked at her for a long moment and then got out a map. She ought to know better, the look said. We protect our own here. But Jess's clothes and manner of speaking seemed to convince the girl she was up to no harm.

The Voorsanger family lived in the foothills on land that looked rippled from above, crests of tree-covered forest and valleys with silver streams twisting through the depths.

On the ground the area looked tired, as if the land were molting. The leaves were changing on the trees, some of them already littering the earth and turning the shoulders of road into brown, soggy resting places.

A dirt road led through a copse to a wide yard and a farmhouse with a long, narrow barn in back. The house was slowly falling to dust. A station wagon sat listing to one side on the lawn. Pulled off the shoulder was a pickup truck with wooden slats in the bed. Mud caked the wheel wells and spattered across the fenders.

When they stepped from the car the air was crisp, clear, with a hint of smoke. Jess recognized the scent of burning leaves. Smoke curled up from behind the barn and they moved quickly in that direction.

Damn but it was cold. Jess wished she'd brought gloves. Stuffing her hands in her pockets would keep her warmer, but she knew it would not look friendly.

A dog barked from somewhere inside the barn. As they

cleared the back of the house a man came into distant view, wearing overalls, a plaid hat with earflaps, and strong leather work gloves. He was throwing leaves and branches onto a fire already piled high and smoking thickly. His breath puffed silver in his face. At the sound of the dog he stopped and brushed his hands together and then turned in their direction.

"Mr. Voorsanger? Excuse me, Mr. Voorsanger."

The man stood motionless for a moment, as if deciding something; then he strode toward them. The front of his overalls was stained a dull brown. He was a tall, older man, grim-faced, with deeply lined cheeks and chapped skin. The lines in his flesh were so deep it looked as if someone had carved them with a knife. He looked worn and serious, a man who expected everyone to work as hard as he did.

When he got near them he stopped; then, looking long and hard at Shelley, he said, "Thought we had a deal. You wasn't supposed to come back here."

"That's my fault, Mr. Voorsanger," Jess said. "I'm the one responsible for bringing her here. We've come a long way to speak to you. If we could just have a moment?"

"That ain't possible," the man said abruptly. "We don't want nothing to do with you like we said before. Nothing's changed. If that's all, I got a lot to do."

He started to turn away, then stopped again at the sound of a screen door banging, and a woman in a faded dress and apron hurrying out of the house. Jess saw his eyes change. "You're gonna catch cold, now, go on back inside," he said to her.

"Just a moment, Ed." The woman had her arms wrapped around herself. She was plump, in her sixties, with shoulder-length white hair and a soft, expressive face. Her eyes darted from face to face, fishing for something. "You here to tell us something about our girl?"

"She needs your help," Shelley said. "I wouldn't have disturbed you if we had any other choice."

"She hasn't . . . done nothing, has she?"

"We're worried about her own well-being."

The woman nodded. "That's the way it is, then. Why don't you come inside? Ed, you go on now. I'll call you when we're done." She looked at him and he didn't move; then finally he walked away, and didn't look back. They all watched him until he had returned to the fire again, and he bent and started throwing leaves and branches to the flames.

"Please forgive Ed," the woman said as the screen door cracked shut and they walked through a mudroom full of boots and hanging clothes, into a large, brightly lit kitchen. "He's watching out for me is all. And it's slaughtering time for the chickens and that always gets him in a mood."

"This is hard for you," Shelley said. "We do appreciate it."

The woman waved a pink-scrubbed hand. "I knew you'd come. I wondered what was taking so long." She smiled but her eyes were dark. She shrugged. "I suppose I figured everyone would want to know where something like that comes from. Not that I got the answer."

"Something like what, Mrs. Voorsanger?"

Cast-iron pots bubbled and hissed on the stove. Next to the stove crouched a deep metal sink, a cutting board, and the gray-pink carcasses of birds. The air smelled of bones boiled clean and white.

"Well, you know." She searched Jess's face with eyes that seemed desperate. "After all this time? You must know what she is?" She turned to Professor Shelley. There was sudden bitterness in her voice when she spoke again. "Oh yes, I remember. My Lord. Nine years and you still don't believe a word."

"I think Jess would like to hear what you have to say."

"I see." The woman stuck out her hand. "Well now, aren't you a pretty little thing? Jess, is it? Forgive my manners. I'm Cristina. Would you folks like some tea? I was just about to make a pot."

Mrs. Voorsanger showed them through the kitchen and

hallway and into a low-ceilinged room. The room had the feeling of unfinished business. The walls were bare except for a large silver cross, mounted over the old fireplace mantel. A faded plastic recliner sat in front of a folding table and large console television, and couches crouched at right angles, the patterns long since blurring into a uniform grayness that was either age or dirt, it was difficult to tell. The arms and backrests, where people rested their heads or put their feet up, were slightly darker than the rest.

The best pieces in the room were matching glass-fronted cabinets, which held what seemed like hundreds of painted trinkets: trolls, elves, fairies and dolls, toadstools, collector plates. Glass eyes winked at them from everywhere, peering over the tops of others. Little figures crouched and smiled as if holding secrets.

"My collection," Mrs. Voorsanger said with pride. "I get them through the mail. Why don't you sit down? I'll bring in a pot of tea in a minute."

They sat waiting on a couch as dust turned and drifted through the still air. "What did Mrs. Voorsanger mean in the kitchen?" Jess asked. " 'Nine years and you still don't believe a word'?"

Shelley seemed to consider whether to answer the question. She glanced to the hall, and when she spoke it was in a soft way, under her breath. "This is delicate, you understand. One of the reasons I took Sarah away was for her own good. The whole family seemed to be suffering from a delusion. I'd heard of it before, a kind of mass hysteria, but I'd never seen it firsthand."

"What sort of delusion?"

"They didn't see her as a little baby anymore. They had come to believe that Sarah was the Antichrist. Thank God they called me first. They might have killed her if I hadn't stepped in."

Dear Lord, have mercy, Jess thought. There seemed to be

nothing else to say. But it would explain a lot: the silence for all these years, the missing sections of file, the reluctance of both Wasserman and Shelley to divulge any family history. The reason Sarah's existing family had been kept a secret was as much for her benefit as anything else.

"I'll help her with that tea," Shelley said. She went to the kitchen. A moment later Mrs. Voorsanger returned carrying a tray with a kettle and two little cups with sugar and milk. Shelley brought out three mugs, poured tea into each, and handed one to Jess that read *World's Greatest Dad*.

The tea was scalding and bitter. Jess forced herself to sip it while she waited, still slightly stunned. This house and these people were familiar to her; there were many like them where she grew up. People used to hard work, simple but strong. Money was tight but there was a code to follow that would see them through. It was hard for her to believe they were the sort that would harm a child.

But it happens all the time. People lose their grip.

"Sorry it took so long. I had to see to Annie upstairs. She won't speak a word for months. . . ." The woman shrugged. She sat very straight on the other couch with her hands in her lap. "Our daughter tries, so very hard. But life just don't come easy for her. And she hasn't been the same since Sarah was born."

"Have you had her examined?"

"Of course. But they could never tell us nothing that would help. So we keep her at home."

Mrs. Voorsanger told them about Annie's difficult childhood. Never seemed to relate to any of the other children. At first they thought she was just simple, and that would have been all right; they could have handled it just fine.

"But soon it seemed it was more than that. When she went through puberty it got worse, but we managed. She was the strangest child. She'd go days without speaking, and you'd think she wasn't even there, and then out of the blue she'd come up with something no one in their right mind could know.

"Then when she was nineteen we found out she was carrying a child. We didn't know who the father was, never did. Just one day she was pregnant and she never would say a word after. Ed got crazy in the head about it. He was going to track the father down and make him own up to what he'd done. But that was just talk. Truth was it could have been any number of drifters, people who took advantage of Annie's feeblemindedness. The boys used to get her down in their basements by offering her sweets. You know she loved cake and lollipops. Then she would come home with her shirt undone and her underwear gone, crying . . . she didn't know what they done. She just didn't understand.

"Most of them boys are gone now. Moved away to Lord knows where. Good riddance."

Jess felt a strange sensation of falling into a life that had been so hard, so cruel. Closets full of arts and crafts, moldering papers in crayon, half-finished ashtrays and lopsided mugs. She wondered if Mrs. Voorsanger hated herself for the nights when she thought of putting the pillow over her daughter's face, just holding it there until she stopped moving.

Mrs. Voorsanger reached for the teapot. Her hands shook as she refilled her mug. "Did you know Annie just up and disappeared? On about her eighth month she walked right out of the house.

"We looked for her for weeks. The police came out and combed the woods, we put up posters in town. Then we get word that she'd been found, up in New Hampshire somewhere, and she's had her baby and won't we please come pick her up? There'd been some trouble, as I imagine she's told you." Mrs. Voorsanger nodded at Shelley. "The hospital where Sarah was born burned right to the ground. It was a miracle they got out alive."

"It took us a while to identify them," Shelley said. "Annie wouldn't talk to us and she had nothing on her."

"Course not," Mrs. Voorsanger said. "Didn't I tell you how she was? She couldn't earn a license and she'd lose her pocketbook if we didn't tie it onto her sleeve."

"So you went up there and brought Annie and Sarah home. . . ."

"They told us not to do it but we did. Ed was furious. But here was this little child, and she was sickly, not expected to live. We tended to her as best we could. Annie and Sarah seemed to have a bond. Annie wouldn't speak to her, half the time she wouldn't even look at her, but every once in a while she'd just get up and go to the crib as if she'd been called. She'd stand there and stare. And the strangest things would happen.

"At first I thought I must be seeing things. Curtains moving without any breeze. The mobile above her crib would start spinning for no reason at all. I remember once I came into the room in the morning and there was this ball"—she made a gesture with her hands—"a blue and gold one, Sarah's favorite. And it was floating in the air over her crib. Just hanging there like some kind of—some kind of little planet. Spinning. And Sarah was laughing.

"There were worse things too. Pictures falling off the walls. Glass breaking. Sarah would have these fits, her face getting all red, holding her breath. And she would get out of her crib before she could even walk. Once I found the crib splintered, wood snapped right in half. Ed himself couldn't have done it without a hammer.

"It got so I didn't like to go into her room, afraid what I might see.

"Then finally there was the time after her first birthday. She'd spilled something and she was screaming and throwing things. I went to punish her and it was like I hit a wall. I couldn't move. Then my throat started getting tight and I couldn't breathe. Things from the kitchen started flying through the air by themselves—knives and forks from the drawers, pots and pans off the walls. And all the time little

Sarah was just staring at me with this look in her eyes. I knew I couldn't handle her anymore. I called and they came and took Sarah away.

"She wasn't even two years old," Mrs. Voorsanger whispered. "And she could do something like that. What was going to happen when she grew up?"

Jess felt sudden memories that were too fresh. The buzzing sounds, her strange disorientation. The lights blowing in the hall. The frozen door locks. Sarah's seizure and the feeling that the air had suddenly come alive.

Mrs. Voorsanger had pulled out a package of cigarettes from somewhere and she was in the process of trying to light one. After a moment Shelley got up and took the match from her trembling fingers.

"Much obliged." Mrs. Voorsanger smiled. She leaned forward and inhaled deeply. "Sorry, do you mind? I quit a year ago. But I feel I need one."

"That's all right," Jess said. "You just go ahead if you'd like."

"What I'd like is to know why you're here," she said. "A person doesn't just come out from Boston to have a conversation. I told my story and now you tell me what she's done."

"We're trying to learn how to make her better," Shelley said. "Sometimes it helps to talk to the family."

"You did that before. It didn't help then."

"She's got a mental disorder, Mrs. Voorsanger—"

"A mental disorder? Is that what you're calling it?" Her voice had become shrill and the cigarette hadn't calmed the tremors in her hands. Mrs. Voorsanger took a drag on her cigarette and let out a great, sighing puff of smoke. Something had been stripped away from her surface, and what was revealed beneath looked raw and frightened. "You see how it's been for us. Then she's taken away and we don't hear for years. Waiting and waiting for something to happen. I knew she wasn't going to just disappear. Something like that doesn't go away."

"One of the doctors believes Sarah has a mental disability called a schizophreniform disorder," Jess said. "It's a disruption of the regular thought process, a scrambling of the mind."

"But you don't believe it, do you?"

The surprise must have been evident in her face. Mrs. Voorsanger nodded. "I got some of it, and Ed too. Sensitive to mood. But it don't take a psychic to know that's just nonsense. Any halfway intelligent person could see that."

"Her problems . . . there's a good possibility that whatever's wrong is genetic. That's why we're here."

"You want to see her mother."

Jess nodded. "If it wouldn't be too much trouble. I wouldn't disturb her, Mrs. Voorsanger, and it might mean the difference for Sarah."

Tears trembled in the old woman's eyes and white flecks dotted the corners of her mouth. A silence filled the room. "It's been hard with her. But what she has . . . it isn't hurtful. It isn't evil."

"I don't believe it is."

Mrs. Voorsanger shrugged. "Go on up, then. We'll wait for you here. You won't be gone long."

The hallway was dim and full of clutter, crumbling yellow newspapers and magazines in stacks along the walls. A set of stairs led up into gloom. The air smelled of mice, and damp things left too long without sunlight.

Jess went up the steps slowly, hearing the creak of old wood, and stopped at the first doorway, looking into a small, square room with a four-poster bed, and a floor dipping to the middle and worn white with age. She stepped carefully, half afraid the boards would give under her weight and send her tumbling through.

She paused for a moment just inside the door, listening. Something seemed to buzz softly, like voices speaking too far away to make anything out.

Annie Voorsanger sat in a rocking chair by a large, curtained window. She was bone-thin and her black hair was pulled tightly back and held with elastic. Wiry strands had escaped their bonds and stuck out around the patches of gray at her temples. As hard as it was to believe looking at her, Jess thought, she must have been barely thirty years old.

Annie's clothes were loose-fitting and made of a stretchy fabric, the kind that pulls on easily. She stared unblinking at the curtains, as if focused on something out of sight beyond the glass. Her face was absent, as if she were a puppet that had been tucked away between performances.

Standing there in the wings, Jess tried to piece things together. A silver cross on the wall, the hundreds of figurines. *Simple, God-fearing folk.* They had been given a daughter who was not whole, a terrible burden to carry. They had asked God to protect her, to give her a decent life even if she couldn't live alone, even if she couldn't tie her own shoes.

But it had gotten even worse with Annie's pregnancy. There would be another child to watch over. God had not listened. Or He had not been strong enough. Was it any wonder Mrs. Voorsanger had seen Sarah as the child of the devil? It all made terrible, perfect sense.

Then why suddenly couldn't she keep her hands from shaking or get her heart to slow down?

Easy now, girl. Those are old wives' tales, witches and demon familiars.

Jess stepped closer and said clearly and firmly, "Ms. Voorsanger? Annie?"

She might have been talking to the air. Sarah's mother was in a place very far from here.

Jess could see something of Sarah in her broad forehead, angular features, and narrow shoulders, in the way she rocked back and forth. There was an intensity to her features made all the more apparent by the slackness of the facial muscles. Annie might have been pretty once. But the life that was supposed to live here was absent.

Jess stepped closer still. The curtains drifted slightly on an unseen draft from the closed window, as below her feet the furnace kicked on.

The room seemed to tick the way a hot engine ticked in silence.

Jess willed herself to be still. "Annie? Annie Voorsanger?"

Nothing. The woman might have been wax. Jess reached out to brush a strand of hair away from her forehead, then thought better of it. "I've come to talk about your daughter."

A blink. The woman's eyes were blank walls of glass. "Do you remember her, Annie? Do you remember Sarah?"

A finger twitched. Movement in the throat; was there life here after all? "I don't want to upset you, Annie. I just wanted to talk for a minute. I've been seeing Sarah back in Boston. She's doing real good. I thought you might want to know. We're taking good care of her."

She wondered if this was cruel, if Annie felt any maternal instinct. If it were her, would she want to know any of this? Jess decided that she would.

"Sarah's been coming along lately. I'm going to make sure she gets all the care she needs, Annie. If you can hear me, I'm going to make sure your daughter's given every chance. She's ten now, she looks like you too. A pretty little girl. Can you hear me, Annie? Do you want me to tell you anything else?"

Nothing—

And suddenly the woman's head was turning, her mouth opening in a silent, wide black O that seemed to grow larger and larger. A screech began low in her throat and grew into a rusty, cracked wail, rising in pitch like the tortured sounds of cats in moonlight. It was an alien voice, one that did not belong here in the middle of a farmhouse bedroom.

The sound came from both outside and within her head. Disoriented, Jess reached out as if to touch her, drew her hand back in shock at the waves of cold air washing across the dusty space.

Annie's eyes jumped and rolled as the sound grew to fill the little room, a mindless howl of protest as her fingers plucked at something only she could see, as she rose out of her chair, and Jess stumbled backward as if pushed by a monstrous, unseen hand.

—11—

They did not speak until the car was back on the asphalt road, headed into Gilbertsville. They had left Mrs. Voorsanger tending to her daughter, Annie's screams slowly quieting as her mother spoke softly, gently in her ear. It had been nothing but a reflex, a simple release of tension, or at least that was what Jess kept telling herself; it had probably been building for a long time.

But she couldn't keep the chills from running up and down her spine, or the quivers from her muscles. It was almost as if she had experienced Annie's fear, had been inside the woman's mind.

According to her mother, that scream was the first sound that Annie Voorsanger had uttered in almost three years.

"So what do you think?"

"I don't know," Jess said. She did not want to look away from the road, but finally she did.

Shelley sat up straight in the passenger seat and was looking at her with the calm and considered gaze of a doctor. "Give me an opinion."

"She's obviously disturbed. Beyond that—she'd need to be examined more fully."

"You can see how it was," Shelley said. There was a gleam in her eyes that hadn't been there before. "Sarah was alone with them and I wanted to get her out as fast as I could. They agreed to give me full legal responsibility and the state signed the paperwork. If she ever got to the point of leaving my care I would contact them."

"Would you have?"

"I doubt it."

Take her, I told you, Mrs. Voorsanger had said, turning to Shelley as they left, as her daughter's screams had finally turned to low moans. *You remember. Care for our Sarah, I said. But never forget what she is.*

And what was that?

A child with the power of the devil in her hands.

"You think they're all insane?"

"I didn't say that. If there's one thing I've learned," Shelley said, seeming to choose her words carefully, "it's that the mind is capable of amazing feats. But what they're asking us to consider here is in the realm of parapsychology. Pseudoscience. You understand what I'm saying."

Something that was not logically possible, according to all the laws of physics. A child of the devil? Certainly not. That went far beyond anything she was willing to believe. A lapsed Catholic, she was not a particularly religious woman. Only in times of great stress had her mind searched for belief in a higher power, and afterward she always felt slightly embarrassed, a little childish, as if someone might have seen what she had been thinking and thought less of her for it.

But there had been studies, she knew, examining just this kind of phenomenon. ESP. Psychokinesis. Some of them were fairly persuasive.

And yet. All those years of training in the science of everything, an unwavering belief in everything explained, rationalized, dissected. Things like this just didn't happen, or if they did there was a logical explanation. Did she believe it now? Could she believe it?

"That wasn't the whole story," Shelley said quietly, interrupting her thoughts. "I want you to understand that we acted in the true interests of the child. There was evidence of physical abuse when we took her in. Bruises, a slight concussion. We think it was the husband, Ed, though it could have been any of them."

"They were hurting her?"

"Something happened to that little girl, and it wasn't falling out of her crib. Remember that when you're thinking about what we just heard."

They reached the airport. Jess ignored the appreciative glances from the two men who filled the plane's gas tank, their eyes moving across her face and breasts like men considering a purchase. She felt a cold dark emptiness, as if she were outside herself looking in.

Soon she was looking down the wing as they turned to circle back over a tiny toy airport and flash of hills, a ribbon of road through green trees and grass, lines of houses drawn in neat patterns and squares. From above, everything looked as if it had been fashioned by giant hands, laid out in neat geometric shapes.

The distance gained was more than physical. There were many times in her teenage years when she had felt the lift of the wings like a sudden unburdening, and the whoosh of air sounded like something chasing her from the ground.

It was still that way, she decided. No matter how hard she tried she could never outrun what was chasing her. She always had to land.

STAGE TWO

—12—

"Maria's given her notice," Dr. Wasserman said, leaning forward in his chair and fixing Jess with an intent and serious gaze.

This time his tic did not show itself, but his nervous energy remained. He picked up a sharpened pencil, tapping the eraser against the resignation letter on his desk, like someone knocking to get in. "It's a tragedy of course, a terrible setback for the hospital. Maria was one of the few I trusted to tend to our more difficult patients . . . Are you all right?" Wasserman was looking at her curiously now.

"I'm fine."

"Did you notice anything when you were here last? Did she seem unhappy, angry?"

"She did seem a little upset."

Wasserman shook his head. "It was very abrupt. I tried to speak with her. . . ."

"I'm not exactly sure what to say."

"You don't have to say anything." Wasserman leaned back in his chair, then forward again, as if trying to get comfortable. "It's unfortunate, but I cannot allow it to adversely affect what we're trying to accomplish here." He paused as if to emphasize his point. "I have to say that Sarah has made a rather remarkable improvement. She's more alert, docile, co-operative. We've adjusted her medication, but I'll admit that your visits may have had something to do with it."

"I wanted to speak to you about that, actually, Dr. Wasserman. I wondered if it might be possible to take Sarah outside the quiet room for a few hours, maybe a couple of times this week. I think she might benefit from a more interactive environment."

For the past several days Jess had been trying to decide how to approach the situation. The one conclusion she seemed able to reach was that she wanted to help Sarah at whatever the cost. It was obvious she would have to do some damage control with Wasserman after the last visit, but kissing ass had never been her thing. *Especially a slimy one.* No matter how hard she tried, she could not get an image of him out of her head: Wasserman sitting in his office after her first meeting with Sarah, grinning at her when she told him she was going to report what she considered abuse. Like a teacher with an unruly student. And now that image had grown, twisted, so that he was leering at her inside her mind, openly mocking.

Go on. Get it over with.

But Wasserman surprised her. There was something different about him today, Jess noticed, something that went beyond Maria's resignation. He seemed more uncertain, a look in his eyes as if he were uncomfortable with her presence. Had something else happened? she wondered. Whatever it was, it couldn't possibly last.

"From what Jean has told me, you visited the family and you have some idea what we were dealing with so many years ago. I hope you can understand why it was necessary to take her away from that situation. And also why confidentiality was such an issue." He sighed and shook his head. "Strange people. I can't say I ever met them in person, but I did talk to her grandmother at the time of Sarah's admittance. The experience was unsettling." He was staring out and beyond her now. "A woman with strange ideas." He focused on her suddenly and smiled, but there was no warmth held there. "Silly, isn't it? Childish superstitions."

"Dr. Wasserman, about Sarah. Now, you've brought me in here to try a different approach, you've agreed to give this a chance."

"What are you getting at?"

"Just that I need you to trust me enough to let me try to get through to her."

"Hmmm. You don't make it easy for me, now, do you? We have rules here for the health of each patient. I don't just make them up to amuse myself. Sarah was restrained for her own well-being, and for the good of the staff. We're all just lucky something terrible didn't happen."

"I'm sorry for any harm I may have done." Jess swallowed to keep the sour taste down. "I did what I thought was right under the circumstances."

Wasserman took a handkerchief from his pocket and wiped his brow. "If she weren't so improved I wouldn't even consider it. But we all want the same thing here." He studied Jess's face as if he would find the answer in her expression. Finally he folded the handkerchief into neat little squares, smoothed the creases, and stuck it back in his pocket. "I'll have her brought up to the play area. You may have an hour in there during each session together if you like. No more than that, I don't want her to backslide."

"Thank you, Dr. Wasserman."

"Just don't disappoint me."

—13—

As her routine and surroundings changed, Jess began to feel more at home in the facility.

On the days she did not have class, she would arrive each morning at nine o'clock. The janitor and handyman, Jeffrey, would let her into the playroom, then take up a quiet vigil in the corner, arms crossed. Apparently he had been told that his duties during Jess's visits would include acting as a chaperone.

Almost in spite of herself, Jess liked the man, maybe because he always seemed to be around, and he seemed to genuinely enjoy the children. He rarely interfered in any way during their sessions. In fact, she often forgot he was even there. Wasserman had insisted that he was trustworthy, if a bit slow, and that whatever they spoke of would most likely go right over his head, so she shouldn't worry about what was said around him.

All that seemed to be true. He did not talk much. After Sarah arrived in the room he would smile at her, and then make a show of studying the bookshelves or cleaning up the toys.

During the first three visits to the playroom, Sarah sat quietly at the little table near the window. They were careful to keep her visits at times when other children were not around. She was clearly more alert, her eyes following movement, but she would not speak again or get up from her chair until an orderly arrived to return her to her room.

Jess spent the hours talking about what had happened during the previous day, or problems she was having with a paper or an exam, or she sketched, or simply took notes on Sarah's condition. Sometimes she felt as if she was getting more out of the sessions than Sarah herself.

On the fourth visit, however, something had changed. Sarah was already waiting for her in the playroom, dressed in a simple blue jumpsuit and standing by the window.

Jess hardly recognized her at first. Her hair had been brushed and held away from her face with a band, and her eyes were alert and bright, though ringed with dark circles like bruises. She looked almost pretty, in a plain, backwoods sort of way.

Her breasts are starting to show, Jess thought with some surprise. *She's so young. Is it just something I hadn't noticed before?*

The air hung heavy and still. Sunlight fell in squares through the wire mesh windows onto the maroon carpet and children's toys. A large plastic tube to crawl through, and a low, yellow plastic slide. More toys lay abandoned along the edges of the room; nothing sharp or heavy, everything plastic and worn smooth from hundreds of tiny hands. Jess noticed the sink the little girl had been playing with the first time she had come here. She wondered about Dennis, the autistic young man in the baseball cap, whether he had anywhere else to go, whether they would ever release him. What had he said to her that first day? *I make her spirit glow.*

The room was empty except for the three of them, Sarah, Jess, and Jeffrey standing motionless now in the corner. Jess caught Sarah's eyes darting left and right. Her eyes settled on the man for a moment, something glowing there, a spark of emotion. Then back to Jess's face.

How long has it been? she wondered. *How long since you've been aware of something other than the padded walls of that cell, or the walls inside your own mind?*

As she stood there, dumbfounded, Sarah crossed the room without a word and took her hand. Her grip was like that of a swimmer clinging to the rocks in deep water.

She convinced Jeffrey to lock the doors and leave them alone, promising to behave herself. He told her he would be right outside, and to call if she needed anything.

"Go ahead," Jess said to the girl, after he had left. "You can do what you want in here, play with what you like. No rules."

Jess let Sarah explore the room slowly. She sat in a molded plastic chair near the door and watched without speaking as Sarah picked up a naked plastic doll, and discarded it; then a set of soft cloth blocks with pictures of animals; then a bright yellow plastic plate and spoon from a child's tea set. The girl moved easily, her visible symptoms almost completely gone.

Jess wondered again why Wasserman had had such a sudden change of heart since he had agreed to move the sessions upstairs. He had hardly spoken with her at all the past week. *Do not allow her to touch you.* From restraints and unsettling warnings to almost complete freedom. Had he simply seen an astonishing improvement and rewarded it? It seemed unlikely, considering his distrust. Why wouldn't he just assume Sarah was playing more games, waiting for another chance to escape?

Sarah climbed up the colorful little slide and sat at the top, then climbed down. She went and looked inside the plastic tunnel. She went to the window and stood on tiptoes, looking out into the sunlight for a long time. Then she turned away and picked up a picture book from the built-in shelves on the opposite wall, and carried it with her to a smaller chair near a child's table, where she sat with it in her lap, looking at the cover.

"I've got a present for you," Jess said. "Some people say ten is too old for something like this. But I say you're never too old for a friend."

She picked up the paper shopping bag she had carried in

with her and took out a worn, well-loved teddy bear. She had removed the plastic eyes and replaced them with two pieces of blue felt, but otherwise he was the same as he had always been.

"This bear's name is Connor. He was mine when I was about your age. He helped me through some hard times. He's yours now, if you want him."

For a moment she was back in the bedroom she had shared with her mother, holding on to that bear with her life, waiting for the bang of the screen door. She never knew if her mother would be alone, or would be half carried, half dragged to the couch by someone she'd met at the bar. On the worst nights, she'd crawl under her bed and sleep curled against the wall in the dust, rather than face what was outside the bedroom door.

Sarah got up and crossed the room. She took the bear and studied its face, fingering the spots that were worn smooth with age and handling. Then she returned to the table and picked up the book again. The bear sat next to her, deaf and blind.

They both sat in silence for a while. "I like it here," Sarah said without looking up.

"Didn't you come to the playroom before I started visiting you?"

"I don't remember." She nodded somberly and made brief eye contact. "I guess maybe."

Her eyes are so very dark, Jess thought. And so sad. "Does that happen a lot, are there a lot of times when you can't remember?"

"Yes," Sarah said, flipping the pages of the book in her hand. "Those are gray times."

"You were sick for a while but now you're feeling better."

"I waited for you to come back today," she said, shyly now. "I knew you would. You were nice to me. You want to help me. I can tell."

"Aren't there others here who want to help you?"

She shook her head. "They give me pills and shots and the

gray comes and swallows me up." She put the book down on the table and went over to the window again, hooking her little fingers into the wire mesh. "It's pretty out there. I like it."

"We'll go out and play on the lawn sometime."

"Can we?" Turning back excitedly.

"As soon as Dr. Wasserman says it's okay."

Immediately Sarah's smile vanished. "He'll never let us."

"Oh, I don't know about that. He might surprise you."

"No way," she said. "But I could leave if I wanted, right now. I could just . . . break out."

"Just walk out the door?"

She shrugged. "If I wanted."

"But they're locked."

"I can break them."

They were silent for a moment. Jess hesitated. "Why don't you, then? Just open those doors and walk out."

"I'm not supposed to." Sarah turned to stare at the large wooden doors. She narrowed her eyes into squints, her forehead wrinkling, mouth tightening into a pucker of concentration. Jess waited, held her breath as if breathing would break the spell. *What am I expecting? The doors to go blasting off their hinges?*

"I can't," Sarah said finally. "I told you. I'm not supposed to do that here."

"All right," Jess said. "That's fine. I'd rather have you stay here with me. Now I want to ask you something. A while back when I was here you had a seizure. Do you know what that is?"

"Not a see . . . see-sure. I only fainted. I do that sometimes when I get really upset."

"Well, maybe that's one of the reasons the doctors want to keep an eye on you. To make sure you don't hurt yourself."

"I wouldn't hurt myself. I just didn't want any more shots."

"You wanted them to leave you alone?"

"That's right." Sarah smiled. "I'm glad you came here. Before you came I didn't care about anything."

"So I make you care again. I'm happy about that."

"Are you really my friend?"

"Of course."

"And you won't tell them what we talk about? You'll keep everything a secret?"

"I promise. Is there anything you want to talk about now?"

"Sometimes I wish . . . I wish I didn't do bad things. So I wouldn't get punished. But I can't help it. It's scary sometimes when it happens."

"Like you lose control?"

"Yeah. It's like my head gets full and I . . . empty it."

"Like a bowl full of gray mush. You just dump it out."

"Yeah!" Sarah walked quickly across the carpet to stand close to her. She lowered her voice in a conspiratorial whisper. "You know what I did yesterday? When they brought me my pills? I pretended to swallow them, only I didn't. I hid 'em under my tongue. Then when they leave I spitted 'em out on the floor and ground 'em up and rubbed the paste under my bed."

"You spit them out. You didn't swallow them."

"That's right." She nodded. "That way my head doesn't get all . . . fuzzy. Only the shots, I can't do anything about those, see? That's why I hate them."

Sensing she was being tested, Jess said only, "I see. That's very clever. You're a clever little girl, grinding up your pills like that."

"No, I'm not. I'm dumb. See, I told you about it, and now you'll tell them. You won't tell, will you? You promised."

"I won't tell. Sarah, can I ask you something? Why do you think they give you the pills and the shots?"

"It's a game, see, a big mean game, they're trying to get something from me and I won't let them have it. And they don't really want it anyway because they're scared."

"Do you know what this thing is?"

"I can't tell you. It's a secret."

"Hmmm. I like secrets. Maybe you'll share yours with me sometime."

"You wouldn't like this secret. And anyway, maybe you're just part of the game. Maybe you're on their side and it's all a big trick. You're gonna put me in the bad room!"

"No, Sarah, I would never do that. I would never make you do something you don't want to do, or put you someplace you don't want to be. We're friends, remember?"

But Sarah wasn't listening. "They want to get rid of me. They're trying to kill me." She walked to the table and picked up her bear, clutching it to her chest. Then she went back to the window.

"I'm going to break out of here soon," she said, looking into the sunshine. She was trembling. "Then they all better watch out. Oh boy, they better."

—14—

The Fingertip Bar and Grill is located just outside of downtown, directly off the C subway line. Barely visible from the street, unmarked and "long and thin as the tip of a finger," it is a favorite of local students looking for someplace a little off the beaten path. Road signs interspersed with the grilles of classic cars decorate the walls like some kind of automotive graveyard. A traffic light mounted over the door flashes green, yellow, and red.

Saturday evening, Jess stepped though into that smoky, alien place, and paused to let her eyes adjust, searching for Charlie. A moment later she spotted the smiling, chocolate-brown face moving toward her from the bar, as jazz swelled and throbbed from somewhere in back. The bar was narrow and deep; drunk students would sometimes confess to getting lost in the depths, and the rumor was that on particular dark nights you could just keep going, that the bar never ended.

"Hey there, girlfriend. Thought you might be thinking about standing me up."

"Never, Charlie. I haven't been out on the town in a while. I forgot how long it takes to get anywhere."

The woman appeared concerned, her powerful features managing to seem exotic and warm at the same time. "You look like death. Come on over here and tell me all about it. We'll get some food into you and you'll feel better. It's not man trouble, is it?"

Jess shook her head and smiled. She followed the swish of Charlie's silk skirt to a small booth against the wall, amazed as always how the crowd seemed to part for her as if by magic. Charlie was a large woman, but lithe and quick on her feet. At twenty-seven, she had a beauty that transcended her size, a breathtaking nobility that others often found intimidating. But she could be refreshingly blunt. They had met in a shared lab class a year earlier, and since then had become fast friends. Jess admired the way nothing ever seemed to get to Charlie.

"If it's not a man," the woman continued, after they settled into the booth and ordered a plate of nachos and two Blue Moon beers from the tap, "then it must be family. I can't think of anything else that would make a girl look the way you do."

Jess wondered how on earth to respond. Normally she was fiercely independent, proud of her ability to thrive on her own. But since she'd returned from Gilbertsville, her evenings had been endless and too quiet. Something fundamental to her own nature had been changed. She felt like a caterpillar that had crawled into a cocoon—though she had no idea what kind of shape she would find herself in when the metamorphosis was over.

She was pleased with the sudden progress Sarah had been making. The girl seemed to be getting comfortable with her and opening up. They were bonding. And she and Shelley had been meeting regularly for coffee to discuss the case. But she was still uncertain about the experience of meeting Sarah's family, and what it all meant. The image of Annie Voorsanger standing up in that dusty, forgotten room, the sound she had made, the sudden, wild look in her eyes, remained with Jess no matter how hard she tried to shake it.

And she was lonely. Late nights were the worst—waking

up in the emptiness of her apartment, Otto gone from his customary spot at the foot of her bed. That was when she had the strongest feeling that some basic part of her had been shaken, some simple truth exposed. Her mind seemed to be humming, voices muttering at a distance too far to be overheard. It was then, and only then, that she would allow herself the longing for another human being, anyone who could fill these moments in time with something other than ghosts.

Finally this afternoon she had decided to follow up on something else that had been bothering her. Now she wished she hadn't. Not until tonight had she been so desperately bewildered, so incapable of discovering her true feelings.

"I've been thinking about my brother a lot lately," Jess said. "The way he died."

Charlie knew about her brother. She knew about the agreement with Professor Shelley and the sessions with Sarah. Charlie knew more about Jess Chambers's life than most people. "I think you've got an angry spirit," Charlie said. Her eyes sparkled.

"What?"

"An urban myth, you might call it. Anyone you've done harm to will come back to haunt you. The gangs believe it. They're careful about who they shoot. Only," she said, leaning forward and fixing Jess with those deeply black, shining eyes, "you didn't harm anyone, least of all your brother. So that's all in your head. Just like it is with those Latin Kings."

"I don't follow."

"Simple psychology," Charlie explained patiently, like mother to child. "Come on, it's an established phenomenon. A gang member who kills without proper justification decides he's cursed. He'll be dead within a year. Why? Not because he's pursued by the souls he's killed, because he takes risks, he exposes himself, he has a guilty conscience. He makes it happen."

"Charlie—"

The woman shook her head. Jewelry tinkled somewhere. "Dear Lord, girl, let yourself go for a bit. I've never seen anyone so wound up. Sometimes I wonder if you're gonna just shoot off right through the ceiling."

The drinks came. Jess let the cold beer wash down her throat, listening to the thump of the music, the loud chatter of voices. She had spent yet another hour with Sarah just that afternoon, going over what little schooling she had received. She had to search hard for any trace of mental illness; Sarah spoke with an intelligence and sophistication Jess would not have believed if she hadn't been there herself.

And then she had gone home to make the telephone call. And that call had rattled her more than she believed possible. Only now, sitting here in the smoky confines of a bar filled with people, did she begin to relax.

"So what you're doing, is trying to calm the dead." Charlie glanced at a table to their right, then back again, the twinkle in her eyes. "What you need is a good, hard fucking."

"Charlie . . ."

"I mean it. It would clear your head. That man over there seems willing to oblige."

Jess glanced at the table, saw the man staring at her and smiling slightly, hunched and broad through the shoulders, heavy jaw and brow.

"No, thanks," she said. "I prefer my own species."

"Your prerogative. But let me ask you. Do you ever wonder why you surround yourself with women?" Charlie nodded. "Me, for example. Professor Shelley. All your other friends." She paused for dramatic effect. "You're afraid."

"Of what?"

"Letting someone in, and I mean really inside, where you can't hide things the way you normally do. The kind of vulnerability that comes from sleeping naked with another human being. They see all your flaws, pudgy thighs, puckered cheeks, moles and freckles and bad breath in the morning. It's just a thought."

"Let's get up off the couch, shall we?"

"Mmm-hmmm. Don't say I didn't warn you."

"Let me ask you something. Can you think of any reason why a woman would suddenly quit a good job where she seemed to be respected and competent?"

"I can think of many reasons. Her boss is a creep. She's found a better job. She won the lottery."

"But she refuses to give an explanation. One day she's there, the next she's not."

"Again, her boss is a creep. Coming on to her or something similar."

Jess tried to imagine Dr. Wasserman putting his arm around Maria's wide shoulders, leaning close to whisper in her ear. The image was laughable. "I don't know."

"Are we talking about someone at that place you've been spending so much time at, when you should have been spending it with me?"

"The woman who worked with the difficult patients. She gave her letter of resignation. And I keep thinking maybe it's connected, the way she looked, the way she acted around Sarah, and Sarah's sudden improvement—"

"That's your problem," Charlie announced, "you think too much." She drained her glass with a tip of her wrist, somehow making it look dainty and sophisticated, and announced, "Tonight is not a thinking night. Am I getting through to you?"

"I called her," Jess said absently, her mind continuing to play over the earlier conversation in a way she hadn't allowed it to before. Maria's voice over the phone line, her accent so difficult to understand, but the emotion unmistakable. "Swiped the number off her letter on Wasserman's desk. You know what she said?"

"I can't imagine."

"That Sarah was 'inside her head.' That she was *embrujado*. I looked it up, it means—"

"Haunted," Charlie said. "And from what you've told me about this poor girl, I'd agree. You're not dealing with some suburban teenager with adjustment problems. This is a girl who probably doesn't even remember what the outside world looks like."

"That's what I don't understand."

"Is that all?"

"Something's not right here, Charlie. We've got a hospital director who until recently acted like he had a serial killer in his basement instead of a ten-year-old girl. We've got a file on said girl that reads like a medical textbook on diagnostic procedures, except when it comes right down to diagnosing anything. We've got a family that for all intents and purposes didn't exist a week or so ago, insisting that their granddaughter is the spawn of the devil—"

"Let's cut to the chase here, Miss Chambers. What you're saying is you've discovered a case for the *X-Files*. I'll be Scully to your Mulder. Have you seen the girl's head spin around? Any speaking in tongues? Projectile vomiting?"

"You're impossible."

"Honey." Charlie leaned across the table and touched Jess's arm. "I am telling you to let it go. Get away for a while and fly to Florida. Take a break and clear your head. We'll all be here when you get back."

"I can't leave now."

"You should. You're getting this confused with your feelings for your brother, everything that happened to you when you were young. You're like a greyhound after that rabbit. But even greyhounds take a few minutes to lie down in the sun."

"She's stopped swallowing her medication, Charlie. I can't afford to take a few minutes. I have to decide whether I break her confidence, or say nothing and risk a setback in her treatment."

"How do you feel? What does your heart tell you to do?"

"That's just it. How can I know when I can't even decide if she's unstable or not?"

They sat and drank for a while in silence. The music

throbbed like a heartbeat. Charlie closed her eyes and moved with it. Then she opened her eyes and said, "Have you thought about talking to someone? I mean, if you insist on playing this silly game of yours?"

"A therapist?"

"Someone who specializes in the sort of thing you mean. Not a spiritualist or medium, but a *gen-u-wine* scientist. Double-blind experiments, the works. Very aboveboard. There's a group right outside of Boston related to the Rhine group in, where is it, Carolina? I only mention it because I happen to be friends with someone who works for them."

"Oh, I don't know, Charlie," Jess said tiredly. "Maybe you're right. I am just trying too hard to make up for something. My brother, maybe."

"Well, honey." Charlie touched her hand gently again. "That might be true. But you ever need that number, you let me know."

—15—

It's possible to help this girl, Jess thought as she made her way back to her apartment in the early morning hours, the sounds and smells of the bar still with her like ghosts in her clothes. *Really make a difference. But the first thing we must accept is that the traditional analytical approach may not work. A good psychologist tries to unlock every door, using any key available.*

And if those keys don't fit, you look for the ones that you aren't even sure exist.

Sitting down at her desk, her head still pleasantly thumping from the beer, she opened up her MacBook and jotted down everything she could think of relating to her feelings about this case. She stared at the words floating on the glowing screen, typed in a few others. There was more to add but she didn't know where it fit. Wasserman and Shelley and their places in all this. Mrs. Voorsanger's strange description of her granddaughter's first year of life. Maria suddenly quitting. And those . . . incidents she could not seem to shake. The way she had felt the first time she had visited Sarah. And the second visit, the shattering light-bulbs, the way the air crackled with a presence unseen but definitely there.

One thing was certain; regardless of the truth surrounding Sarah's supposed paranormal abilities, Sarah herself believed them. Her frustration after her attempt to open the locked playroom doors was proof of that.

The question remained; should she tell Wasserman Sarah had stopped taking her pills?

For most of the following Monday, Jess's thoughts were occupied with more mundane things. Lately she had allowed her grades to slip, something she had never done before, and she concentrated on getting to class on time and taking good notes. Her class with Professor Shelley did not meet until Thursday, for which Jess breathed a sigh of relief. She did not know what she would say to the woman yet. Lately Professor Shelley had seemed preoccupied. Perhaps the visit with Sarah's family had upset her more than she let on.

After her last class ended, Jess made a quick sandwich and grabbed her laptop and book bag. She walked the three blocks to the Brookline Library through an early evening chill, seeing the imposing stone and brick building as if for the first time, though she had been there many evenings in the past. Now it seemed to dig itself into the hill, or rather rise up out of it like some Gothic stone castle, and she wondered why she hadn't seen it that way before.

Inside it was warm and bright. Recent renovations had put the sparkle back into a space that had grown tired and worn. At the reference desk she asked for a stack pass, and slipped down into the lower level, where she stashed her bag in one of the cubicles nestled beyond rows of musty books. It was a good place to sit and think, suspended over the back alley and silent as a tomb. The light in the stacks was dim and thick with dust, but the cubicles were made of a much friendlier wood, and built into the side of the building like bubbles in a submarine.

She left her book bag in the cubicle and returned to the main floor. Computer monitors lined the walls beyond the information desk. She found a free one and began a search. Soon she had gathered an impressive pile of books, which she stacked on the cubicle desk. She began to scan through them, starting with the earlier titles. Some were based upon specific cases of hauntings and "expert mentalists," and those she set aside; others were filled with technical experiments on dice throwing and remote viewing techniques.

A full hour later, she had begun to get discouraged. The books were filled with outdated experiments and philosophical ramblings. Then she picked up a book called *The Reach of the Mind*, and the name on the cover made her pause. J. B. Rhine. At the Fingertip, Charlie had mentioned the Rhine group. Curious, she opened to the beginning of the book, and skimmed down the first few pages. *More philosophical bullshit.* Jess flipped farther into the book. There she found something that gave her pause.

> The effects of narcotic and stimulant drugs (on ESP and PK) are like those produced on higher mental activities. Large doses of narcotic drugs force performance in tests to drop practically to the chance level . . . the drugs do not, on the other hand, nearly so quickly or so seriously affect the efficiency of the sensorimotor functions.

Sarah's comment about her head being "fuzzy," the "gray days" that came upon her and blanked out her memory. A symptom of drug therapy, especially the heavy one employed by the Wasserman Facility. She remembered how Sarah had blacked out during their second visit, how Maria had moved so quickly to administer the injection. How the big woman's hands had trembled as she held the syringe up to the light and bent to the unconscious girl's arm.

A simple sedative to calm the heart, Jess had assumed at the time. But now she wondered whether Maria had had more sinister intentions. The woman was obviously superstitious. It would not be too large a stretch to imagine that she had come across this passage in Rhine's book, or something similar, and, fearful of whatever imagined threat she believed

Sarah held for her, decided to take matters into her own hands.

She read on, through descriptions of tests on students and supposed "sensitives," through the piles of data and the secondhand accounts of paranormal events. The book seemed desperate to prove something, but in the end she found nothing that convinced her of the existence of anything other than coincidence. And yet something was beginning to form in her mind, the raw substance of a possible answer. She flipped through another of the books about alleged poltergeist phenomenan and psychokinesis, looking for something she had read earlier.

Finally she found it, a passage about a young woman named Esther Cox who had lived at the turn of the century. Esther became the center of attention when a supposed poltergeist began terrorizing her family's home. Loud banging noises occurred at all hours. Boxes flew around the rooms. Water boiled in the girl's presence. Fires burned all over the house, resisting efforts to put them out. Esther's sister had a boyfriend, and it was rumored that this boyfriend had tried to rape Esther one night, and the strange activity had begun at that point. A best-selling book on the subject was written by a man named Walter Hubbell.

Esther was described as a plain and psychoneurotic girl under eighteen years of age. She lived at home in poverty, sharing a bed with her sister. A girl who had already exhibited signs of mental instability; a rape or attempted rape could likely have pushed her over into a full-blown psychosis. She might have caused the pranks herself, Jess thought, and not even been consciously aware of it. In fact it was very likely. Most supposed poltergeists were connected with adolescents in some way. Strange events in "haunted" houses always seemed to occur when the teenage son or daughter was around, and disappear when they left.

Put it together with what we know to be true. There was a biological theory, lately advanced, that introduced the idea of gradations of mental illness. Many researchers believed that a group of genes were responsible for the majority of mental diseases such as schizophrenia, and that it was possible to inherit one or several of these genes without becoming a full-blown schizophrenic. This person would become a "schizotypal personality," and would exhibit a milder form of the disease. Such a person would be suspicious of others, prefer isolation to groups, would be preoccupied with unusual ideas such as UFOs or belief in the paranormal.

And anyone or anything that encouraged those beliefs would only serve to reinforce them.

Which led her back to Sarah. A girl who had very likely inherited one or more of the "schizophrenic genes" from her mother. A girl with developmental problems, regressed to an earlier childhood stage, experiencing delusions of grandeur, omnipotence, a powerful need to have control over herself and her world. At such a young age, she had been taken away from an abusive family. Isolated. Poked and prodded. And naturally those rumors, the stories her family had told, would persist. You couldn't stop things like that, even in a medical environment. All it would take were a couple of superstitious orderlies. . . .

Convinced that she had finally found what she was looking for, Jess packed up her bag and returned the books to the reference room to be reshelved. Sarah was not a true schizophrenic, of that she was sure. She had not been misdiagnosed, exactly; it was simply a matter of degree. The girl could have a milder form of the illness, which would become more or less severe depending on the circumstances, hence her remarkably quick "recovery." She would be suspicious of people trying to help her, exhibit odd behavior, even fits. At the same time she would seek out attention, crave acceptance. She would believe herself to be gifted, even psychic, and she would perpetrate any sort of prank or trick to prove it to others.

As she walked quickly through the deepening twilight,

leaves crunching under her feet, Jess tried to imagine that Wasserman would not have come to the same conclusion. Impossible. He was an expert in the field; surely he would be familiar with the latest theories.

Then why had he treated Sarah so roughly? Why had he kept her from the proper treatment for this type of disorder? Why had he isolated her, put her in restraints, treated her so heavily with drugs? And most of all, why had he brought in a young graduate student and risked exposing all the mistakes he had made?

But those were questions for another time. Right now Jess felt as if some great crisis had been turned away, an abyss looked into and then avoided. She would concentrate now on continuing to gain Sarah's confidence and they would see from there.

First thing tomorrow.

—16—

The private helicopter landed at Downtown Manhattan Heliport (DMH) at 6:43 p.m. An attendant scurried free and opened the passenger door, and then held his hand out to assist those disembarking. A white-haired man and a blonde woman in business attire climbed off the fold-down steps and nodded to the attendant. They looked like wealthy middle-aged lovers on a date, but they were not. Far from it.

The man, who carried an attaché case and wore a very expensive blue silk suit and red tie, slipped the attendant a bill while the woman hurried inside, clutching her jacket around her shoulders. The evening air was chilly with a breeze coming off the water. The attendant was pleased when he had the chance to look down at his hand; the bill was a fifty. He hurried after them, to see if there was anything else he could do.

The DMH is located on Manhattan's East River, and provides its users with breathtaking views of the New York and New Jersey skylines. The heliport's main terminal contains an operations control center, pilot and VIP lounges, and a passenger waiting area. Because of its proximity to Wall Street, it is often used to transport documents for investment and law firms and large banks, and the occasional high-powered business meeting is held in a pair of private rooms above the lounge, overlooking the water.

The man's name was Steven Berger, and the woman was Philippa Cruz. Berger, as the head of business development for Helix Pharmaceuticals, was the fund-raiser, the salesman. Cruz was the brains. At the tender age of forty-two, she was the lead investigator and head of the project team, with an M.D. from Harvard Medical and a Ph.D. in biology from Duke. But she did not fit the stereotype of a geeky researcher; today she wore a pin-striped Brooks Brothers power suit, impeccably tailored, with clean lines and the timeless look of quality. Her straw-colored hair was cropped short and groomed in a rake-fingered, mussed style.

Berger might have been accused of trying a bit too hard to project money and importance. To Cruz, it was effortless.

They arrived at one of the private function rooms and were shown inside, the first of their party to appear. Berger and Cruz had met others here on several different occasions, so they were familiar with the layout. This time, a table had been set for six, though there would be only two other guests.

"Something smells delicious," Cruz said. The air held the scent of curry and wine. She removed her jacket and draped it over one of the mission-style wooden chairs, and then drifted over to the wide stretch of windows and stood next to one of three lush, potted Boston ferns. Lights blinked on in the deepening dusk. It was a hauntingly lonely, breathtaking scene, one that she rarely had the time to appreciate properly. She rubbed at the goose bumps on her arms.

A waiter knocked on the door and then entered, asking them what they would like for drinks. Berger ordered a Bombay, while Cruz ordered a Manhattan. "How appropriate," Berger said when the waiter had gone. Cruz smiled.

"Only one," she said. "I want to make sure we remain focused. This promises to be an interesting evening."

Steven Berger placed his attaché case on the table. He removed his wire-rimmed spectacles and rubbed at the indentations in his nose, then set them back again. "An interesting evening," he said quietly, almost to himself. And then, "You really think we've got things moving in the right direction again, eh?"

"I'm sure of it."

"So you can assure all of us that there won't be any more . . . accidents?"

Instead of answering immediately, the blonde woman turned and stared back out at the water. "Did you know that when a person breaks his neck," she said finally, "the severed nerves don't actually die? They form this scab called a growth cone, and that cone pushes ahead like a blind man trying to find his way in the dark, fumbling around with these tiny strands called philipodia. Eventually these strands come up against a barrier and just stop. They're at a dead end, and so it goes. Our friend remains in a wheelchair, drooling across his lap. But the *potential* is always there, waiting to be tapped."

"So how do scientists help give the philipodia a helping hand?"

"They've recently discovered that the key is very likely a group of proteins called EPH."

"Always proteins," Berger muttered. "You'd think we could just eat a steak dinner and be done with it."

Cruz didn't seem to notice him as she continued. "Different EPH proteins either attract or repel nerve strands, and in that way they help guide the philipodia along. So what if you could get rid of the particular version of EPH protein that repels or blocks nerves? Well, scientists at Melbourne have tried it, and guess what? Mice with broken backs are jumping up and down five weeks later. Nerves have completely regrown. It's a miracle."

"Yes, yes," Berger said. "A miracle indeed!" He often got caught up in the woman's enthusiasm in spite of himself; she was breathtaking in her passion for science and the infinite possibility of mankind.

"Jesus healed the sick, walked on water, rose from the

dead," she said, turning back with her sharp predator's eyes gleaming. "At the same time, a giant ball of flame rose each day in the east, and then fell again in the west. Who's to say which is the more significant event? Why is one considered miraculous, the other accepted as scientific just because we understand the mechanics of it? My point is, it's possible to perform many so-called miracles, if we understand the mechanism of action."

"Ah, I see. But some might say that the intentions of God are not for man to discover these things. That we are going down a path that can only mean our ruin."

"Small minds," Cruz said.

Berger chuckled. "Perhaps they possess too much of the bad sort of EPH. You're not going to get too philosophical with our guests when they arrive? I don't think my heart can take the suspense."

A knock on the door and the drinks were brought in on a silver tray, along with bread and a bottle of chilled wine.

They held their tongues for the waiter to leave. "No," Cruz said, after the door had closed with a soft click. "I'll try to keep it as straightforward as possible. Small minds, as you say."

"Let me ask this once more. If we begin the testing again, you'll have total control?"

"This is the tightest molecule we've ever designed. Think of it like a thermostat, giving us the ability to dial things up from zero to a hundred, and back down again. It's an excellent candidate. I believe we're starting some extensive testing tonight, perhaps even as we speak."

"That's good enough for me," Berger said. "Now, the key elements here are to make them understand what we've discovered, the data we already have, and the breakthrough we've experienced recently. I want them to see the potential. So don't get preachy. These people are simply interested in the bottom line."

"You're the expert in that," Cruz said. She picked up a

small loaf of dark bread and ripped it in half, dipping a chunk into a bowl of garlic oil. The smell was delicious. She hadn't eaten since that morning, and now she attacked the bread like piranha in blood-threaded water.

A few minutes later the others in the party arrived; first an older man with Nordic features and a slight limp, then an Asian carrying a small, wrapped gift, which he handed to Berger with a nod and a smart bow. They all made small talk while the two waiters took drink orders, and then they sat down for dinner.

The meal began with a mesclun salad with grilled fruit and edible flowers, and then a small pumpkin-curry soup, followed by a very rare filet served with a garlic butter sauce, asparagus almondine and wild rice, and finally a black plum sorbet. The party ate with enthusiasm, remarking on the weather in this part of the country, and the situation in the Middle East, and the state of airline travel. The waiters came and went, bringing fresh drinks.

Finally the meal was complete. "Please excuse me," Berger said to the others.

He got up and went to the waiter at the door. "We're about to engage in something more confidential now," he said. "Please, do not disturb us until I call you. And lock the door."

After the waiter had left, Berger went to his attaché case and removed a small black device. He scanned the table and chair legs, moving carefully around the personal spaces of his guests, then went to the window and traced a pattern around the edges. Finally he examined the potted plants, and the door frame.

"Very good," he said, and put the device back in his case and removed a small silver DVD player. "Can't be too cautious. You have the nondisclosures I faxed you? Excellent. Let's begin, then. I'd like to show you something very exciting."

For the next five minutes the four were glued to the DVD

player's seven-inch screen. Nobody said a word; the events playing across the liquid crystal display were words enough for anyone.

After it was done, the Nordic-featured man said, "It could have been faked."

"I assure you, it's absolutely authentic," Berger said. He was unable to keep the small smile off his face. "You've seen some of the initial data in the encrypted files I sent you, but we've kept most of the details back for security purposes. Here's another copy with a bit more revealing information."

He pulled photocopies out of his attaché case and handed them to the two men. "Most of the technical readings and results are there, as well as the history of the company. As you can see, we've been at this for quite some time. We have a real expertise in small-molecule design and cell-signaling. It's taken us years, but we feel that we finally have a viable candidate in this particular case to proceed with confidence."

He glanced at Cruz. This was getting beyond his own comfort zone. It was time for the technical side of the house to take over.

She stepped in smoothly. "The building blocks of life," Cruz said. "DNA gives way to genes, genes give way to proteins. Proteins are the worker bees, you see. To unlock the greatest secrets of mankind, all we have to do is figure out how and why these proteins do their jobs. Then we can decide how we can make them work for us." She tapped a graphic in the file the Asian man held open in his hands. "Our research is focused on discovering and developing these small-molecule drugs my colleague has referred to, those that can regulate cell-signaling and gene expression. But it's not a simple thing to do. First, you need to understand how the human machine is built. As you probably know, the most critical processes of life—metabolism, cell growth and differentiation, gene transcription—are handled by signals carried from the cell surface to the nucleus through a system of molecular pathways. Are we okay so far?"

The two men nodded at her.

"Good. We understand quite a bit about some of these genes' proteins and pathways, but others are still a mystery. In fact, most of the genes in the human DNA strand do not seem to serve any apparent purpose at all. We call them dormant or junk. Some scientists believe that they function in a way we don't yet understand, or they served an important purpose somewhere back along the evolutionary chain but are now simply residual, the equivalent of male nipples.

"Then, of course, there are the subtle differences that make us unique from each other. These are the genes that belong to only you"—she nodded at the Nordic man—"or you." She smiled warmly at the Asian, who seemed to be drifting. "Or more specifically, to your family. There aren't many that are different. We're all pretty much the same animal."

Berger made a subtle cutting motion with his hand. "This is all very interesting," he said. "Would you talk a bit, please, about the opportunity we're offering?"

"Almost there, thanks. I was about to tell these gentlemen about the psi gene."

A silence descended upon the group. "Please go on," the Asian man said. Now she had his attention. Suddenly she had everyone's attention.

"We've discovered a particular subject—the subject you just viewed on that video—who was born with a rather remarkable gene. This gene, which is either dormant or does not exist at all in most people, actually produces a protein, which acts in a particular way, on a particular cellular path. This mechanism of action has to do with the transfer of heat at a microscopic level, and it allows the subject to influence her natural environment physically through thought."

"Amazing," the Nordic man said. "The psi gene, you say?"

"From the word *psychic*. Psi encompasses a lot of different things—telepathy, clairvoyance, psychic healing, precognition, to name only a few. But what we're concerned with here is what's commonly called psychokinesis—"

"I'm not sure I understand," the Asian man interrupted. "What exactly are you offering us?"

Berger motioned for Cruz to sit. "The investment opportunity of a lifetime," he said. "The possibilities here are limitless—literally as far as your imagination can reach. Government and military applications, certainly. But medical, corporate, and even nonprofit entities could benefit tremendously. This is, quite literally, a revolution waiting to happen. But to get there, we're going to need more capital. Research and development is tremendously expensive, as you both know."

He took out another two packets from his case and handed them to the men across the table. "This will explain in greater detail what we're going to do, and what we need from you. I'll talk about that in a moment. But first, I want to show you one more video clip. This one is a little more . . . impressive. I think it will give you a good idea why we're so excited about this opportunity."

Steven Berger flipped open the little screen once again. The small party gathered around it to watch.

This was Berger's favorite part. He kept stealing glances at the two men, at their faces, full of wonder, awe, and disbelief. Even Cruz was riveted, though she'd seen it many times before.

The scene played out across the little screen. Nobody spoke, moved, even breathed until it was over.

After another five minutes the screen went black. They sat back in silence for a long moment.

"Take this information back to your people," Berger said quietly. He handed both of them a Helix business card with his name and private contact information across the front.

"We'll be entertaining partnership offers from as many as seven major players." He let the pause go just long enough, waited for the beat. "I'll begin the bidding at five hundred million."

Across the table, Cruz tore off a fresh piece of bread. Smiling to herself in satisfaction, she bit into it with a vengeance.

—17—

Sarah awoke with a scream lodged thickly in her throat. It had come again, the dream that used to plague her night after night. The howling machines with metal tubes and wires swarming across her face, webbing pinning her down, the smell of metal and burning flesh. Needles dripping clear fluid. The screams. Darkness, and she was lost! It was hot, so hot she was gasping for air, and she knew she had brought this upon herself, that she was the cause of the burning.

Dream images faded into a pattern of pink, swirling dots. She swallowed and blinked, fighting against the fear that rose up inside, fighting against her own mind. *I know where I am. I'm in my room. Not in the bad place.*

But how could she know for sure? The room was pitch-black when she slept. They had kept it that way on purpose to punish her at first, and as she slid deeper into her own private darkness they hadn't bothered to change things. Not that it would have mattered then.

But her world had shifted now with all the swiftness of a flash flood. She thought of the woman who had been coming to see her, and it gave her heart a forgotten surge of hope. She allowed herself a moment to wonder what it might be like to be normal. But what did that really mean?

To be like the others she used to know before the gray fog came, Aimee who talked to herself and Shawn who picked his hands until he bled?

No. They were different too.

She squeezed her eyes shut tight and waited for the voices, but they did not come. Her mind had been unusually clear lately; she could function without the fog creeping up on her, and that made her feel uneasy. She was not used to such freedom, such long stretches where she had nothing but her own thoughts as entertainment. Maybe she should start taking the pills again? What would they do to her? Would they stop having to give her the shots? Would she have to go back to the bad place?

She heard a sudden noise. Something shifted nearby. Memories floated to the surface and she was transported to another time, another place. Disorientation. Nothingness. Whispers of words too faint to understand. Smoke touched her face, heat singed her skin.

Her arms and legs were held down. She stretched out her finger and fumbled for something, anything to tell her she was still alive. Somewhere in the distance she thought she could hear screaming again. Terror flooded her body and for a single moment she thought she might lose control.

When the lights flickered on she was blinded and hopelessly disoriented. The flashback had been vivid and had almost put her over the edge. She blinked as shapes swam into focus, and held on with all her might, biting back her scream.

"You're awake," the doctor said. She flinched. He was standing just inside the door. "Good. It's time we talked this out. Long past time, actually." He bent to undo the straps on her wrists, hesitated. "There are three men right outside the door. You'll behave?"

She nodded. His skin was slick with sweat. She had never seen him with a single hair out of place until now, and it disturbed her more than his expression.

She studied him as her pounding heart shook her thin frame. His face had changed for her, and something deep inside had broken because of it. His face, a source of warmth and comfort for so long, was now cold and the light had gone from his eyes.

She reminded herself once again that she was the cause of the change. She had been very bad. She had done something so terrible, so unforgivable, that it could never be taken back. Never.

The straps fell away, and she sat up on her narrow mattress. This room had a dresser in it, and a lamp on a table by the bed, but the walls were bare. An upholstered chair faced her. There was a window across the room, with a shade pulled down and taped tightly to the window trim, to keep any light from entering. She knew there were heavy bars on the other side.

Dr. Evan Wasserman sat down in the chair across from her and crossed his legs, being careful to keep the creases in his pant legs straight. He smoothed the fabric with his palms and folded his hands in his lap. He patted down his hair with one hand. Then he looked at her, his gaze searching her features. His eye twitched. She could not tell whether he was satisfied with what he found there.

"Modern Catholic thought holds that each person is sacred," the doctor said. "The church believes in the inherent dignity of the human form. Do you know why that is?" He did not wait for her to respond. "The idea is grounded in the belief that man is made from the image of God. The human form is the clearest and most obvious example of God living among us."

He pulled out a white napkin from his pants pocket and dabbed at his face. "It's rather hot in here. We should have lowered the temperature. But this is an old building, you see, and the controls are not very accurate. If one were to lower the thermostat here, the lower levels would become uncomfortably cool. Do you know why I mentioned God? This is important. I want you to listen carefully." He leaned forward in his chair, hands in his lap again. He twisted the napkin as he spoke. "I mention these things because I want you to understand what you've done. By murdering another person you are, in essence, killing a piece of God himself. You are committing a mortal sin, one that cannot be undone. And, perhaps worst of all, by taking another person's life you are acting as God. That. Can. Not. Happen." He twisted until something ripped. His eye twitched at her. "You have something inside you that can be dangerous. That part you must keep tightly bound. The rest are parlor tricks. You must always remember that."

She was trembling. Wetness streaked her face, and she wiped at the snot running from her nose. A single, choked sob escaped her lungs. "I didn't mean . . . to . . . to . . ."

"But you did. You lost control and two people died. You forgot that whatever God has cursed you with, you are no different than anyone else on this earth. No different. You live, you breathe, you shit and piss, and you are here because someone else has willed it to be. I have willed it to be!" He stood up abruptly, knocking the chair backward against the wall. "This, above all, you must remember. *I am in charge.* I decide what you do and when you do it. You will not shut me out anymore."

He was breathing heavily now, and his eye twitched violently. She stared at him through swimming tears, as the light refracted into a multitude of colors and blurred his features. She wanted him to go away now, *please, leave me alone.*

Wasserman took a step closer. "I say all this because we will resume our lessons tonight."

"No!"

"You must learn control. The world demands it. *God* demands it."

"I won't do it! You can't make me!"

The lightbulb in the lamp blazed brightly for a moment, popped, and went dark.

Wasserman glanced over at the lamp, and at the cord that had been unplugged from the wall since he came in. He stared down at the little girl on the bed, and chose his next words very carefully. "Your new friend. You like her, don't you? I want you to understand something. She comes under my supervision, and only as long as I say so. Would you like to continue her visits?" He waited for her nod. "If you don't cooperate, she can never return to this place. You will be alone. We will lock you away downstairs, and you will never see the light of day again. You will never be allowed to see anyone *except for me and the person who delivers your medication.* If you do not learn to control yourself, you are not fit to rejoin the rest of the human race. The risk is too great. This is why we must continue, tonight."

Fear bloomed deep within as her emotions battled each other. Above all, she did not want to return to the Room. She did not want the needle. Did not want to begin all over again. What if she could not hold herself in, what if it happened again? She could not bear to think of that, the smell of the burning, the screams.

But to refuse would mean the end of all hope.

"You have the opportunity to make amends," Wasserman whispered, leaning over her. "You have taken lives, but now you have the chance to save one."

For a moment, his face was full of naked fear. She realized that this part of what he was saying was very important to him, as important as life and death. She didn't know why, but she thought that maybe she had found something else she could use.

Finally, she nodded. Wasserman smiled, reached out as if to pat her head, then thought better of it. "Good."

He opened the door. Three large men in open white lab coats entered the room. They regarded her as a zookeeper might study a dangerous animal. Weapons were strapped to their waists; she could see the bulge there, and caught the flash of black as they moved.

"She's cooperating," Wasserman said. "But I'll want you to follow at a safe distance. Should something happen, you know what to do."

They strapped her to a gurney and rode up in the creaking elevator in silence. Her stomach cramped and burned, her pulse raced as they rolled down the familiar hallway toward the Room. She studied the patterns on the ceiling and tried not to scream.

They prepped her quickly. A nurse bent over her to administer the shot. Panic overwhelmed her, and she tried to twist away. *No needles!* But it was too late. Prickles of fire ran up through her shoulder, through her body. "Stay calm," the nurse said. "This is going to make you feel a little strange. That's normal. You're going to do just fine." She touched Sarah's wrist. The light pressure of her fingers tingled. Then she was gone.

They pushed her into the Room. The gurney's wheels squeaked as they slipped across the black padded floor. She could see the black ceiling, could feel the emptiness, the weight of the air. The walls swallowed sound. People spoke through layers of cotton. There were many of them around her now. Wasserman's voice cut through the rest, directing everyone to their various duties.

She felt herself trembling, sickness welling up inside as her pulse thumped in her throat.

Wires were placed about her face and temples, monitors attached to her fingertips. Faces loomed over her, filling her sight, quickly replaced by others.

The prickling fire had spread through her limbs, her neck, her tongue. She felt something building deep within her body and began to feel the familiar itch of pending release. With it came another wave of terror.

They left her alone. The door closed. She was plunged into utter blackness.

She could not hold it back now. She screamed.

The Room swallowed the sounds with ease, and everything else that came after.

—18—

"We've had a problem," Dr. Wasserman said.

Shelley had called that morning as Jess was sipping her tea at the window, watching the trains. She borrowed Charlie's car and rushed there as fast as she could, arriving in under twenty minutes. She knew it was serious enough, calling this early.

Now he was walking quickly and she had to trot to keep up. "It was in the playroom—Sarah was accidentally brought in when the other children were present. You're the only one she seems to respond to now, not that any of us had great luck before. . . ."

Jess had never seen him in this state. His tie was pulled down and his shirt looked damp in back. He looked like a man on the edge of a very dark and very deep drop, who was looking for something to grab hold of before it was too late.

She could hear the sound of raised voices through the thick concrete walls as they moved quickly down the hall. By the time they reached the playroom, she could tell that the current disruption, at least, did not involve Sarah. Still, she had to pause for a moment to stare openmouthed at the scene that greeted her through the half-open doors.

Toys were scattered everywhere. The slide was overturned; a tattered, one-limbed doll lay against its base. Books had flown like fluttering birds across the room. The little plastic table had been upended and the legs popped off.

The bear she had given Sarah lay just inside the door, a mute eyewitness to the tragedy.

Light flashed in her eyes. She glanced across the room at the right-hand window. Behind the wire mesh ran a long, splintering crack, winking in the sun.

The commotion came from the corner farthest from the door. Two white-shirted counselors were slowly closing in on a disheveled, hysterical figure.

"She touched him," Wasserman said. "Dennis does not like physical contact of any kind, as I think I told you."

Dennis was backed against the wall. His baseball cap was tilted to the right and upward, his shirt untucked. His hands were up and pawing the air and his head whipped back and forth like that of a dog trying to free itself from a choke collar. His voice was a constant, piercing scream. *"Nononononononono . . ."*

"Where's Sarah?"

"We managed to get her back downstairs. It took three men and almost fifteen minutes. She scratched one of them badly. I believe he's gone for the first-aid kit."

"I want to see her."

"She needs to calm down. I'll go with you in just a moment." Wasserman stepped into the room and raised his voice to a commanding pitch. "You there! That's not the way to treat him. Step away, give him air."

"Onetwothreefourfivesixseveneightnineten. Twoandtwoisfour. Threeandthreeissix. Fourfivesix. Seveneightnine."

The two counselors slowly moved off. Dennis continued to scream numbers in a wild, high-pitched stream. Jess remembered her brother's similar episodes. Sometimes they wouldn't even know for sure what had set him off, only that he had felt threatened by something. Her mother would have been drinking, most likely, though she hadn't been doing that as much when he was still alive. Somehow he had always seemed to know when she did. He tried to draw it out of her by force.

What did we used to do? Talk softly to him, talk him down . . .

Wasserman spoke in a calming, quiet voice. "There, there, Dennis, no one's going to hurt you. We're all friends here. Friends, Dennis." He moved slowly closer, hands at his sides. "There, now, that's better. . . ."

She took the bear and slipped down the hall to the elevator. Downstairs, she told Jeffrey behind the desk that she was here to examine Sarah. She let him examine the temporary pass Wasserman had given her after her first visit, even though he had seen it many times. Finally he led her through the dreary corridor to Sarah's door.

Now that she was away from the scene upstairs, she allowed her anger to boil to the surface. How could they have made such a stupid mistake? To leave the girl with a group of other children when she hadn't seen another child in God knew how long . . .

When Jess caught a glimpse of the poor girl, crouched against the wall, she was glad Wasserman had not followed her down here.

Sarah's eyes were already beginning to glaze over. A long, thin scratch divided one cheek. They had slipped her back into her restraints and the drugs were at work on her already. But Maria was gone. So who was giving her these heavy sedatives?

"Sarah, fight it," Jess said, over by her side. "Fight it. Do you hear me?" She unbuckled the jacket and slipped Sarah's arms out, then lifted the girl to her feet. Sarah muttered something incomprehensible.

Jess made a sudden decision. "Hold on, we're getting you out of this place," she said. She piloted them to the door, hit the buzzer with her palm. *Come on, you son of a bitch.* A moment later the door swung open and she pushed by the startled

Jeffrey—"I'm taking her back upstairs"—and through the hall, half carrying, half dragging Sarah to the elevator.

Upstairs she poked her head into the hall, which was empty. "You stay with me," she said, holding Sarah's chin and looking her in the eye. "You focus. Do you want to see the sky? Do you want to feel the breeze outside?"

Sarah muttered. Her eyes rolled and focused and rolled again. *What the hell am I doing?* Jess wondered, carrying the girl down the empty hall. But Sarah needed something to shock her from this trance. If it went too far she might never come back out again.

Noise still from the playroom; Dennis had calmed down a little, but not much. She went for the doors, and didn't see anyone until they were on the front steps, blinking in the bright sun.

She sat Sarah down on the top step. "Now you listen to me." She took the girl's chin in her hand again and tried to make contact with her eyes, tried to force her way through the soft glaze and hazy sun. "I know you're scared, and angry, and hurt. They treated you like an animal in there when you had a good reason for what happened. How were you supposed to feel, with all those people looking at you?"

Sarah moaned. She pulled her arms into her sides and rocked, head cocked, eyes squeezed tight.

"You didn't deserve to be treated like that. You didn't mean any of it. You only fought back to protect yourself. Am I right, Sarah?"

Sarah twisted her head away. "Leave me 'lone."

"I'll go if you want. Do you really want to go back to your room? Do you want them to lock you up again?"

"No! I don't!"

"I want you to fight that gray feeling that's trying to fill you up. I want you to push it away. We've come too far to go back and I don't want to lose you. Can you do that? Can you open your eyes?"

"I don't want to!"

"Then you'll miss it. Can you smell the air? It's cool out here. There's grass and some trees in the yard. There's a squirrel by the fence, he's standing up and holding something in his paws. He's chattering at us. Can you hear him, Sarah?"

Slowly, her eyes still squeezed tightly shut, Sarah nodded. Then she opened her eyes to the sun and struggled to her feet. Spreading her arms wide, she stood there for a moment, then stepped away into the grass and stumbled to her knees.

Jess felt a curious chill creep over her that had nothing to do with the wind. Sarah's face had suddenly gone absolutely smooth and a smile touched her lips as she knelt in the grass.

She bent and grabbed two handfuls and pulled, digging her fingers into the dirt. She rolled on her back and wriggled herself into the earth.

A strange sound the girl made. It took Jess several moments to realize Sarah was crying and laughing at the same time.

The sun slipped behind a cloud. Jess sat on the steps and watched as Sarah sat up and swayed like a snake, eyes closed, cheeks streaked with dirt and tears. "I don't feel too good," she said in a slurred voice.

"They gave you a drug. It's supposed to calm you down. It will make your mouth feel a little dry and your head kind of full. You're going to feel calmer and you might get sleepy."

"I don't like it."

"What happened in there, Sarah?"

She opened her eyes. "Nothing!"

"You mean you don't know, or you don't want to tell me?"

"I didn't do anything."

"I don't believe you did anything on purpose. You were scared."

"You weren't there. In the Room. I needed you!"

"If I'd known they were going to bring you to the playroom today, I would have come sooner."

"I looked for you out the window."

"Did you break the glass, Sarah?"

"I don't know! I just wanted to get out!"

"And then what happened?"

"I tried to talk to that boy, to help him. But he wouldn't listen. He started screaming, and he tried to take Connor. Then they came to take me away. You don't know what they do! They grab you hard and they give you shots and tie you up. They take you to the bad place. I didn't want them to do that anymore. So I pushed them. I . . . pushed." Sarah smiled and closed her eyes again, drifting. "I pushed . . ."

"You fought them."

"That's when the glass broke. They made me do it."

"You didn't mean to."

"I'm stronger now. I've been practicing. Do you want to see?"

"No, Sarah. I don't want any more fighting. No matter how bad things get, violence is not the answer."

Sarah opened her eyes again. "You don't know anything. I'm not going to let them tie me up. If they try it again I'm going to make them dead."

"Sarah, I know you're angry. You have every right to be. But they're adults, and they're bigger than you. No matter how hard you fight them they're going to win."

Jess saw the man in the guardhouse down the driveway watching them. He raised something to his mouth and spoke into it. Then he stuck it back into his belt and started walking up the driveway.

The gates were shut and the fence ran unbroken around the perimeter of the building. There was no reason they couldn't be out here. Still, for some reason she felt threatened.

The temperature had dropped noticeably. Jess noticed Sarah following her gaze to the guardhouse and the man walking up the drive. She hugged her arms to her chest and rubbed her fingers. "We should go inside now," she said.

"No!" Sarah staggered to her feet, shaking her head. "You lied to me! You don't want to help me at all! You're just like them!" Her face was twitching, its slack, sedated look giving way to something else. She was fighting hard against the drugs coursing through her veins. Jess wondered at Sarah's strength while at the same time she felt her own heart rate increase, the hair on her arms beginning to stand on end. The strange disorientation she had felt during her first visit returned as the temperature around her plummeted still more, as her icy breath plumed around her face.

A shimmering in the air, as behind her she heard a door open; a shout.

She turned through the sudden, drifting mind-fog; saw Wasserman and three others there on the doorstep, two of them in uniform. "Wait!" Wasserman cried, his face bleached white, his lips a purple, bloodless wound. "Get away from her! Get away!"

Jess turned back again through a slow-motion dream. Sarah stood on the lawn under gathering shadow, her arms tight at her sides, her hands balled into fists. Her body trembled as a sudden wind grew and whipped through her hair.

"Get back!" someone else shouted from far away. "She's not under yet!"

The man from the guardhouse started running. The two men in uniform rushed past Jess and jumped at Sarah's trembling, shuddering form. They met, collided, rolling, Sarah's feet drumming the ground as the seizure ripped up and through her.

Darkness met, joined, spread over their heads. A deep rumbling began below their feet.

And then it was as if the very air exploded. Jess threw herself to the ground, covered her head with her arms, as everything around her shuddered and rocked like blows from the fists of a giant.

Cries from the men still on the steps; she looked up,

shocked, unbelieving, as something began to fall and the men ran, as the rain of great black stones thundered down on the roof and walls of the Wasserman Facility and shook the earth.

—19—

The familiar larger brick and stone structures that made up the city had long since given way to smaller, private homes by the time Jess Chambers reached the Dorris-Edgecomb Nondenominational Church. Her hands clenched on the wheel as she thought about what she might be giving up by coming here. It was night and the lights were dark, but she had called ahead and she knew they would be waiting for her.

The Church was an old clapboard structure that had once been in the Episcopal fold, before the church board (controlled by several prominent members of the business community and a great deal of money) led a small mutiny and convinced the congregation to go independent. At the heart of the dispute was the church's growing belief in what they called the "new science."

The Organization for the Study of New Science had been on their own and a licensed nonprofit by the state for over ten years now. They were interested in not only the spirituality of man but also man's potential to evolve as a spiritual and physical being, to stretch the boundaries of accepted scientific phenomenon. The OSNS believed in life after death; they believed in man's capacity to overcome. They also believed that the full power of the mind had only begun to be explored.

Jess had learned most of this from Charlie, who had insisted on setting up a meeting for her that very night. She was driving Charlie's car too; another favor insisted upon and finally accepted.

The leaves had turned and the air had a late-fall bite. Stepping from the car, she thought of afternoon walks home from school in Maine, haying time in the fields, apple picking, and wood-burning stoves. For a moment she slipped into the false comfort of memory, and struggled to hold on to the mood, for she did not know when it would come again.

Most of her usual remembrances were filled with drunken neighbors and yapping dogs chained to dirt tracks between mobile homes. The grass would be worn to crackling wisps of spotty brown. Other families would hang their laundry there to dry, until the fall days turned so cold they would go out one morning to find the shirts and socks all frozen stiff and hanging like cardboard from the line.

When she knocked at the big church doors there was no answer. It was not until she moved around to a side entrance that she had any luck. A short, scruffy young man with curly blond hair and a goatee introduced himself as Ronald Gee. Gee moved as if he were intent on slipping through space with the least possible resistance. He led her through a short hallway to a set of narrow stairs leading down to a white-painted door with a sticker that read PSIGN: WE KNEW YOU WERE COMING, and a smaller sign that hung from the doorknob, EXPERIMENT IN PROGRESS. Music bled faintly through the walls.

"Shhh," Gee said, finger to his lips. She couldn't tell if he was serious or not. His mouth held a permanent half smirk. "They're creating a mood. It was no good earlier but they might have it by now."

He pushed open the door. The OSNS had strained the basement of the church well beyond its original design. Tables and file cabinets lined the walls and middle space, the rest filled with laboratory and electronic equipment: microscopes, computers, and related peripherals, and other unrecognizable machines. A large refrigerator/freezer occupied a corner. Shelves held jar after jar of medical specimens. Unrecognizable objects floated in milky fluid.

It was impossible not to feel cramped. Jess felt everything crowding at her, demanding her attention. She felt like ducking her head, though the ceilings were at least ten feet.

At the far end of the basement was a tiny observation room she had not noticed at first. Gee led her closer. Through a plate-glass window, a man and woman faced each other with their hands clasped across a wooden table and their eyes closed. The woman had a blood pressure cuff attached to one arm and electrodes fastened to her forehead.

A tall, slender man stood just outside, watching a set of monitors with a clipboard in his hand. Classical music played from somewhere out of sight.

The woman opened her eyes. "Close the door, Gee," she said. "I can't think with all that going on."

"Close it yourself. I'd like to see that sometime. One of you sensitives actually doing something."

"Cut it out, Gee," the tall man said, coming out and looking at Jess. "We're all familiar with your opinion." He introduced himself as Patrick Elwes and spoke with a slight lisp. He was olive-skinned and serious, with round, frameless glasses and dark hair cropped tight against his scalp. His face was handsome and boyish, at odds with the rest of him.

"You're Charlie's friend. Dr. Chambers, isn't it?"

"I'm not a doctor. Quite a setup you've got here."

Patrick smiled in an awkward, pleased way that reminded her of a proud parent. "We make do. They won't let us in any other place in town. Scared of the publicity."

"So what is it?"

"Excuse me?"

"Gee's theory."

"Oh. Gee is of the opinion," Patrick said, "that table raising, levitation of any kind actually, is beyond the scope of psi. Gee is what we call an informed skeptic."

"Which just means that I'm withholding judgment," Gee said loudly. "Isn't that what proper experimenters do?"

She motioned toward the two others in the observation room, who were pretending to watch each other but kept glancing at her and then looking away. "Are they all right?"

"I think they're playing hard to get. Bilecki is a sensitive; she may already know all about you. The other one is James something. I just met him myself today."

"What were you doing over there again?"

"Table levitation. Attempting it anyway. We can't even get Bilecki's heart rate up, and her beta waves are too flat. It's no good."

"I knew it," Gee said. "Parlor tricks. We should get David Copperfield down here, it'd be more entertaining."

"That isn't what Miss Chambers has come here to see. I believe she has something very interesting to share with us."

They waited, watching her. Jess took a deep breath. "What has Charlie told you?"

"Only that you may have had a genuine psi experience. It really isn't that unusual," Patrick said. "You don't have to feel that you can't discuss it. We treat that sort of thing very seriously here. It's what we do."

"I really don't know what I have to tell you," she said. "If I was sure, I wouldn't have come. Let's just say I wanted to explore my options."

"Have you read the book *The Reach of the Mind*, Miss Chambers?"

"I . . . skimmed it."

"Rhine is a legend. The man who started it all. He coined the terms parapsychology, psychokinesis. What we call the Reach."

"Which is what, exactly?"

"The interaction of the mind with physical space. Mental energy. Mind over matter, you might say." Seeing her skepticism, Patrick explained, "It isn't as far-fetched as it might seem. Cases are continuing to surface, documented cases involving hundreds of scientists across the world. There are plenty of frauds out there trying to make a buck, but there are others. True sensitives."

"Like Bilecki here?"

Patrick smiled. "When the conditions are right, she's quite remarkable. It's rare to find a subject able to perform on command. So, what is it you've seen?"

"I don't really know. But levitating tables can't begin to describe it."

A sudden silence descended upon the group. Looking at the faces surrounding her, Jess said, "Maybe I shouldn't have come. I'm sorry."

Patrick studied her, the way she held her briefcase in both hands. "It would be better to talk in private," he said.

—20—

"Charlie tells me you're a flier," Patrick said, lighting a candle near the upstairs door.

They had retreated into the deserted church. Gentle moonlight glowed through stained glass. The candlelight flickered across the backs of empty pews, sparked against something hidden within the shadows of the altar.

"I have a license, yes."

"What's that like?" he asked almost dreamily, his voice echoing back as he walked away from her along the wall, lighting more candles. As it grew the light gave life to the carvings, made the walls and stained glass figures dance like merry ghosts.

Jess felt a little off balance. She wasn't sure exactly what she thought of Patrick Elwes, but something about him made her want to hurry to catch up.

"Like freedom," she said. "At its best, weightlessness. Like a dream."

"And at its worst?"

"A way of avoiding things, I suppose. An escape, when running away isn't always the best choice. And sometimes it's a little hairy, especially in bad weather."

"I've always wanted to learn to fly."

"You've been up before?"

"No, never. I'm scared to death of it too. Isn't that crazy?"

"There are worse things to be afraid of."

Patrick nodded, turning back to face her. "How right you are."

They sat down next to each other in the front pew, Patrick with his long legs stretched out in front, Jess with her briefcase clutched on her lap.

Jess had the faintly unsettling feeling, half dream and half memory, of kneeling in front of an altar much like this one when she was a little girl. Her mother had dragged her to the Congregational church one Sunday morning to offer some kind of penance, the details of which had gone over her head. But she remembered a feeling of quiet dread mixed with embarrassment, as if they were interlopers at a private party.

Today she felt like speaking in whispers, as if they might be disturbing someone here in this empty house of God.

"I hope you don't mind the candles. I find it peaceful. And when it's not so bright, the neighbors don't notice the lights on and call the police." He smiled. "There's a rumor going around that the place is haunted. We like it, actually. It keeps the attention away from what we're doing."

Jess was trying not to stare at his eyes, which she had noticed were two slightly different colors, hazel and a light misty gray. They held the candlelight in their centers like tiny flickering suns.

The effect was distracting. She wondered if something had happened to him when he was young that had affected the pigment. He had a very slight accent that she couldn't quite place, or perhaps a speech impediment that he had spent many hours trying to erase.

"Heterochromia iridium," he said.

"Excuse me?"

"It's the scientific name for two different color eyes. Relatively rare in people, but it happens pretty frequently in other species. Science used to believe eye color was controlled by one gene, but it's been established as polygenic.

It's an inherited trait. Most common cause is a mutation of the PAX3 gene on chromosome 2q35."

"I'm sorry. I was staring, wasn't I?"

"No problem." Patrick smiled. "Hypnotic, aren't they? Helped me get away with a lot more mischief when I was a kid."

"They're beautiful. So, how do you know Charlie?"

"We grew up together. She was always trying to get me to go out with her, but I refused." Candlelight flickered in across his features. She could not tell if he was being serious at first. "Actually, I suppose you could say I had a crush on her. She lived just down the block and was a year older. A real exotic beauty."

"She's told you all about me?"

"Only a very faint idea of why you might come. And about your flying airplanes."

Jess considered how to begin. "This doesn't leave the room. It involves a patient I'm helping to treat and so any information I tell you is confidential. Can I trust you with that?"

"Of course."

"This person—a young girl—has been treated for a schizophreniform disorder for several years. While in this girl's company I have been witness to several strange events. Lightbulbs exploding. Drops in temperature. Jammed door locks. These things seem to happen when the girl is upset or under stress. I have spoken with several members of the girl's family, and they insisted that similar events occurred almost from the moment of her birth. And then, this morning . . ."

"Go on."

"We were outside the hospital. She became upset, didn't want to go back inside. There were men there who tried to restrain her, the hospital director as well. It got very dark, very cold—this happened extremely quickly—I don't know how to say this. Large black rocks—chunks of ice and stones, actually—began to fall from the sky like rain. And it was clear to me that somehow, this girl was causing it to happen."

There was something almost sacrilegious about saying it in a church. Patrick didn't seem to notice. He had a way about him that was very serious, very intense. "What did the hospital director have to say after this occurred?"

"Storms had been forecast all day, severe weather warnings. The stones matched the ones used to landscape the hospital grounds. A tornado of some kind, a minicyclone—"

"The ice," Patrick interrupted. "Did it melt quickly? Were the stones themselves warm?"

"Yes."

"And the temperature had dropped, you said?" She nodded. Patrick said, "I see." He pulled out a notepad from his jacket pocket. "Do you mind? It's easier if I write this down. We'll go over it later." He held the notebook in his palm and scribbled something with a stubby end of a pencil. "Hmmm. So the director, he's asking you to believe that this storm came up out of nowhere, picked up a hailstorm of stones without doing any other damage to the grounds, and dropped them on the roof. Without damaging a single other person or object within a ten-foot radius?"

"I don't know half of what he said, to be honest. I was pretty shaken up, and I suppose he was too. I don't know if he believed it himself. But you have to understand that Dr. Wasserman is a man of science."

"So am I." Patrick edged slightly closer. She could not look away from his eyes, such strange eyes. "You know how ancient man worshipped the sun as a god because they could not understand the meaning of such a great, shining presence in the sky? Or that before they understood mental illness they believed in possession of the body by spirits?"

"I'm not very good at this, Patrick. If it wasn't for this girl . . . you might call me one of your skeptics."

"I'm only trying to make a point. I want you to entertain

for a moment another possibility. This is quite scientific and utterly reasonable. Suppose that there are functions within the mind we have yet to understand. Perfectly rational, explainable abilities if only we knew how the process worked. In some cases these abilities are more advanced, more developed, the same as musical talent or physical coordination. A person might even be able to improve these abilities, strengthen them with practice."

"I'm listening."

"The human brain contains over seventeen billion cells. *Seventeen billion.* These handle approximately one hundred million messages per second. There are many different areas of specialty inside the brain itself, and we understand the functions of a bare fraction. What are these other cells doing? Is it fair to assume that we have no idea? That we cannot even speculate? Look at your airplanes. And yet they're so primitive compared to what we've been given. If you told anyone that you could build a machine with seventeen billion parts and make them all work fluidly together, and explain what each part does and how it does it, do you think they would believe you?"

"Being in here inspires you, doesn't it?"

"It just serves as a reminder of what a gift we have. And it keeps me humble. There are many mysteries in the universe, and I've chosen to focus on just one of them, because to take them all on at once would be impossible."

They were very close now, knees touching.

Deeper in the shadows above the altar was a life-size statue of Jesus on the cross. Patrick saw her looking at it. "We believe now that he was very likely a sensitive. Certainly telepathic, clairvoyant, quite possibly psychokinetic. It would explain a lot—his knowledge of future events, the power to heal, even walking on water."

"Rising from the dead?"

Patrick smiled. "We've chosen to leave that particular miracle to the imaginations of the parishioners." He touched the briefcase she still held on her lap. "This girl you've told me about, she may have a gift, a portion of the brain more developed than the average person. We've studied that here, and we've come to a few conclusions based on scientific method. One, these psychic abilities do exist. Two, they follow specific physical rules. And three, they are not as rare as you might think. But they are variable, much like personalities, and for the most part they are minute, measurable only in a laboratory setting."

"But not always?"

"Stories like yours have been told for centuries. A mother who suddenly has the strength to lift an overturned car. A grandfather clock stopping at the exact moment of someone's death. A rain of stones. Generally they happen only once or twice in a lifetime, and so it is very hard to document them. A person who can perform at such a high level over time is extremely rare."

"You asked me if the stones were warm."

"If you'll recall from your early physics classes, it takes energy to create motion. If something is being levitated, raised into the air, some force must be accountable for it. What we've concluded here—and it's been documented in South Carolina and other places—is that psychokinesis involves some sort of heat transference at a microscopic level. In any successful PK experiment, the air temperature drops while the surface temperature of the moving object rises."

"I'm not sure I understand."

"Neither do we," Patrick said with a smile. "We don't understand the process. But what is heat except the movement of molecules? Isn't it possible that during a psi event, a person is somehow able to borrow motion and energy from moving particles—perhaps at the atomic level—and use that energy to affect a change in the environment?"

"Anything's possible." *Just don't ask me to believe in the bogeyman.* That would be next, Jess felt suddenly sure; she was careening down a path with no brakes and no map, without even an idea of where she might be at the end. *I've never believed in anything my eyes couldn't see. Maybe it was the way I grew up. Maybe it was Michael's death. But I've got to believe the world has a set of rules. And this goes way beyond anything the world has ever shown me.*

But that wasn't really true, was it? Didn't she know just one split second before Michael ran out in front of that car, wasn't there a single moment in time where she knew what was going to happen? Or was that just hindsight?

"In your little girl's case," Patrick was saying, into the deep and heavy silence of the church, "she would have been pulling heat energy from the air and using it to exert force upon the stones. The resulting temperature drop causes moisture in the surrounding air to form ice almost instantly, even as the stones heat up. How did she do it? It's difficult to say. There's been a lot of study lately on brain wave activity and microparticles. But the fact is, we don't know for sure."

"Would you take CAT scans in a case like this? MRIs? EEGs?"

"Absolutely."

Jess touched her briefcase and unsnapped the clasps. With slightly unsteady hands she withdrew the yellow folder. "This is her file," she said. "What I've been allowed to see of it anyway. I'd like you to take a look and tell me what you make of it."

Patrick took the folder and withdrew the contents, spreading it across his lap. He studied in silence for a few moments, his eyes moving quickly across the pages of notes and reports. Then he held a transparent film up to the flickering light. "Here, you see a slight enlargement of the cerebral ventricles," he said, pointing at a gray area. "And here. But no visible reduction in the hippocampus or hypothalamus. In fact, I'd say it's enlarged."

"In other words, if they were looking for a neurobiological sign of schizophrenia, they didn't find it."

"Mmm-hmm. And yet there are abnormalities."

Suddenly he stood up and went to the candles at the altar, holding the film up to the light and pacing, peering, his voice rising in excitement. "There's definitely increased activity here. Let me see the rest of it." He returned and fumbled through the records with more urgency. "You see, look at these readings. The patterns are positively abnormal. Ordinarily you would have a beta wave reading if the person was awake, delta if they were in deep sleep. Occasionally you might see an alpha or even a theta in a state of hypnosis. But in this case it isn't either, but rather a combination of the two, even when she's supposedly awake. And in several instances"—he punctuated this with a tap of his long finger on a graph—"there's a spike, a surge of terrific proportions. It's as if someone jump-started her brain with a car battery."

"Have you ever seen anything like it before?"

"Not like this." Patrick seemed to lose himself for a moment. "I'd heard stories, seen hints, but nothing like this."

He turned to face her, leaned down, and smacked both hands on the back of the pew. He grinned. "Do you know what you've done? If what you've told me is true, and these records are accurate? Something we've been failing to do for years, with people like Bilecki, thousands of them."

Patrick clapped his hands together like a child. The sound was like a gunshot in the silent church. "You've found us our Holy Grail."

—21—

Jess Chambers dreams she is in a large, cavernous building.
The lights are all off, but emergency bulbs allow her enough
light to see. Red light glints off polished metal doorknobs,
shines dully from the stone walls, and turns the wooden
trim as black as blood.

She pauses to listen. Monsters are chasing her, and she does
not know which way they have gone. Paranoia creeps like
stealthy dark figures into her mind. She feels them around
every corner, watching her from every door frame. She hears
them running after her. But she is searching for something,
and she cannot leave until she finds it.

Jess hears her mother's drunken voice echoing through the
empty stone corridors; crashing into things, knocking over a
lamp that shatters all over the floor, laughing and shouting.
Glass tinkles and crunches. Others hissing at her to be quiet.
A door opens somewhere close by. The sound of voices becomes very loud. Jess presses herself into a shadowed doorway, listening in a near panic as the footsteps become louder.
She has nowhere to go. If they find her they will take her
away and lock her up.

She reaches behind her and turns the knob, stumbling
into an open room. White carpet shows bloody footprints
leading across a sea of broken and dissected toys, past a toy

sink and through a plastic tunnel. Something seems to catch in her throat. What has she been looking for?

She hears a noise over by the bookcase. A little boy stands with his back to her, his blond hair curling over his collar. Both arms are raised and she sees the blood running down his wrists and dripping onto the carpet.

Michael? she says. Her brother turns. Blood pulses from holes in both palms. The look on his face is one of sadness. She sees her mother in him. But something is missing. She does not see any trace of the autism that has plagued him from the moment he was born.

Then the look changes. Suddenly she is afraid. Michael frowns, little furrowed brows coming together in a pantomime of adult emotion. He raises his hands higher. The door swings shut behind her with a bang. Papers pick themselves up off the carpet and whirl through the air. Michael's shoulders shake, his eyes roll backward into his head.

The plastic tunnel shivers, rocks, lifts into the air. Books slam against the walls and flop like broken birds. Glass shatters in the window with a crack like a lightning storm.

Toys batter her face as a wind picks up and whips through the room. Glass shards flash like little silver arrows in the sun. Fists pound at the door, voices shout her name. She looks at her brother and sees the light of revenge in his eyes. She realizes too late, she hasn't been running away from them, after all. She has been running away from him.

Miles away, a little girl opens her eyes to inky darkness. Her throat is tight, her limbs slick with sweat. The dream remains with her, of a woman, and a little blond boy, and blood. Lots of blood.

She tries to turn over, but her wrists and ankles are strapped down.

Voices come to her like ghosts now, murmurs in an alien tongue. It is difficult to separate them from the things that happen inside her mind, these other voices that come and go and bring the dreaded gray fog. She isn't sure right now whether any of them are real, or whether she is truly lost inside herself.

The gray fog is a method of control, a weapon in battle, maybe the only one *they* have.

She used to think about what might happen if someone came for her. She has only the faintest memories of a woman who might or might not have been her mother. Would this person care for her, would she take her away and soothe the voices, take away the pain? Would someone please, please help?

She knows the woman in the dream she has just had, knows her face. But the truth is frustratingly out of reach. She was here recently. What has happened? *Please, remember.*

But it does not come. There is only the dream, the terrible, bloody dream.

Her head pulses slowly, throbbing with the pain of a thousand pinpricks. She is lost, and alone, and too weak to move. She lets out a single, choked sob, and lets the gray fog swallow her whole once again.

She keeps her heart jealously guarded, and does not let it beat too loudly for fear that they will hear it.

—22—

Jess awoke into darkness close and cool, got up, and shuffled into the kitchen, hugging herself in the soft tick and hiss of early morning heat as the radiators sputtered to life.

Okay, so suppose Patrick is right. Suppose for one moment that they're not all off their rockers, that there actually is a portion (where? how?) of the human brain that is capable of exerting an effect on the outside physical world, simply by a particular sequence of thought.

The question then became: where to go from here?

Of course, Patrick wanted to see this miracle child right away. He was already mapping out a plan to test her, record the results, contact the people in Carolina and elsewhere. But it would not be that easy; there was Wasserman to contend with, for one. And it was important to consider what was best for Sarah.

There was also the question of how far this talent could reach. There was still a big difference between levitating parlor tricks and the ability to bring the very walls down around their heads. *A rain of stones. Or something larger.* A little girl with a mind like that could be very valuable to the wrong people.

Jess sat clutching a cup of tea at her kitchen table, while Otto rubbed his fluffy tail against her bare legs. Outside the window it was still dark, though it must be approaching dawn; she had not heard the trains running for a while now, and the traffic was almost nonexistent. Soon it would pick up as people resumed their daily lives, rushing into work so they could hurry up and go home again.

As she sat there in the empty kitchen, the silence hit her like a backhanded slap. For some reason she thought of Patrick's face, and she stood up and went to the sink. Not good to think about him now. She needed to focus.

When she used to wake up like this as a child she would sneak out onto the front steps, hug her knees to her chest, and look at the stars. The stars were always larger and brighter in the country. If she tried very hard, she could find the answers there. The night sky gave her perspective. She would feel impossibly small in a universe of endless planets. Somewhere up among the stars, she felt sure, someone was looking back at her.

At the window now, she leaned over and craned her neck to see if she could see the sky. She felt a moment of numb heat in her palm, before something bit down hard.

She yelped and yanked her hand away from the still-hot coil on the stove, then pressed her palm to her mouth. Already the skin was throbbing. *Damn it.* Unreasoning anger welled up inside, the product of too much stress and lack of sleep, and as she turned to run her hand under cold water from the tap, her half-full mug of tea slid off the kitchen table and shattered on the floor.

She stood for a few moments in disbelief. Brown liquid had spattered across the linoleum, up the front of the refrigerator and cabinets.

Someone pounded on the floor from the apartment below and shouted at her. She swore to herself and went about cleaning up the pieces of ceramic, being careful not to cut herself on the sharp edges. Otto padded over and licked at the tea with a pink tongue. She grabbed a wet sponge from the sink and wiped all the surfaces down before he made himself sick on milk and sugar.

When she had finished cleaning up the mess, she soothed her burn with an ice cube from the freezer. By then the sky had lightened with the coming dawn.

The day was not off to a very good start. First the dream, then this. Somehow the shattered cup seemed to symbolize where her life had gone. And she still had to come to some sort of decision about Sarah. What was she going to do?

Just because you don't understand something doesn't mean it isn't there. How do you think Isaac Newton felt? Or Ben Franklin?

Okay. All right. But we're losing track of what's important here. Inside this hypothetical situation was a very real little girl. A girl who was confused and alone and very probably scared to death. No matter what happened, Jess would not allow a witch hunt. That was far too dangerous.

Perhaps Shelley could help. Jess looked at the clock by her bed. After four; she considered calling anyway. Instead, she dialed Charlie's number. She was surprised when Charlie seemed to be expecting her. She did not even mention the hour.

"Patrick's a good boy," Charlie said. "He may be a little intense, but he's honest."

"I know, Charlie, but do you trust him?"

"Absolutely. Listen, you trust *yourself*, girl. Then let the rest come."

"Where would I be without your advice?"

"I suppose you'd be happily married to a millionaire."

"I'd die first."

She could hear Charlie grinning through the phone. "Well, maybe you'd settle for a slightly mad scientist with a fetish for the paranormal. He's single, you know."

"You don't say. He is kind of cute. I think he's carrying a torch for someone else, though."

"Why don't we all get together for drinks when this is over?"

"I'll think about it."

She hung up smiling, then thought about climbing into bed for just a few more minutes. Maybe there would be a chance for some honest sleep after all.

—23—

Sarah lay on an examining table, arms and legs hanging limp, eyes vague and unfocused. Straps held down her wrists and ankles; Wasserman had insisted upon them, though they were hardly necessary, Jess thought. They had pumped her so full of tranquilizers it would be a wonder if she could move a finger.

"She'd stopped taking her regular medication," Dr. Wasserman said from their place by the door, as they watched the young doctor do her work. "We found them under her mattress. I don't suppose you know anything about that?"

Jess glanced at him. "I had no idea."

"That's how these things happen. The brain is a very delicate thing. The slightest change in chemistry, and you've lost all that you'd gained."

Jess had the feeling that Wasserman was speaking for his own benefit as much as hers. But he seemed to have regained his footing, looking calmer and more self-possessed than the last time she'd seen him. She had expected more resistance from him than she had received; when she had pressed for a fresh opinion on Sarah's condition, then asked to be present at the exam, he had not only agreed but seemed almost glad to have her. His only requirement was that it occur on-site.

The doctor undid the restraint from Sarah's right leg, then

stretched it and released. Then she tested Sarah's reflexes lightly, tapping the bottom of her foot with a hammer.

"I want to make something clear," Wasserman said. "I must admit you seem to have connected with her in some way. But that doesn't excuse the fact that you've gone against my wishes on two separate occasions. I'm only allowing you in here because Jean insisted upon it."

So that was it. Her urgent phone calls had done some good, after all. Professor Shelley had missed last Thursday's class, leaving only a note taped to the lecture hall door saying she was ill and giving the week's reading assignment. Jess had been unable to reach her. She had left several messages on the professor's machine, but did not know until now whether she had received them.

The doctor looked into Sarah's eyes with a penlight. She raised Sarah's lids and lowered them, frowning; flashed the light on and off, on and off. She felt about Sarah's skull and neck, ran her fingers carefully through the girl's hair, searching for scars. "We'll need to do some more scans," she said. "MRI, EEG, CAT. I want to absolutely rule out a lesion. Are you sure she's never had a serious fall? Some sort of disease or swelling in childhood, an infection?"

"We've tested for all that already, years ago," Wasserman said. "Do you have a firm medical opinion?"

"Well," the doctor said, "from what you've told me I'd say it was some sort of muscular contractions caused by damage to her temporal lobe. A lesion such as that would explain the schizophenic-type behavior, as well as the seizures. Though I can't see anything right away that would bear that out . . . is this level of sedation really necessary?"

"She's tried to harm herself before. And when I've tried to bring her out she's begun to have the convulsions again. Right now this is the only way I've been able to keep her still."

"All right. It will make testing her more difficult, but not impossible. I'd like to start with the EEG. We'll look for an abnormal pattern, and then, if nothing shows up, I'd like to go to the CAT scan. Maybe we can uncover a pocket of fluid somewhere that's causing a pressure."

They set up an IV glucose drip to deliver a continuous stream of medication and keep her relaxed and docile. Jess requested and received permission to have a cot set up next to Sarah's bed; for the next several days she left only to go to class, and to go home to shower and feed Otto. She saw Jeffrey during her first visit every morning and evening, when he came through to clean. He would smile at her in that soft, gentle way of his, and it made her feel safe to know he was nearby.

One night she sat in semidarkness. The smell of the fresh flowers she had brought filled the room, but it wasn't enough to kill the sharp scent of disinfectant. The smell of hospitals. When Michael had been struck down she rode in the back of the ambulance with her mother, screaming through the streets while her brother's tiny, crushed body lay strapped to the gurney. The EMTs had worked over him like machines, fast and furious and calculating. But she had known even then that it was too late; whatever had lived in him was gone. She had felt it go, like a soft breath of wind.

She reached out and took hold of Sarah's hand. The flesh was cool and dry. "I know you can hear me. Please, try to come back. I'll do whatever it takes. Give me one more chance."

She felt a gentle pressure. Sarah's hand curled in hers. Her eyes were closed, and now her mouth turned downward in a gentle frown, as if she were puzzling with something.

The next morning Jess woke up to find Sarah looking at her from the bed. She didn't move for a long moment, and then she rolled over and stood, brushing at her wrinkled clothes. "Look who's here," she said lightly, rubbing at her face. Her mouth tasted stale and sour. "I'm glad you could join us."

"I heard you talking to me last night. I just didn't want to wake up yet." Sarah's eyes were bright and clear. A moment later Jess saw the reason; her IV had come loose during the night. Fluid dripped out to stain the sheets.

"You were scared?"

"Just tired. I'm always tired after . . . you know."

"Honey," Jess said, moving to the edge of the bed and sitting down, "can you tell me what happened that day we went outside? Do you remember?"

"I don't want to."

"It's important that you try."

"No!"

"Okay. But you're not alone. I want you to know that. Maybe I haven't given you much reason to trust me yet, but I'm on your side."

Sarah looked intently at her for a moment. "You were thinking about something sad last night."

"I don't remember anything like that."

"It was about your brother."

"How do you know about Michael?"

"He died a long time ago. I'm not him, you know. He's not here anymore."

Jess felt a chill hand against her heart. She couldn't have overheard anything; she hadn't been talking to anyone. How long had the IV been disconnected? An hour? All night?

"Well," she said, "I guess I underestimated you, didn't I? I suppose Dr. Wasserman knows something about it by now. You overheard him talking, maybe? You can learn a lot by eavesdropping."

"I wasn't eavesdropping. You told me the first time you came to visit."

Jess sat down on the edge of the bed. "But how did you know I was thinking about him last night?"

"I just knew." Sarah let her head sink back into the pillow and closed her eyes. Dark circles ringed their edges. "Sometimes these things about you come into my head. It's like you're speaking to me, only there's no sound."

Poor thing. Jess was overwhelmed with pity. She looked so young. You don't deserve to be here, she thought. You deserve a family, someone who understands you.

They sat silently for a moment. Jess took her hand. Just as she thought Sarah had drifted off, she spoke in a sleepy voice, her eyes still closed. "Do you have a mom?"

"Sure. She lives in Florida, near the water. It's where her parents live, so she can be close to them."

"Do you see her a lot?"

"Not very much. Florida is a long way to go. And we don't get along very well, Sarah."

"Why not?"

"Well, we don't agree on some things. There are parts of her I don't like very much."

"Like what?"

"She drinks a lot. And she's very angry most of the time. Sometimes things happen where it's nobody's fault, but people just can't accept it that way. And sometimes a person reminds you so much of someone or something else you've lost that whenever you're with them, you get sad."

"Like what happened with your brother?"

"Yes, exactly like that."

"Oh. You're lucky, though," Sarah said. "I wish I knew my mother."

"Sometimes parents aren't what we'd like them to be. They might be too sick to take care of their children, or they might even be dangerous. In that case it's better if they aren't around."

"My mother wanted to keep me with her. I know she did."

"Do you remember her?"

"Sometimes I do. Sometimes I dream about her. Why did she leave me here? Why doesn't she come get me?"

"Oh, honey. I'm sure she would if she could."

"You don't think she's scared of me?"

"Why would she be scared of you? I'm not scared of you."

"I just want to be like everyone else."

"Being different can be a good thing. If everyone were the same, what a boring world it would be!"

Sarah was quiet for a minute. "Will you go get Connor? I want him to stay with me."

"Sure I will."

When she spoke again, her voice came drifting back from the depths of sleep: "I dream about her a lot. . . ."

Jess waited until Sarah's breathing deepened. She slowly disengaged her hand and stood up.

She was surprised to find herself shaking. Whether it was from anger, sadness, or something else, she couldn't tell.

—24—

Shelley still wasn't in class the next day. The guest lecturer told them she would be out for at least another week. After the session ended, Jess reached her by telephone. "I'm sorry to bother you at home, but it's important."

She thought she sensed a moment's hesitation. "All right," Shelley said. "I'm feeling a bit better today. It's time we met again anyway. Why don't you come here? It's a nice day and the leaves are turning. We'll sit out on the deck and have a drink."

She jotted down the address. Charlie was using her car to go shopping in Natick, and so Jess took a taxi into Chestnut Hill. She knew the neighborhood, and was prepared for the quiet, tree-lined streets and stately homes tucked among the gentle hills, but she was nevertheless surprised when the taxi turned into the driveway of what was obviously an estate of considerable size. Iron gates swung open to admit them up a gently sweeping drive, and around tumbling juniper and rock displays to a sprawling Tudor mansion with perfectly manicured lawns and flower gardens that were just beginning to droop and curl in the crisp fall air.

She avoided the imposing front entrance as Shelley had instructed over the phone, instead following a flagstone path that led down a slight slope and around the side of the house. Several big hunks of rough-hewn granite formed steps that ended at a rear door.

Feeling out of place, she hesitated before ringing the bell, half expecting a somber-faced maid or English butler. But Shelley herself answered, looking as if she'd just splashed her face with cold water. Her flesh was puffy and very pale. "Come on in," she said, "I was just making something to eat. Are you hungry?"

The house held a deep, expectant silence. They walked through a hallway lined with a patterned wine runner and hung with oil paintings, into a spacious, well-lighted kitchen. Stainless steel Viking appliances offset warm wood tones, and an oak-topped island in the middle of the room kept a sink and dishwasher.

But what held Jess's attention was the contents of the full-length granite counter to the right of the cooktop: whole oat bread, a cube of white, fleshy tofu on a cutting block, a container of what looked like seaweed, and a plastic bottle full of greenish liquid.

"I've been meaning to ask," Shelley said, busy inside the huge refrigerator, "how you managed to pay for school. It doesn't sound like you had much help from your parents."

"A full scholarship to the University of Connecticut. I waited tables there for spending money."

"And now?"

"The man who taught me to fly airplanes died when I was a junior. He left me his plane, along with his wishes that it be sold and the proceeds set up as a scholarship fund."

"You were close?"

"He was the only person I trusted as a child."

On afternoons after school, when she knew her mother would be drinking, she would listen at the foot of the driveway for the sound of the plane. She would linger at the farm down the street, watching him do his graceful loops and spins, wishing she could be up there too. Sometimes, if she was lucky, he would land and take her up again.

"I hope I'm not being too personal. I just wondered." Shelley had turned from the open refrigerator with a container of orange juice. She looked very frail in the yellow light, years older. Jess caught a glimpse of the swelling showing in her wrist, and what looked like a particularly nasty rash up the inside of her arm. Something clicked like tumblers falling into place inside her head, and she wondered how she hadn't seen it before.

"It's not important," was all she said.

"As a matter of fact, it is. Evan and I were very concerned with who we picked to help with Sarah. It's important for us to know what makes you tick. To be perfectly blunt."

"She's not a schizophrenic."

"I know." Shelley put the juice down on the counter, turning away from the sudden silence. "Actually, I'm not very hungry after all. Why don't we go out and sit on the patio?"

They walked through a room dominated by a huge Steinway grand piano, decorated with an antique oriental rug in deep earth tones, a Chippendale walnut chest and china cabinet, a Tiffany clock, through French doors, and onto a stone deck that overlooked the lawn and gardens. The air was pleasant but cool, the distant trees peppered with orange and yellow leaves.

"That's better. A little sun always lifts my mood." Shelley settled into a cushioned deck chair. "Have a seat."

Jess took a chair opposite. "What was all that on the counter?"

"Macrobiotics. It's supposed to help clean out my system." She waved her hand. "Diet, meditation. You try something new. I have good days and bad days. More lately of the latter, I'm afraid."

"You're sick, aren't you? Is it cancer?"

"Acute lymphocytic leukemia. You know, I never thought I

would go this way. It's not the kind of exit you wish for when you're a little girl. And I thought, if I could cleanse myself, if I eat well and pray . . . it sounds silly when I say it out loud."

"Not at all."

"I won't go without a fight," Shelley said. "I've been living with this for ten years now, and it doesn't get any easier. My father was CEO for the largest steel company in the country. I've seen the best specialists in the world. But money can't solve everything. You go into remission, you think you've beaten it, and then it comes back to bite you harder than ever."

"I'm sorry."

They sat in silence while a gentle breeze rustled the leaves at a distant edge of lawn, while flowers bobbed their multicolored heads. There had been a frost last night; when Jess woke up it had been written across the window, the crust of ice on the inside so that when she'd dragged a nail across the pane it had come back flaked with snow.

"I've tried to keep this as quiet as possible. I like my privacy. I assume you'll respect my confidence."

"Of course."

"Anyway, enough of all that. You didn't come to talk about my life. You're here to talk about Sarah." Shelley turned to look at her, and for a moment the pain was so naked, so obvious, Jess had to keep herself from flinching.

"I always knew it would come to this," Shelley said. "That's one reason I fought Evan so hard to bring you into our confidence. I needed someone to uncover everything, bring it into the light, and you were the perfect choice, for a number of reasons. But I hope you don't blame me too much for letting you in slowly. You had to do it on your own terms, in your own way. Do you understand what I mean? When you're faced with the fact that something you've believed all your life is a fiction, a silly superstition . . . the belief dies hard. It did for me."

"I deserve to know the whole truth. You owe me that."

"And you'll get it."

"If you knew that what her family said was true, why did you let Dr. Wasserman lock her up? Drug her? Treat her for a disability that didn't exist?"

"It wasn't that simple. Remember that there is a history of mental illness in her family, she did show many of the classic indications—"

"With all due respect, that's bullshit. And you know it."

Shelley stared out over gently rustling leaves. "There are other factors involved here. I truly wanted to help her. I thought maybe we could help each other. But there are things you can't know, things that make it all but impossible. Especially now."

"Then tell me."

But Shelley was no longer listening. "I've spent ten years trying to forget that night, the night she was born. I was the first thing she saw, coming into this world. . . . Can you imagine what a doctor looks like to a child coming into the light for the first time? Hooded and gowned, mask covering her face? What a human being looks like to someone who has never seen one before? I know because she let me see. I saw through her eyes."

"I don't think I understand."

"I don't know how she did it, how it happened. But I can't ever forget that. It isn't easy seeing yourself as a freak. Huge. Misshapen. All those features you look at in the mirror each day, turned into something alien. The next thing I remember was the firemen pulling me out, the hospital coming down, and I kept asking them where was the monster, where was that *thing*?"

They had gone all that way to New York, they had spoken with the family, they had listened to the stories that seemed too fantastic for belief, and never once had Shelley said a word about any of this. All Jess could think of now was Maria's voice on the phone; Sarah, inside her head. *Embrujado*. Haunted.

Betrayal stung her like a slap to the face. "Sarah's not the devil. She's just a little girl."

"Let's assume she's the product of some random genetic mutation. But do you think it's a coincidence that my cancer began nearly ten years ago? I had no family history, no previous symptoms. I contracted what is almost exclusively a childhood disease, caused by changes in the cells of the bone marrow, changes that have been linked to high doses of radiation or exposure to toxins. Somehow she lashed out at me—I felt it—and she did something to me. She changed me. At the cellular level.

"When she was barely a minute old, I saw her tear a building apart. What do you think she's capable of now?"

Jess had no idea what to say. During the taxi ride she had gone over and over in her head how she would present her case, and again and again she had come up against the same problem. Shelley was a pragmatist. She would never believe it.

And now here she was, saying that she believed every word. Worse, she had known about Sarah's talents from the beginning.

"My God, listen to me," Shelley said. "I'm a doctor, for God's sake. But it happened. It happened."

"I don't know what she's done to you, or what she's capable of doing. I can't answer to any of that. But we're responsible for her, as a human being. She deserves a chance to live her life. I want to take her to see someone who has experience with this sort of thing, a parapsychologist—"

"Evan's under a tremendous amount of pressure, more than you can imagine. He'll never go for something like that. And he'll never let you take her out of the hospital alone."

"Then you'll have to help me."

"Impossible."

"You brought me into this for a reason. You wanted me to reach her, and I have. I can't believe you would stop now. Imagine if she were your child. She's just a little girl, no matter what you say she's capable of, what she's done. She scared, and she's alone. We owe her this. *You* owe her this."

"I don't owe her anything."

"How can you say that? She's spent most of her life behind the bars of that place. She's been drugged and restrained to keep her docile. You put her there. You sentenced her to that prison. And if you don't help me right now, if you don't give me the chance to get her out, I *will* go to the authorities for child abuse charges. Then it will all be out in the open. This will be over, one way or the other."

"It will kill her if you do it that way. You know that, don't you? The media pressure, the people falling over themselves to get at her. She'll be destroyed, just as if you'd held a gun to her head and pulled the trigger."

Jess had gained her feet. She found that she was breathing hard, and her throat felt tight. She fought to regain control of herself. "Then help me now," she said. "Help me do what's right for her."

For a moment she thought Shelley wasn't going to answer her at all. Various emotions passed across her face like ghosts. And then something seemed to move like a shudder through the professor's body, and she nodded.

"This isn't because of any threat of exposure. I'm beyond that now, understand? But you're right, I did bring you into this for a reason. It's time to force the issue, one way or the other. Evan's gone too far with her and it has to end.

"I'll call him to set up a private meeting off-premises for Sunday afternoon. They'll be at minimum staff then. Do you know Jeffrey? I helped place him there, nearly ten years ago now. He's an old patient of mine, in fact. He trusts me, and he'll do what I say. He'll help you get past the guard."

She stood with effort, pain etched across her face. "I can't go with you. I hope you understand. From then on, you're on your own."

—25—

"Okay, Sarah," Patrick said. "We're all friends here. I want you to try to relax."

They were huddled around the table in the tiny observation room of the church basement: Patrick, Gee, Jess, Sarah, and Connor the stuffed bear. It hadn't taken them long to get there. Jeffrey had seemed more than willing to cover for them, and he was good at it. In fact, he had done much more than that, getting Sarah upstairs and into the back of Charlie's car without drawing suspicion, and providing a distraction for the man at the gate so that they could get out without anyone noticing a thing.

But Jess was already looking at her watch. She couldn't be sure how long Wasserman would be gone, and what would she have accomplished if they were caught?

What she hadn't counted on was Sarah's resistance. The girl had been willing to go with her, eager to see the outside again. But when she explained what they were going to do, Sarah grew upset. No, Jess thought, it had been more than that; she had become frantic. It took everything Jess had to convince her that she would be all right, that these were friends who wanted to help her. Even now, she looked ready to bolt at any moment.

The empty worship hall hung like an expectant audience above their heads. Already she was regretting the decision to come. She was trying to reason, to find alternatives. Shelley had simply buckled under the terrible pressure of her disease, and was spending the rest of her life trying to deny the fact that her body had forsaken her. As for Sarah's grandmother, she was crazy as a shit-house rat; and what about all those strange things Jess herself had witnessed? There were explanations, there had to be. Perfectly reasonable solutions. If only she could find them.

Yes, the whole thing was crazy. What could possibly happen now, here under the lights and the intensely scrutinizing eyes of Patrick and Gee? And how could she put Sarah through this? She had told the girl that they were her friends, but what did she really know about this group, other than what Charlie had told her? They were certainly odd, but whether it went further than that, she couldn't tell.

She felt like a wrecking ball gathering speed and coming loose through its swing. This carelessness wasn't like her. *Damn it, you should have checked things out more carefully. You know better than that.*

But there hadn't been time. And it was too late now.

"We're going to run a few tests, nothing serious, but I'm going to have a look at your brain waves, and we'll record your heartbeat and blood pressure and respiration. There's nothing that's going to hurt, and nothing to be afraid of, okay?" Patrick fiddled with the contacts that had been taped to Sarah's skull. He was very gentle with her, adjusting the cuff around her upper arm. "Can I talk to you for a moment, please?" He gestured Jess out into the larger chamber and closed the door.

"This isn't going to work if you can't calm her down," he said, when they were out of earshot. "She can feel your nervousness. I can feel it. There's something on your mind. Let's get it out."

"I was just wondering why, if this sort of psychic phenomena is as widespread and proven as you say, we all haven't heard about it."

Patrick looked at her oddly for a moment. His lighter-colored eye seemed to bore into her, searching for her private heart. She felt uncomfortable and crossed her arms. "You have, you just don't know it. Let me tell you something. In 1985 the Army Research Institute was commissioned by Congress to study aspects of psychic phenomena. In their subsequent report they said that the data they had reviewed constituted genuine scientific anomalies for which no one had an adequate explanation. There was no scientific answer to what they had seen. And yet nobody listened. The report was buried, along with four others that said the same thing. In 1989, Radin and Ferrari at Princeton used meta-analysis to evaluate 148 different die-casting experiments performed during the last fifty years. They eliminated all except the most scientific and rigid of the group. What was left still proved the existence of psi with the odds against chance of more than a trillion to one.

"The truth is, the Defense Department has been conducting secret parapsychological experiments for years. Psi isn't a belief anymore. It's a proven fact. The data is there."

"So what are you telling me? There's some sort of conspiracy?"

"Absolutely."

An intercom clicked into life. "Come on," Gee said loudly from inside the observation room. His round, scruffy face peered through the window in the door. "Let's get the show on the road. I gotta get home and watch *The OC* on Tivo. It's a new episode, you know."

Jess wondered for a moment how it might feel to get her hands around Gee's skinny little neck.

"Calm yourself," Patrick said. "We're coming." To her, more gently, he said, "We've got to get Sarah to relax, to enter a premeditative state more conducive to psi. She's too tense, there's something upsetting her. But you have her trust. We can't do it without you. What have you got to lose?"

Jess held her breath, let it out slowly. "If she shows any signs of discomfort, seizure, anything at all, we stop. Immediately. All right?"

"You're the boss."

She had to admit, even before they began the serious testing (if such things as die-casting and random number generators could be called serious), that there was a feeling of heavy expectation in the air. Sarah seemed to sense her change of mood, as soon as they rejoined the others. Now she tugged at Jess's hand, and whispered in her ear, "I don't like it here."

"Do you want to leave?"

"Do you?"

"Not just yet. Are you scared?"

"I don't like tests. I don't want anything bad to happen!"

"Then we'll just make sure it doesn't."

"I had a dream last night," Sarah said. "I was in a big room and I was really mad. And I was hurting people."

"Recording," Gee said, bent close to a nearby glowing screen. A machine nearby started spitting out jagged lines on paper. "I'm getting betas. She's ready to roll."

"All right," Patrick said. He was standing in front of a bank of electrical devices with quivering needles and gauges. "Blood pressure slightly elevated, within normal parameters. Heartbeat coming down. Let go of her hand, Sarah, that's right, you can hold Connor. We won't bite you. I'm detecting a slight magnetic or electrical field. Overheads, Gee."

Gee turned a dimmer switch. The narrow room was transformed with a soothing wash of pink light.

"Can you tell me any more about your dream?"

"There were people coming after me and I was running, I was looking for my mother but I couldn't find her, and I hid in a big room and they were going to catch me. . . . I was doing things. I couldn't stop."

"I had a dream like that too. My brother was in it. But then I woke up and I realized it was just a dream. And dreams can't hurt you."

"But I was so mad!"

"We all get angry sometimes. But anger is something you can control."

"I don't like tests," she said again. Her fingers clutched at Jess's wrist. "No needles?"

"No, honey," Jess said. "I promise."

Patrick had returned with a set of headphones to the chair where Sarah sat, and he picked up a pair of halved Ping-Pong balls and began to tape them carefully over her eyes. They had lined the tabletop with pillows in order to make her more comfortable, and now he helped her climb up on them and lie down. "This is called the Ganzfeld approach," he said, into the strange pink light. "It's simply a way of allowing the mind to concentrate by reducing the amount of sensory stimuli. We'll turn on some music, and all I want you to do is relax, and try not to think about anything."

To Jess, he said, "I was thinking about the contents of that file. The people who put that together were aware that something unusual was going on with her. You don't take those kinds of tests, you don't record that kind of data without a reason. Gee, tweak the frequencies, will you? I'm getting some feedback."

"It's not me," Gee said. "Everything peachy here. Sure it isn't coming from your head?"

"Very amusing," Patrick said. "Pay attention, please." To Jess, he said, "So what else is our good hospital director hiding from you? That would be my question. If I were asking the questions, I mean."

"I guess it's lucky for him you're not."

Patrick left the room briefly and touched a button on a CD player. They were surrounded by gentle piano and strings. "Sarah, you're going to feel sleepy, you're going to feel like you're floating. I'm going to put these headphones on you to make that easier. Jess, why don't you take a seat? Gee, what are we reading?"

Chopin rolled and swelled within the basement chambers. Sarah lay on her back with her eyes closed, holding Connor while Patrick and Gee tended to the machines, conversed quietly, and took notes. Finally Jess pulled Patrick aside. "This isn't working."

"We're getting normal readings."

"That's just what I mean. Whenever something happened, something unusual, Sarah was in an extremely agitated state. I don't think you're going to get anywhere by hypnotizing her."

"So you want to piss her off?" Gee said, coming over. "I could give it a shot."

"We're going to start running her through a series of escalating steps. This is just to allow her to reach an alpha plateau. . . ."

"I dunno, though. She might melt my brain or something," Gee was saying. "Maybe I'll pass."

"Hush," Patrick said. "Why don't you check her readings, Gee? You're the best at it." When Gee had turned back to the bank of machines, and a second printer buzzed into life, he said softly, "He knows this isn't a joke. It's just his way of blowing off steam."

"I'm sure."

"Really," Patrick said. "If he hadn't come here, he'd be working on his Ph.D. at Duke. We're lucky to have him. But he's never been much of a people person, an only child and all that. His parents were both physicists and they were gone a lot. I don't think he had much of a social life."

"I'll be damned."

Patrick turned to a small monitor where an animated flipping coin played out across the screen. "This is a random number generator, fully automatic data recording. It uses radioactive decay times to provide electronic spikes at several thousand times a second. Heads is one, tails is zero. The computer chooses randomly, with the chance of one or zero being equal over time.

"We're going to ask her to influence the pattern. I'd expect hits in the range of fifty-three to fifty-five percent over time, if things go well."

"That doesn't seem terribly significant."

"The odds against it are billions to one. Now, I'd have done a blood test but I'm afraid I'd frighten her. Do you know what she's been given in the past to control her mood?"

"Sodium amytal, mostly."

"Sodium amytal, hmmm. Rhine used that exact drug to practically eliminate psi effects during his tests at Duke. Your director knows exactly what he's doing."

"We're getting alphas, but they're slipping," Gee said. "You better hurry. She's gonna fall asleep."

Patrick took a deep breath. "I want you to get her up and bring her out here. Gently, now, you can take off the Ping-Pong balls and blood pressure monitor but don't loosen the contacts, they'll reach. Don't make her nervous."

They sat down facing the random number generator and Patrick refastened the blood pressure cuff, Sarah trailing wires from her skull. She was still clutching Connor, but her eyes kept closing and she seemed deeply relaxed, as if in a trance. Patrick explained to her that the coin flipping across the screen was a computer image that corresponded to the numbers one and zero, and that she must try to make the image come up heads. She must try to think of the number one, or the image on the coin. His voice was slow and deep and soothing. Jess could not tell whether Sarah heard him or not.

They sat back and all watched the screen. The coin would bounce, flip, then bounce, flip again; after a while it seemed that tails was coming up more frequently. Two in a row. Three. Six.

Finally a long, straight line of tails had flashed across the screen. Sarah frowned. She sat up a bit straighter in her chair and stared at the flipping coin.

"I'm getting betas," Gee said. "No, wait, hold on, something's happening here—we've got alphas with very high peaks—it's like Mt. Everest over here."

"She's fighting herself," Patrick said, voice quiet and tight with excitement. "You see that, Gee? It's a reverse pattern."

"I see it," Gee said. His voice had lost all traces of sarcasm as he collected a steady stream of spitting paper printout. "You gotta look at these betas, I've never . . ."

"It happens sometimes," Patrick was saying, almost to himself, "people fight their own minds and do the opposite. If she's afraid of what she might do, if she's trying not to make it happen—"

"Whoa," Gee said. "Hold on. Jesus. She's off the chart."

Sarah was sweating lightly, her eyes wide open now, her little brow furrowed, mouth tight. A steady line of tails streamed across the computer screen.

The screen shivered; blinked. The temperature in the room had dropped. Jess felt the hairs on her arms rise up to meet it. Once again she was confronted with the familiar feeling of electricity, of a charge like an invisible presence in the room. The atmosphere had subtly changed; she held her breath and watched the air shimmer before her eyes.

The computer monitor began to smoke. A wisp curled like a gentle ghost-tongue around the plastic housing and drifted away; then the smoke grew black and thick.

"Dear Christ Almighty," Patrick said. "Gee, get the extinguisher. Gee."

Ronald Gee stood frozen as sparks jumped within the depths of the machine. The screen flickered and blinked again and went dark. Jess reached for Sarah's arm. Her fingers brushed the girl's skin and the effect was like walking across a thick carpet. She gasped. Every hair on her head prickled as she felt the charge enter her and wait, coiled.

Sarah trembled, clenched, as flames licked at the monitor

and the smell of melting plastic filled the room. The temperature kept dropping. The room was frigid. Someone called out and the words were lost within the buzzing that rose up like the flight of a thousand bees.

"Let it go!" Jess shouted at her. "Into me! Just let it go!"

Sarah turned to look blankly at her and for a moment fear rose up and an oily sickness turned Jess's stomach, and then the girl looked away and a cry like a splitting inside forced itself from her lips as a series of small cracks and then explosions came in quick succession from across the room.

Sarah slumped; then her body jerked once as Jess gathered the girl into her arms and felt the coiled charge jump from her hands and dissipate into the air.

"Oh, baby, sweetheart, it's okay, it's going to be all right . . ." she whispered into the girl's muffled sobs, her body tingling, muscles suddenly weak. She stroked Sarah's hair, smoothed the sweat from her brow, pulled the electrodes from her skin as her own tears spilled out over her cheeks. Sarah curled into her lap like a small child and rocked, shaking. Jess clutched her bony ribs, rocked her, rocked. "It's okay now, I'm here. . . ."

Jess heard the hiss of the fire extinguisher and from somewhere far away she watched Patrick spraying the monitor's smoking husk with white foam. The air was thick with a choking, acrid smoke.

Only then did she glance around at the place where the explosions had come from, and saw the rows of specimen bottles shattered across the shelves, their contents lying among the dripping ruin of glass and bottle tops like dead things, evidence at the scene of a crime.

—26—

She was in the empty church, standing with her arms wrapped around herself for warmth, as the afternoon sun trickled through stained glass and painted the polished floor in reds and yellows beneath her feet. She had wrapped Sarah in a blanket and laid her down in the backseat of Charlie's car, had smoothed the fine black hairs away from Sarah's forehead until the girl's breathing deepened and she slept.

Her heart broke for the girl. Who had been there to protect her, all these years? Who had been there to hold her when the darkness crept in, to explain that whatever affliction God had given her, whatever this curse was (and yes, Jess thought, it was a curse), it didn't destroy her humanity?

Her words, whispered before she knew what she was saying: *"I'm here for you, Sarah. Everything's going to be all right. I promise."*

She stood now among the shattered remains of her confidence, struggling to find something whole, something she could hold on to and use. But everything needed to be rethought, reevaluated. The world was different now, not on the surface but underneath, where it really mattered. For some reason, her thoughts kept going back to Michael's death; had she wanted it to happen? Had there been a part of her, however small, that had wanted it all to end, had she reached out at that moment and pushed him away when she should have been pulling him in close?

A voice spoke from somewhere like a chittering devil: *You were happy when he died, weren't you? Happy to have the burden relieved?*

Her helpless gaze fell on the statue of Christ, hanging cold and lifeless in the shadows of the altar. A half-remembered children's prayer rose unbidden to her lips, a prayer for forgiveness, for absolution. For strength. What sort of God would make a world like this? she wondered. Where children were given terrible burdens to carry, left alone, abused, even killed?

Everything had happened so fast. It baffled her. When had she become so attached to this girl? Surely she felt sorry for Sarah, felt as if she should do all she could to help. But when had these feelings blossomed into real responsibility, into something even more?

A noise came from the direction of the door. Footsteps offered into silence. A moment later Patrick stepped up next to her, smelling sharply of smoke and chemicals and light sweat. "She's still asleep. I suppose you have someplace to take her?"

"She needs to get back to the hospital before she's missed."

"Are you sure—"

"What else can I do? Another hour or two, they'll arrest me for kidnapping. I can't do anyone any good from jail."

"You're questioning yourself."

"Of course I am!"

"I want you to know that everything you're doing for that girl is honorable. You're the only one who's really tried to help her. You're the only friend she has right now." Patrick's excitement was palpable. But he was fighting hard to hold it in, probably for her benefit. He slipped an arm around her shoulders. The movement did not seem inappropriate.

For a moment she allowed herself to lean into him and regain her balance. She looked up into his face, felt him lean in as well, his lips brush hers. Then he pulled away.

"I apologize," he said, a look very close to shock on his face. "I shouldn't have done that."

"It's all right. I—"

He was shaking his head. "No. That was crazy. I'm taking advantage of an emotional situation. It's just that I've witnessed something I've waited my whole life to see. It's overwhelming. I'm sorry."

He turned and walked down the empty church aisle, pacing, a ball of nervous energy. She watched him go, not sure what to think of anything. Had she wanted that to happen? Had she been sending out some kind of signal?

"She's at the right age," he said finally, turning back. "Puberty often triggers psychic phenomena. We call it the poltergeist effect. But once she's older, these phenomena may very likely grow easier to control. They may even disappear." He studied the light and the patterns falling from stained glass. "I'm sorry for my part in this. I got carried away, I didn't think about how it might affect her. She's scared to death of it, I know. But you've got to understand what this means to me. She's revolutionary. She's one of a kind, all that you told me and more."

"Just don't you try to exploit her, Patrick. I won't allow it."

"You misunderstand me." He turned back, and she searched his eyes for honesty. "The important thing now is to teach her. She's going to face skepticism, fear, mistrust. She's got to learn to hold on to her anger. She has to learn that psi isn't a curse, it isn't something to fight, to be ashamed of. What she's been given is a gift, a blessed, extraordinary gift."

"You're forgetting the fact that she's been involuntarily committed to an asylum and they aren't about to let her just walk away."

"They haven't been playing straight with you. They know exactly what they're doing, and I'm willing to bet there are more people involved in this than you think. Look at the tests they've run, the missing information. Look at her file. They're going to try to push her. They may just push her too far."

"What do you suggest we do?"

"She could disappear tomorrow. I know people who could make it happen. There's a network, you understand? People just like us, who want to help, who could teach her how to live with this gift of hers. More of them than you think. Anywhere in the country, a new name, a new beginning. She'd be in good hands, capable hands."

"You're asking me to break the law. And what's the difference between you and the people I'm trying to get her away from? Do you honestly expect me to believe you won't end up pushing her too far too?"

She was struck by the intensity in his eyes. Patrick reached into a pocket of his coat. He showed her what he held in his hand; a shapeless lump of blackened plastic and metal. "It's the number generator's CPU. We tested the circuits before you came; there was nothing wrong with the machine. She melted it down to nothing. Do you see that? Do you understand what this means?"

"Electricity," Jess murmured. She took the lump from him and held it in her hands; it was still slightly warm. "That's what it feels like. Some kind of electrical charge."

"I don't know what it is. But I want to find out. This is a once-in-a-lifetime chance. There have been cases, once or twice a century, of people with a talent like hers. Uri Geller was one, though even his abilities were never truly proved beyond the shadow of doubt. But we all have the possibility inside us, I'm sure of it. It's just a matter of learning how to unlock the right doors."

"Why are you doing this, Patrick? What's made you search these things out, what drives you?" *Do you understand, I have to know before I can possibly trust you?*

"You don't want to hear that story. It's really nothing special."

"If I didn't, I wouldn't have asked."

"All right. But don't say I didn't warn you." Patrick gestured at the empty church, at the rows of pews, as if it would make her see. "My father was a minister. I grew up in churches, spent more time in them than I did at home. But my father loved God more than he did his children. At least that was the way it felt. I was always trying to impress him, make him notice me. But nothing worked.

"Then one day, I was about eight years old, I ran away from home. I didn't get very far at first, it wasn't a real attempt, but I remember getting lost in the woods behind our house. Those woods were deep. It got late and I remember being very frightened by the dark. And finally I remember someone speaking to me. It was my father. He said, come home, son, come this way. And I just followed his voice until I saw the house again.

"When I got to the front steps my father opened the door. He didn't say a word, he just held out his arms. There had been people out looking for me, but my father had just stayed behind. He said he wanted to be there to guide me home.

"After that, my father and I had a special bond. I understood him and he understood me. And I never forgot that night. You don't forget something like that."

"Where's your father now?"

"He died when I was seventeen. Diabetic shock. They put him in the hospital overnight, said he'd be out the next day. But I knew he was never coming back. I knew. Have you ever felt anything like that? Not a hunch, or an educated guess. When the moment comes you're sure, you've never been so sure of anything your entire life. It becomes a part of you, a certainty."

"I don't know." Tiredly. *Yes.* She thought of childhood dreams, headlights, and the scream of car's tires, of nights waking in a choking sweat. Memories surfaced like creatures from the deep. *Maybe I have. Maybe I just don't want to admit it.*

"We're holding in our hands the key to a new kind of life, Jess. A higher life on earth. More spiritual, more peaceful, more connected. Mind over matter. Imagine the possibilities. I truly believe that it's just within our reach."

"Maybe so. But you're wrong about Sarah's being able to learn to control it. She's barely able to hang on for the ride. And if you push her, if you try to dissect her like some kind of lab specimen, you'll be no better than anyone else."

The door slammed open at the other end of the church. "Two hundred beats per minute," Gee announced, trailing paper like white fluttering birds. "Blood pressure through the roof. Her EEG was off the charts. Temperature dropped thirteen degrees, enough heat energy to lift a truck. Big one too, one of those semis with the eighteen wheels."

"Good Lord," Patrick whispered almost reverently. "And she was still on sodium amytal. Imagine what might have happened if she were clean?"

"I'm imagining it," Jess said grimly. "Is that supposed to make me feel better, or worse?"

"Give me the word," he said with urgency, facing her, holding her wrist gently between two fingers, as if he was afraid to touch her. "Just tell me and I'll have it all planned by tomorrow. She'll be free to live her life as normally as possible, I promise you."

"I can't do that. I have to go through the proper channels. It wouldn't be fair to her. It wouldn't be fair to anyone involved."

Patrick looked at her for a beat. He nodded, and did not look too disappointed. Did he know something she did not? Or had he just anticipated her response?

"All right. Here's my home number. Just tell me you'll think about it. It's a standing offer. For now, take her back, go home and get some sleep. You look like you could use it."

She tried; oh, how she tried.

But back in her little apartment that evening, with the October wind whispering to get in and Otto pacing restless by the door, Jess could not think of sleep. Not now, not here, maybe not ever, with the feeling of Patrick's kiss still haunting her lips. She didn't know what to think of that, of him, of anything. When she closed her eyes the walls pressed in close and she couldn't breathe, could not find herself among the voices clamoring to be heard.

Finally she set up a blank canvas on the easel at the window, mixed her paints at the sink, turning yellows into reds, swirling and dipping, smoothing, finding her place. *A rough bristle will do*, she thought, *tonight is calling for broad, bold strokes.* It was necessary to clear her head. She wished briefly she could be up in the night sky, above the clouds and under the full moon. But this late the airport would be empty, planes tied down and covered for the night like slumbering metal beasts. And she knew from experience that the need was only her desire to escape, something she had to fight against, especially now.

Her mind was free to drift back in time. She had been left alone more and more often after Michael's death, as her mother searched for answers at the bottom of a bottle. An orphan of alcoholism. It made her more self-sufficient, but also took from her a portion of her childhood. She became the adult in a family of two. At times her mother would not come home at all, and she would have to fend for herself. It made her grow up too fast, kept her from forming a solid foundation upon which to build her life, left her with a shaken self-confidence, left her as an overachiever, a person who pushed herself to the dropping point and then pushed some more. If she had to run a mile for gym class, she would run two; if she needed a B on a test to get by, she would get an A. There were no markers for her performance, no limits set. So she set her own, always trying to prove something. That she was better than this life.

Understanding your weaknesses is the difference between a person who is led by life and a person who leads, Jess told herself. She bathed the canvas in a base of gray, a touch of lighter orange near the top to simulate the color of a coming dawn, as the 2:00 a.m. train rattled by down below. More paint, thicker strokes. White and dark playing off each other, creating shadows and light, texture and depth. The night she had returned from college her freshman year, Christmas Eve, filled with the hope of a new beginning; her mother on the phone, I've started going to meetings, I'm getting with the program. The tree was up and decorated for the first time in years. The living room was clean and bright and empty. Waiting on the sofa, angry, then worried, then finally hours later her mother at the door, slurring her words and stumbling, the sound of a man's voice. *Get the fuck out of here, my daughter's home. . . .*

So she knew. The point was, she knew something of how Sarah felt. Unable to trust, to ever feel truly secure. Sarah felt like the world was out to get her. And why shouldn't she? Jess searched for that common thread and clutched at it. She knew it was important to have a bond with the person you were trying to understand. You had to walk in her shoes.

And yet the differences were immense. At least she had been able to escape, to choose another life, to make her own decisions. Sarah had been a prisoner from the moment she could think. Her frustrations and her anger had built over years of barred windows and institutional walls.

And finally those emotions were manifesting themselves physically. The walls were coming down. Even now, after all she had seen, Jess found it hard to believe. But the proof was before her eyes, in shattered lightbulbs and a rain of stones and a piece of electronic equipment melted into oblivion; even Connor the bear, singed where Sarah had clutched him. She thought of the case of Esther Cox and her poltergeist, pots and pans flying off the walls, water boiling in pails, beds shaking and thumping up and down. Before she had believed it to be a clear case of psychotic delusion; now she believed otherwise. And what about Uri Geller, world-famous metal bender extraordinaire, who had been continuously denounced as a fraud and a cheat by the scientific establishment? Did she believe now that he too, along with countless hundreds of others, was the real thing?

Her painting was too dark. A storm was coming. Frowning, she dabbed white paint, lightening the clouds and searching for moonlight. The angles of shadow were wrong, the moon was not overhead, but behind . . .

The proof was in more than just those things too, she thought as she dabbed paint and searched for an angle of imaginary moonshine. Little more than a month ago Sarah had been a catatonic invalid, and now she spoke, thought, imagined, dreamed. *You had something to do with that*, Jess told herself, and from that thought arose pride, an unreasoning hope, and a long-dormant faith. It was one of those thoughts that came easily in the stillness of early morning. Where one impossibility exists, why not two? Hell, why not all of them? Why couldn't Patrick be right in insisting that they stood on the edge of a new era of mankind?

It was a lot of weight to put on the shoulders of a single

little girl. Jess put down her brush, clenched and unclenched her hands, remembering the feeling of the charge inside her, how it had coiled in her belly and then leapt from her palms like a living thing. Was that how such a power felt? Like a muscle tensed and quivering for release?

Jess knew she had found herself again. She had put her feet back firmly on the ground. She could go on, she could finish this thing now without second-guessing herself. But there were so many questions left unanswered. What were Wasserman's real motives? And Professor Shelley. What was her role in all of this? There was something more behind Shelley's confession that she needed to get out.

Give me the word. She'll be free, I promise you.

No, Patrick, she thought, *I won't do that. I won't entrust Sarah's life to another set of strangers that take her and disappear.* But there were organizations that would listen to her case. The state licensing board, mental health charter, even the American Medical Association, if it came to that.

For a moment the feeling thrilled her, filled her with hope and a sense of coming struggle. She would have to go up against Wasserman again. She would have to be very careful.

But Shelley was still Sarah's court-appointed guardian, and that carried a lot of weight. And Shelley would have to do something when the truth was out in the open.

She would have no choice but to listen now.

—28—

Three men and a woman stood in a small room filled with electronic equipment and leather bucket chairs. The room resembled the cockpit of a submarine with a viewing window that opened up over a vast, black space that appeared as deep as an ocean trench.

At the moment, all eyes were on one of the flat-screen monitors bolted to the wall, where a flurry of activity had reached its end. The sound was low, but the quality was such that they had no trouble hearing everything.

On the screen, several technicians moved into view, eclipsing the figure on the floor save for one pale hand and part of an arm. They watched in silence as the hand flopped once, like a fish out of water, and lay still.

"That's better," Philippa Cruz murmured, flipping through the pages of her chart and jotting down more notes. "She's like a light when the power's cut. I think we've got something, right there. Run it back and play it again."

The monitor blinked gray static before the camera picked up the little girl again. She was surrounded by a fine, white mist that made it difficult to see. At first this had been a very unsettling thing to witness. They knew now that it was caused by the rapid acceleration of subatomic particles and the wicking of moisture and heat from the air, which in turn caused an intense drop in temperature and condensation to form in the surrounding space.

Simple physics, Cruz thought. *Just like anything else. There are no miracles, only science.*

When discussing the phenomenon of the psi gene and its effects with others, Cruz had found it helpful to present it in terms of conventional versus microwave heat. Most people are at least somewhat familiar with how a microwave oven works when heating food. Conventional heating requires contact by an object with another warmer one, like a pan on a hot stove. Energy is passed between the two in the form of heat. Microwave heating does not require direct contact, but accomplishes much the same thing.

To put it another way, Cruz thought, to push someone, most people would have to reach out their hand and make physical contact. A person with an active psi gene could accomplish the same thing through a process that utilized wave energy.

There was much more to it, of course, so much that they still didn't understand. But they were getting closer. Blue light leaped in staggering jagged flashes across the screen as the scene played out once more. Cruz glanced at several other monitors displaying heart rate and brain wave activity at the time the video had been filmed. Right here, they had administered the inhibitor; see how quickly it had taken effect. She counted less than thirty seconds. It was remarkable.

She made more notes. "Have you been taking blood samples at precisely the right time?" she asked. "You know how important this is. Within three minutes before and after the event, and no later."

Evan Wasserman bobbed his head. He had combed his thinning hair back and used a light oil to calm the wisps that tended to float in a halo about his scalp. "It's all in the latest report." He handed her a file.

What a strange bird, she thought. He was so anxious today, as if anticipating something tremendously important. She hadn't seen him in person in over a month; she hadn't had to be so personally involved in the testing until recently, which was fine. She preferred the lab setting. But now that they were so close to a breakthrough, she needed to be on-site.

Her boss's dependence on this man was a mystery to her. At one point, Wasserman's influence over the girl and his ability to persuade her to cooperate had made him useful to them, but now that they had a viable drug candidate his usefulness was mostly gone, and he had to know it.

He was so jumpy she thought perhaps he was finally breaking down. She had always supposed it would be a matter of time, but with the added pressure they were all under, there was actually a reason for it.

She thought back to the dinner meeting at the heliport. It had gone spectacularly well. After viewing the second video clip, the two men had fallen all over themselves to express their interest. They were efficient brokers and already Helix had received partnership inquiries from three other companies, and an outright buyout offer from one.

Clinical trials were expensive; prostituting themselves was a necessary evil when they needed to come up with another five hundred million. To get that kind of money they would have to produce more concrete results, of course, and eventually demonstrate the new compound's effectiveness in another subject.

But from the looks of this latest video, they were well on their way to something truly special.

"Hmmm . . ." Cruz flipped through pages. She noted something else that excited her a great deal. "Expression is tight as a drum. PSI-526 blood levels jumped over three hundred percent by half an hour after dosing, and then we dialed it back down to almost nothing. That's very good."

"Talk dirty to me, my dear," Steven Berger said, smiling up at her from his seat on one of the bucket chairs. "'Tight as a drum.' I love it." His thick head of white hair was very carefully groomed today, and he had an extra bounce in his step. He had insisted on coming here, even though he didn't have much to offer in terms of expertise. He simply wanted to be a witness to their future. Here was a man who was motivated by greed, and had no problem letting everyone know it. And yet he held a certain poetic sense of the moment in history.

Berger certainly had a reason to be giddy with their recent success, even if he didn't understand the technical details. Structure-based drug design was always a slow process; much of the work done under the microscope and through computer-assisted modeling, and potential molecules had to be tested, tweaked, and tested again. It was necessary to identify and validate the drug target using functional genomics, chemical genetics, and proteomics, and it required an encyclopedic knowledge of biology, chemistry, and genetics.

But the potential payoff was huge. The purpose was to throw out the old hit-or-miss way of drug discovery in favor of the intelligent and informed design of synthetics. If you studied the structure of a protein carefully enough, you could create a molecule that bound very tightly and selectively to its target, thus creating more potent and effective results.

Designing a drug that would tightly control the psi gene's expression was essential, of course. It was no good to just turn the gene on and let it go like a runaway train. They had already seen what could happen without an effective "off" switch, and the accident and the deaths that resulted from it had forced them to shut down testing for nearly a year. The next attempt had yielded a compound that, along with the other drugs she had received as a precautionary measure, had caused a nearly complete catatonic state. The new compound had brought her out of it, and so far it looked like a winner.

But this was only the first step, and Cruz knew it. The psi gene was carried naturally by one in approximately five hundred thousand people in the world, as far as they had been able to estimate. There were markers to help identify them, but it was still a very small pool. To create something truly revolutionary, they needed to take the next leap forward. They needed to be able to deliver that gene into the general population.

Cruz stepped closer to the observation window. With the lights off inside the adjoining room, she could see nothing clearly now except her reflection. But she knew what lay beyond the specially coated glass. It was, in essence, their safety valve, constructed shortly after the fire incident. Wave energy interacts with various forms of matter that absorbs it, reflects it, or passes it through. This was why they had lined the testing room with a material that first absorbed that energy and then served to disperse it.

The whole thing was perfectly contained. And they had several other rooms just like it, along with better equipment and more space, at a facility in Alabama. Empty now, and waiting for them to arrive.

"You want dirty talk, imagine this," she said, studying the mirror images of her own ice-blue eyes, her nose, the rather sensual curve of her lips. "A stripped adeno-associated virus is loaded with the cloned psi gene and a transcription factor. This is injected into anyone you like; a construction worker, scientist, doctor, member of the U.S. Marine Corps, perhaps. The virus acts as a gene delivery vehicle into muscle cells, where it waits in a dormant state, until we decide to 'turn it on.' We do this using a small-molecule drug that activates the transcription factor, and which can be taken orally. The level of gene expression depends on the amount of the small-molecule drug administered, giving us complete control over the result."

"I don't know exactly what you just said, but I liked it." Berger sat up in his chair. "Evan, did you get all of that?"

Cruz turned to Wasserman, who had paled visibly. "Exogenously regulated expression of a transferred gene," he said. "Can you really do it?"

"U Penn researchers did it years ago with erythropoi-etin," Cruz said. "They demonstrated sustained and pre-cisely controlled expression in rhesus monkeys over a period of months, with only one injection to deliver the gene. The regulating drug was in oral form, a simple pill, dial it up, dial it down. Easy as pie."

"Incredible," Wasserman said. "But you *can't do that* in this case. You know what it will mean. A member of the Marine Corps? You're talking about a weapon." He turned to Berger with his hands out and palms up in a gesture of supplication. "Steven, you can't be serious."

"Why not? Every single person in the world would kill to have an ability like this. The military applications alone are limitless. And we'll be the only ones able to give it to them. At a fairly hefty price, of course."

"No, no, no." Wasserman moaned. He shook his head. Beads of sweat had broken out across his brow. He looked ill. "Listen to me. You haven't been here when it's been let loose, you haven't seen all of what she can do. You haven't seen her lose control."

"We've seen the tapes."

"That's not the same!" Wasserman shouted. The sound was deafening in the cramped space. "I was there, I saw the damage firsthand. I saw those men die, I heard their skin crackling, for God's sake. What if that kind of power fell into the wrong hands? It could make the atom bomb look like a firecracker."

"Hold on now," Berger said. He was still smiling, trying to placate. "The system we're talking about is very tightly regulated, that's the beauty of it—"

"I won't let you do it," Wasserman said. "This has gone far enough. I can't let . . . my own—feelings—" He stopped. "I found her," he said. "I earned her trust the first time around. Don't forget that."

"And without our help, you would have been moldering away in an adjunct position at the local community college by now," Cruz said. "A place like this, there's a lot of over-head. We've bankrolled you for too long, let you have your way, working everything from your own location. It's a wonder anything's been accomplished at all."

"All right, Phillipa." Berger waved his hand. "Let's not get carried away here. . . ."

A knock came at the door. Wasserman's eye twitched frantically. He swiped at a trickle of sweat rolling down his cheek. "Come in," he said.

"Sorry to interrupt," the big orderly who stuck his head in said. "But we've spotted the woman you asked about coming in at the gate."

Wasserman blinked. "She's here now?"

"May already be inside."

"All right. Thank you. Please take her directly to my of-fice to wait for me."

The orderly left. All three of them stood in silence, con-sidering each other, each realizing something irrevocable had happened and not sure where to go next.

"This conversation isn't over," Wasserman said finally. "I have to see to something important. I'll be right back."

After the door closed, Cruz and Berger exchanged a look. It had happened a bit more abruptly than they might have liked, Cruz thought, but it was time now. In fact, it was past due. They had made all the progress they could with her here, and Wasserman was a liability.

Alabama was waiting. Now all they had to do was tie up a few loose ends.

"Would you like to make the call, or shall I?" Berger said.

—29—

The guard at the gatehouse was not one of the regulars, but Jess had seen him once or twice before. He waved her ahead in Charlie's car with barely a glance at her temporary pass, and a smile that was a little too friendly. She stopped and backed up. "Excuse me. Is Dr. Wasserman around?"

"Don't know that he's arrived as yet, but I just got on duty ten minutes ago. Say, I know you, I never forget a face like that. You wouldn't want to grab a drink with me when I get off shift, say, around five o'clock?"

She smiled vaguely. "I've got a class."

"No kidding? That late, huh? You in school? I would've thought you were another of them specialists. People coming and going, I gotta open the gate every goddamn three minutes—"

"Sorry, I'm sort of in a hurry."

"Some other time, then. Be seeing you."

Good Christ Almighty. She parked in a space behind the hospital and went around to the front. No point in letting Wasserman know she was here too quickly.

But inside the doors she noticed an unusual silence. The playroom was empty. Her footsteps were too loud in the deserted hallway.

At the elevator, something made her pause. There were

four floors in this building. The third, she knew, held bed-rooms for the children. But what was above them? She stepped in and pressed the fourth-floor button, but nothing happened. She noticed a slot for a key next to the button. *Curious.* As she was jamming the button hard with her thumb, an orderly she didn't recognize hurried around the corner and stuck his arm in the door to keep it open. "You there! The doctor wants to see you in his office as soon as possible."

She thought of protesting. The orderly was big, heavy through the shoulders. He had her by the elbow. "Come on, Miss Chambers. Right this way."

He knew my name, she thought. They were looking for her. Why? Did Wasserman know she had taken Sarah out of the facility? *Of course he knows.* If not, it could only be a matter of time; though Jeffrey had done his best to get them out without being seen, cameras could have caught some-thing, someone would have talked.

The orderly steered her down the hall into Wasserman's office and closed the door. She found herself alone with the memory of him. Desk swept bare, coat hanging in the cor-ner, a lingering scent of shoe polish and Old Spice after-shave. For a moment she saw him at home in a spotless and slightly outdated apartment, decorated to hide the absence of a woman's touch. Wasserman was bright and proud and completely socially incpt. She wondered briefly if he had trouble finding dates and thought his awful aftershave would help.

All right, okay, let's put this time to use.

She cracked open the door and checked the hallway; empty. The file cabinets were locked. She found the key in the center drawer of his desk. She found the patient files kept alphabetically by name and flipped through them. Her fingers paused for a moment on Brigham, Dennis, and she thought rather fondly of the poor, sad boy in his baseball hat and white socks; and then she moved on to *H*.

Sarah's file seemed no fatter than before. Jess scanned it quickly and saw nothing that hadn't been there the first time. She replaced the file and tried the other drawers on his desk. Locked. A wire end of a barrette would do the trick. *You're getting in pretty deep.* But judging from the behavior of that orderly out there, things couldn't get much worse. This might be her only chance.

She found a barrette in her shoulder bag, crouched, and slipped the lock in twenty seconds flat. Inside the top left drawer was an assortment of pens and pencils, a tape recorder, three pads of legal paper, a Snickers bar wrapper, a half-empty bottle of bourbon, and in the back, a handgun, curled like a blackly oiled snake. She checked it; loaded. *What the hell is that for?*

No time now. In the bottom drawer were more file folders done up in plastic slipcases and rubber bands. One of them was stamped PROJECT SV-ALPHA. Sarah Voorsanger? Jess took it out and carefully undid the rubber bands, slid it away from static-free plastic. Here were the missing PET scans from a number of intensive tests using radioactive dye to study glucose metabolism and regional cerebral blood flow. Several areas were circled in red marker and labeled.

PET scans were expensive, and the use of radioactive tracers in children was unusual. There were scans from more than fifteen separate tests. She slipped one into her bag.

There was more: the missing family history, transcripts from interviews with Cristina and Ed Voorsanger, a medical diagnosis on Annie Voorsanger . . .

And then this, the last. A series of charts that seemed to track medication levels. But they were nothing she recognized.

The sound of a doorknob made her skin prickle. She slid the drawer closed but did not have time to lock it.

"What the hell do you think you're doing?" Wasserman stood red-faced in the doorway, wearing a white starched shirt with rolled-up sleeves. He was sweating profusely. .

"Get away from my desk. Do they teach snooping in graduate school, Miss Chambers?"

"Excuse me. I dropped my barrette—"

"You're out of line. I know you took Sarah off the premises yesterday afternoon. That was a very stupid thing to do. It went against my explicit orders, it violated countless number of state and federal laws, and it put my patient in danger."

"Dr. Wasserman, surely you know that something unusual is going on with her. It's not ethical to continue drug therapy in her present condition. Anyone can see that she's perfectly lucid and capable and she's being held against her will. Now if you'll just listen to what I have to say—"

"Don't you preach ethics to me. What sort of treatment I choose to administer does not concern you any longer. You're through here as of this minute."

Jess felt her control slipping a little. "Why didn't you show me her complete file, Doctor? Is there something you don't want me to see?"

She was learning a great deal about Evan Wasserman now, and what she saw didn't suit him. Anger made his eyes red and piggish and his underarms itch. She could tell by the way his shoulders twitched.

He was moving now, around the desk, close enough to her so that she could smell his breath. "This experiment is over. I will see that you are reprimanded and that your school records show this as a permanent black mark. You're a fool, Miss Chambers, if you believe the things others are preaching. Sarah Voorsanger is a very sick young woman and her delusions are barely being held in check. I'm sure she would be better served if you were out of her life."

Bullshit. "If you would just think this through, I'm sure we can—"

"I've done enough thinking. Give me your temporary staff pass."

"I forgot it at home," she lied. "The guard out front knew who I was."

Some emotion surfaced briefly in his face and he seemed to fight it down. For a moment she wondered if he would frisk her. "I want you to turn it in to Jean Shelley as soon as you get back to school. She'll have some words for you, I'm sure. Good-bye, Miss Chambers."

She refused to give him the satisfaction of watching her slink out with her tail between her legs. "What are you afraid of, Doctor? That I've found out the truth?"

"The truth about what, for God's sake?"

"Sarah, and what you've done to her. You had to know I'd see something sooner or later. Why did you allow me in here? There has to be some reason."

"I'm not going to listen to another word of this non-sense." Wasserman marched over to the intercom on his desk and pressed the button. "Andre? Come in here please, and escort Miss Chambers to her car."

"I can find my own way out," she said. "Thank you."

As she walked toward the half-open door she caught movement in the hall. A white-haired man in a navy blue suit; not an orderly, or a patient. Too well dressed. He smelled of money. A family member? She glanced back at Wasserman and caught him white-faced and sweating, eva-sive, like a man exposed in a lie.

He closed the door behind her. She heard a lock click into place.

In the hallway, the man had disappeared. She hurried to the corner, but then the big orderly was coming toward her again.

"Excuse me, Andre, isn't it? This is embarrassing. I was wondering, that man in the blue suit? I met him last week but I can't remember his name."

"Out," the orderly said. "Right now."

He followed her all the way to the parking lot, folded his arms, watched her from the walkway. She got into the car and sat for a moment in silence, and resisted the childish urge to pound her fists against the steering wheel. Sarah was still inside somewhere, alone and probably scared to death, and there was no way to reach her.

Jess thought about their return trip from Patrick's church, poor Sarah awake now and staring absently out at a crimson wash of autumn leaves, poor, lonely Sarah; *something terrible is going to happen. I know it.*

Nothing's going to happen to you.

I don't want to go back. Am I ever going to get out?

We're going to find a better place for you. I promise.

If my mom can't take care of me, I want to live with you. Will you please help me?

A stiff breeze lifted brittle leaves from the corners of the parking lot and sent them tumbling end over end. She could hear the dry hiss of their passage. It sounded like the whispers of a thousand ghostly voices. She took a deep breath and let it out. *Goddammit, Wasserman, this isn't over. I swear it isn't.* She put one hand on the PET scan inside her bag. Maybe, just maybe, she had something.

Thank God for Charlie's car. The orderly was still standing and watching her as she left the parking lot. She resisted the urge to give him the finger, and waved genially instead. If he was aware of the sarcasm, he didn't show it.

—30—

Jess Chambers drove Charlie's car too fast through crowded city streets. She cursed at stoplights and tested the brakes on more than one occasion, earning the glares of her fellow motorists. But all that went unnoticed.

She was thinking of the changes in Dr. Evan Wasserman since she had first met him, only weeks before: the breakdown in his control, the cracks appearing along his formerly smooth surface. *What are you hiding, Wasserman? You're scared to death of her, aren't you?*

But that wasn't it exactly. This was what really bothered her, his discomfort aimed not entirely at her but *somewhere*. She turned onto Washington Street and drove through Brookline, moving away from traffic, using this time to calm herself again and think. The man in the blue suit, Wasserman's face when he caught a glimpse . . .

Important pieces were missing. She needed answers, and there was only one other place she might find them.

This time when she rang the doorbell there was nobody to answer the door. She went around the back of the house, stepping carefully past pruned juniper hedges and pine bark mulch. The smell of freshly watered soil touched her nostrils, and with it came a feeling of calm, of peace. She flashed back to fields of rustling corn, the smell of turned earth, of September rainstorms. It washed away the stink of the city.

Professor Jean Shelley sat in front of a garden table on the grass. On the ground was a large, silver bowl and a folded towel. She kept her back and neck rigid under a cotton sweater, watching birds flit to the feeder. Jess stood for a moment transfixed. From this angle, she could see clearly how swollen Shelley's wrists and ankles were, how worn she looked. Death comes gradually and then all at once, like headlights around a corner at night.

Shelley turned her ghostly face slightly but did not look at her. "I thought you might come back. I'm sorry I didn't answer the door but I'm not feeling well enough at the moment."

"You should have someone here with you."

"That's thoughtful, but I prefer to be alone."

"I won't stay long."

"Then please, find a seat." Jess took a chair from the deck and set it on the grass. "Good, good. Now how did your little trip turn out?"

Jess told her about the afternoon at Patrick's church and the events immediately following: the meltdown in the computer, her recent visit with Wasserman. "I spoke with him this morning, actually," Shelley said, when she had finished. "He told me you were no longer welcome at the hospital. He wanted me to speak to the school administrative office and have you expelled."

"Did you?"

"Of course not. I don't think you've done anything I wouldn't have done, in your shoes, and I feel guilty enough for my part in this. But you've been missing classes. I know your grades are starting to slip. You need to be careful not to let this consume you."

Jess opened her shoulder bag. She took out the PET scan and handed it over. "It's from Sarah's private file," she said. "The one I didn't get a chance to see. Can you tell me what it means?"

Shelley looked at the scan for a long moment, and put it down on the table between them, where it sat like an unwanted visitor. She seemed to be struggling with something. "Let it go," she said. "It's out of your hands now. Go back to school, take back your life. Be young."

"I can't do that, Professor."

They were silent for a moment. Jess burned with impatience, but let it simmer under the surface, waiting for the right time.

"Let me ask you a question," Shelley said. "Forgive me for being blunt, but I've been thinking about this since you came to visit before. That man who taught you to fly. Did he try to . . . touch you? Do something inappropriate?"

Jess was surprised by the question. She considered what to say. "Yes. Once he did."

"And you stopped him?"

"I thought it was disgusting, it made me angry. I was hurt. I was old enough to know about what he wanted to do."

"I wondered. His gift of the plane seemed like an offering. Only once, though? He never tried again?"

"No. He seemed genuinely sorry, like he had slipped. But we never talked about it and I didn't go see him much after that. Things were different between us. Something had changed."

Shelley seemed satisfied with the answer. She nodded. "Sometimes we take too much responsibility for others, don't we? We assume that they'll act as we do, with decency and respect. And when they don't we take it upon ourselves, we take in their sins and we try to erase them from memory in any way we can."

"I guess so. But it isn't as simple as all that."

"Isn't it?"

"Professor Shelley, I saw a man today with Dr. Wasserman, he was well dressed, white hair, short and stocky. I hadn't seen him before. Do you know what he might have been doing at the hospital?"

Shelley didn't seem to hear her. When she spoke it was with distance, and tinged with a dull anger. "I don't think I'll be going back to school," she said. "I've been feeling very nauseated lately and my strength is gone. I just don't see the value—"

"Professor, please. You'd said before I'd have the truth. Tell me what's going on."

"Do you know anything about acute lymphocytic leukemia? It's a brutal disease. Your bone marrow makes too many immature white blood cells. These cells never develop into lymphocytes, as they should. Here are the symptoms. First you feel a shortness of breath, exhaustion. Your skin is too pale. This leads to bruises and cuts that do not heal. Finally, there are infections, as the dwindling number of white blood cells can no longer fight off germs.

"First-line treatment is chemotherapy. Next is a bone marrow transplant. I tried both. There is no third option."

They sat in silence for a moment as a breeze rippled through the flower heads and rustled the trees. A smattering of red and orange leaves drifted down to settle upon the ground.

"Evan has always suffered from a lack of self-worth. It's important you understand that. His father had run up a tremendous debt and he was determined to show that he could overcome it. In trying to save the business, Evan accepted a very generous sum of money to help study Sarah and catalog the results. But he couldn't get her to cooperate. There was . . . an accident. Two men died in a fire. Sarah felt responsible. She withdrew from him, fought him; he was frightened to death of her and what might happen if she lost control again. And he was beginning to feel the pressure. I finally convinced him that if we brought in someone who could relate to Sarah in a slightly less professional manner, connect to her as a friend and mentor, we could use that to our advantage."

"You have some sort of hold over him, don't you?"

"We have a history. I met him in grad school, there was something briefly between us, he thought it was more. He's still in love with me, even after all these years. I suppose I use it, just like anything else."

"What did you think would happen when I found out the truth?"

"That you would have won her trust by then, and that I might win yours in the end. That's it."

Jess watched a pigeon strutting across the grass, looking out of place here. Two people, dead. It made better sense to her now. Wasserman's evasive manner, his slow disintegration, the fear in his eyes. But something important was still missing. "Where did the money come from that kept the facility afloat? Who is the man in the blue suit?"

"Does it matter? People are interested in her for the same reasons they have always been interested in things like this. Power. They don't care where it comes from or why. They just want it."

Bitterness tasted sour at the back of Jess's throat and she swallowed it away. "You lied to me from the beginning."

Shelley shook her head. "I never really lied, Jess. I just didn't tell you all of it. As I've said before, you wouldn't have believed me."

"You should have given me the chance."

"Maybe so. But it's water under the bridge, isn't it?"

"You're still her legal guardian, you can move her. All you need to do is petition child and welfare services—"

"You haven't been listening to me. It's out of our hands now."

"But goddammit, why?"

"I'm tired," Shelley said. "There are too many others involved now. Sometimes you have to bow your head and admit defeat. Maybe you don't believe that. But you're young."

"What are they going to do to her? They're going to keep pushing her until she breaks, aren't they?"

"Now, don't you jump to conclusions. I'm sure she'll be

treated gently enough. The Wasserman Facility is still a licensed institution, Evan won't want to risk—"

"So you're not going to help me," Jess said. Anger made her cheeks feel hot and her skin prickle. "Goddamn you. You're a coward."

"I want you to understand something, all right? I'm not an evil person. I'm not uncaring. I did what I could for her, and what I thought was best for all of us. But I don't have much time now, and I've got to make a choice. I have to choose how to live the last of my days. I can't be bothered with this anymore."

They sat in the silence of the afternoon. Jess rose to her feet and blinked back tears of frustration. Betrayal stung like acid. Shelley had been a mentor, someone she had trusted. *No way. You're not going to see me break down.* She turned to go.

"There's one other thing you'll want to know," Shelley said, stopping her in her tracks. "Remember I told you that there were signs of abuse on Sarah? Hitting little kids wasn't the only thing Ed Voorsanger was doing at that house. When Evan ran some genetic tests we found out that Ed was Sarah's natural father. He never admitted it and his wife wouldn't hear a word. Of course Annie never talked about it, never talked about the rapes, the sexual and physical abuse she must have been suffering from her father for years. She couldn't. But those tests proved it to be true.

"After that was when things really began. Suddenly Sarah became very interesting to a lot of people. It's in her genes, Jess, some sort of mutation, and something like that can be isolated. It can be enhanced. Replicated."

Jess turned away again. She walked in stunned silence across the spotless stretch of lawn, toward manicured shrubs and pine mulch, into the shadows of the house. She tried to keep her mind from dwelling on the images that had sprung unbidden into her head.

"You're fighting something you can't possibly win," Shelley called after her. "You can't turn back the clock. Even if you saved her, do you really think it would stop whatever pain you feel? Do you think it would silence those voices in your head?"

"Good-bye, Professor Shelley." The words felt strange in Jess's mouth. "God be with you."

—31—

As she left Shelley's drive, trees looming over the car like threatening hands, Jess calmed herself enough to think. She thought about how the psychiatric system might deal with a child that was out of control. Foster homes, juvenile halls, outpatient facilities couldn't hold her; this child was not only violent but utterly beyond the realm of anything humanity had ever seen, or could understand. Where would they put a child like that?

Buried, she thought, they would bury her where no one would ever come looking. In a maximum-security mental ward, for instance. Psychiatry preferred to bare its soul behind closed doors. But then why bring in anyone from the outside? Why risk the exposure?

An answer to that had already been given. Wasserman's desperate attempt to save the hospital had led to his involvement with some very bad people, and he had done everything possible to reach Sarah again and pull her out of wherever she had retreated to in her mind.

But that wasn't all of it. Jess still couldn't rationalize Wasserman taking such a huge gamble. He had to know the chances were good that she would find out what he was doing and expose him. There was something else happening here, but she couldn't put her finger on it.

She thought of Annie and the abuses suffered at her father's hands, the years of silence and the birth of an unwanted child. A genetic mutation. Annie carried it, and her father did too; mixing those genes again had produced something far beyond the capabilities of either of them.

Was that it? A twisting of genes, a double helix bent in upon itself, triggering the awakening of something long dormant and nearly forgotten?

Perhaps. But thinking of it in that way reduced Sarah to a lab experiment. She was more than that, much more.

I could petition for a hearing through Child and Welfare. I could call the police. But by the time anything was done, if anyone listened to her at all, she had a feeling Sarah would be gone. One way or another.

As she crossed the bridge and pulled into traffic on Cambridge Street, she glanced in the rearview. A dark blue Crown Victoria ran like a sleek, smooth shark three cars back. She had seen the same car ten minutes earlier. She watched as it turned into traffic and merged into her lane. Two men in the front seat, looked like maybe one more in back. Difficult to tell.

She turned left onto Harvard Avenue as the light blinked to yellow. The Crown Victoria swung across the intersection and through the red, causing others to slam their brakes, honk, and gesture out their windows. *Boston drivers.* She was worried now, but not much. Yet.

She debated whether to swing into the liquor store lot and see if the Crown followed, but decided to keep going. Traffic was always heavy here, with cars parked along both sides of the street and little stores lining the sidewalks. Thrift shops and unfinished wooden furniture stores attracted the college crowd. People darted and bobbed and weaved in and out of doorways. Nobody was paying any attention to the cars in the street.

She had shopped here herself, buying a lamp and rug and three prints for her walls recently. She had even bought used clothes once from the place on the corner when money was particularly tight, the smell of mothballs and dust mixing with her general discomfort at wearing other people's things.

Okay, the Crown's still there. What to do?

Two cars back. She was being paranoid. *Let's just see.* When it was her turn, she stopped dead at the green light on Commonwealth. The car behind her began to blow its horn. She heard someone shouting out the window. *Hold on, girl, easy.* She drummed her fingers on the wheel. People were suddenly paying attention. A couple stared from the doorway of the McDonald's. The man smiled at the crazy woman sitting in the middle of the street, with the line of cars behind her all honking now.

The light turned yellow, then red. She floored the gas. Charlie's car shot out across the T-tracks and into oncoming traffic. Brakes squealed. She swerved right onto Commonwealth and missed clipping the bumper of an oil truck by inches. More horns and shouting; she ignored them, corrected the car into the proper lane, and risked a glance back.

The Crown had tried to swerve around the cars in front of it by bouncing over the right-hand sidewalk, but it was blocked by the flow of pedestrians. The man in the passenger seat threw his door open and yelled at them to move, move out of the way *now*. He wore a white shirt and a tie and something black and threatening was clipped to his belt.

Jess turned back to the road and kept her foot on the gas. She swung the wheel hard, swerving around cars that were moving much more slowly. A light up ahead, but it was green, thank God, and she swept around a car in the left-turn lane and through the intersection.

Here the street turned steep, running up the crest of the hill and down the other side. A glance in the rearview told her that the Crown had not yet managed to catch up. She swung a hard left onto Washington, shuddered over the T-tracks, and flew past the Whole Foods Market. Another green light, *someone looking down on me right now, yes, sir.*

She forced herself to slow as she approached the playground and the Washington Square intersection. Red light this time. A short distance down Beacon on her left was her graduate school, and her apartment. She could not go home now, she did not know what might be waiting for her there. Another glance in the rearview told her that the Crown was nowhere in sight.

The library had an underground garage. When she reached it she pulled down into the lower reaches and switched off the engine. Metal ticked in silence. She heard the echo of a car door slam, the sound of footsteps moving away from her. A man's voice speaking to someone else in unconcerned tones, both of them drifting away. She sat and caught her breath.

Inside the library she made her way back down into the stacks to a far corner of the lower level. A quick scan told her the area was deserted. She pulled out her cell phone.

A woman answered on the third ring. Jess could hear another voice in the background, a child's high, clear, breathless laughter. She closed her eyes and leaned against the cool wood of the study cubicle.

"This is Patrick."

"It's Jess Chambers."

Suddenly his voice was attentive, crisp. "Hold on." The phone, muffled by a hand; muttered voices, then silence. "Tell me."

"I found something in Wasserman's desk, a bunch of PET scans of Sarah's brain. They've circled what looks like an area of heightened activity in the parietal lobe. Does that make any sense to you?"

"Sure, sure it does. The parietal lobe deals with the sensations of touch and pain, as well as a feeling of where the body is in space and what surrounds it. Sensations in general, so that if a person has damage to the parietal lobe they lose the ability to feel."

"Would it follow that a person with an enhanced parietal

lobe would have increased sensation? Perhaps a heightened sense altogether?"

"We don't know that. But it sounds to me like your hospital director sure thinks so."

"It's not just him. There are others involved in this." She told him about the man in the blue suit, everything Shelley had said just minutes earlier. "I think they're following me, Patrick. I saw a car full of men and I managed to lose them, but they were after me from Shelley's house. She's sick, but she's lucid. I think she was telling the truth. I don't know what we're up against here. Patrick, what do we do now? What the hell do we do?"

"I've done a little digging," Patrick said. "Called in some favors. I want you to understand that this is coming through several sources, and I have no way to know if it's accurate."

"What is it?"

"A little background first. Just bear with me here. The human genome was entirely sequenced a few years back by the NIH and a private company called Celera Genomics. Scientists found that the genome contains less than thirty thousand genes. The function of the majority of these genes is unknown. Only a fraction of the human DNA sequence codes for a protein. The rest is dormant, and some people think it is vestigial or may have some future use."

"English, please, Patrick."

"There are rumors of genetic experiments by a pharmaceutical firm," he said. "My sources say they've been working on isolating a particular protein produced by one of these normally dormant genes. It's supposed to produce a psi effect, Jess. And these same sources tell me they're testing it right now."

"You think this has to do with Sarah?"

"I think you've gotten yourself tangled up in the middle of something very bad. Put it this way. The men in that car following you weren't looking to deliver a Publishers Clearing House check."

"Why would they do this to her?"

"Think about it. If they were able to isolate this protein, they might be able to reproduce the same effects in anyone. Imagine the possibilities here. Scientists able to wake up a long-dormant portion of the human DNA strand and induce psi capabilities whenever and wherever they choose. The military, hell, the *business* implications are enormous. It's cutting-edge genetics, Jess. Billions of dollars are at stake."

"This is crazy. She's just a little girl, Patrick."

"I know. I know she is."

"I won't let them hurt her."

"I talked to my people and they're ready to go," Patrick said. "She can disappear, I swear. Just say the word."

Jess smelled the dust of old books and coffee and she drifted through shades of memory. The window glass here was gray and sticky, like the glass of a phone booth, smeared with children's fingerprints. Eating a chocolate bar while her mother talked on the phone, talked forever on the phone, hurry up, Mama, we're late for school.

Professor Shelley's face drifted into her mind. Her mother's face too. Jess felt the sting of betrayal once again. She opened her eyes, allowed herself a moment to grieve for something lost, a connection grasped at and missed. A fleeting recognition of a turning point, and a decision that had already been made.

There might still be time, before they figured out what she was planning to do. But she had to move, and move fast.

"Let's get her out of there, Patrick. Get her the fuck out. Let's give her a chance."

—32—

Professor Jean Shelley sat upright in a straight-backed cane chair in front of the table and the window that looked out upon her garden. Jess Chambers was gone. The house was empty.

She tried to soothe herself enough to eat from the bowl of miso soup that steamed in front of her. It was no longer easy to do, this simple ritual of spoon to mouth that so many took for granted. She looked down at the swirl of soup and the fleshy gray squares floating in it and the smell nauseated her. She thought of hundreds of thousands eating Big Macs in their cars and dribbling mayonnaise down their fronts and wanted to scream.

Outside she watched a hummingbird flit to the feeder, tucking its long slender beak into an opening and darting away again. She had suction-cupped the feeder to the glass because she liked to watch them dance during the evenings, their nervous vibration of wings translated into a calming, fluid movement by the shadows of the trees in her backyard. Now that she could no longer play the piano without cramps in her hands, this was what beauty she had left.

A bit of a breeze made the shadows dance along in silent partnership, as beyond in the dusky light the multicolored flowers ducked and bobbed their heads. Soon they would be gone. It was fall, and they were dying too.

Next to her chair on the floor was the silver bowl. She kept it close to her because sometimes when the sickness rose up inside she couldn't make it to the bathroom in time. Lately there was blood. She kept a folded towel next to it that she could use to wipe her mouth, though she had not yet been able to do it today. The towel held a delicate lace pattern along its edge. Seemed like such a waste, dirtying a perfectly good towel on something so useless.

From where she sat she could see the dust beginning to gather on things—the tabletop, the picture frames on the shelf above the telephone, the windowpanes. For a long time she had fought the dust and then she had given up when the pain and dizziness had become too great. She had someone who would come in for a couple of hours a day to help her cook, but she would not hire a cleaning service to come in and vacuum and dust for her. In her mind that was a luxury reserved for single old men. It would be too much for her pride to bear.

She thought again, as she had countless times the past few months: *I will not give up. I will not let it win.*

Outside, the heads of the flowers dipped and turned like an audience at a play. The breeze was light and the air was warm. She thought about getting up and opening a window, but the idea of it overwhelmed her and she remained in her seat. Best to just sit and enjoy until she had gathered her strength for what was to come.

After twenty minutes she was ready to begin. She stood up, her swollen joints protesting loudly. She left the bowl of miso untouched, and walked slowly under the lovely carved-wood molding into the sitting room. She had cleared this room of all but a series of yoga mats in various bright colors and a low long table against the far wall, where she kept towels and bottled water at room temperature.

This was going to be a difficult session, she knew. But it

was necessary to prepare. There would not be any more chances to do so, and she needed to be clear and focused for what lay ahead. She ground her molars together against the pain as she worked herself into the lotus position on a mat in the center of the room, and faced the bank of windows overlooking the patio.

The sun gently touched her face. She let the warmth wash over her, soothing her breathing until it became slow and deep. She folded her hands against her lap, her mind an empty shell, focused inward on her heartbeat. In a state of deep meditation she could slow that beat to less than fifty times per minute.

Tibetan Buddhism concerns itself with the power of the mind over the physical body. The belief is that everyone is linked, and everyone has the ability to influence the world through thought. A great Buddhist master had once said, "To study the Buddha Way is to study the self, to study the self is to forget the self, and to forget the self is to be enlightened by the ten thousand things." This was a goal Shelley had struggled to understand. She had studied the Dalai Lama's teachings very carefully. She had visited Tibet three separate times. She had hiked through mountain peaks in pursuit of enlightenment, of spiritual peace. But this riddle remained beyond her reach.

She worked in silence, stretching and loosening her body, calming her heart and mind. A sheen of sweat clung to her skin. She did not like the smell of sickness that came from it. She should not be noticing the smell at all, if she were successful in clearing her thoughts. But the impurities must work their way through her pores.

She imagined a war happening at the cellular level, white blood cells maturing as they were supposed to do, and moving as one to attack the blast cells and drive them out. This visualization was the important part. This was truly mind over matter.

When first diagnosed she had visited countless doctors,

believing in the miracle of Western medicine. Many of them had been friends or colleagues. She had subjected herself to countless prodding and pokes and treatments. Nothing had worked; the leukemia had always returned, more aggressively than before. Finally she had begun to look elsewhere to find some kind of hope.

Physician, heal thyself. She had thought that true devotion would lead to inner peace, a journey that would lead to the loss of self that brought the elusive ten thousand things. She would learn to focus her mind into an efficient killing machine, eradicating the mutating cells as they swept through her blood. Through all this, she thought, she would be able to lose her fear. After all, what did anyone have to fear if the only truth was what the mind created? And the mind had the power to change everything?

But the fear was still there. In point of fact, it had grown, slowly eating her up inside like the cancer that ate away at her guts. It distracted her, kept her from focusing on what she must do. Perhaps, she thought, she was not truly devoted after all.

So she turned to something else.

From the very beginning she had tried to understand the truths of Lamaism in a different light. *Everyone is linked, and everyone has the ability to influence the world through thought.* She had come to believe this to be literally true. She had no doubt about what had happened to her. That night so many years ago she had felt something alien worm its way inside her body. Some kind of energy had been released that had forever altered her genetic makeup.

First chemotherapy had failed. Then the bone marrow transplant wouldn't take. Spirituality alone hadn't solved anything. As far and as wide as she had looked, there was no other option. So Jean Shelley had created one.

They still didn't know exactly how Sarah did it, but effect had something to do with electromagnetic energy. It seemed that whatever had caused her leukemia could cure it as well.

At least, that had been Shelley's hope. And in fact, Sarah's strange power had put her into remission twice. Each time the cancer had returned, but already she had lived for six years longer than even the most optimistic doctors had predicted.

Both she and Evan had tried very hard to teach Sarah the importance of making amends for your mistakes. They had made real progress at first, until the fire. After that, they had lost her. She had come to hate all doctors, anyone who had anything to do with her life in the facility. In her mind, they had betrayed her. She had to be sedated every time Shelley was in the room, and then she had retreated deep inside herself.

Jean Shelley's death was coming. She had one last chance, but it was all getting so complicated now. She had worked so very hard to play everything just right, teasing Jess Chambers along, letting Evan think what he needed to think to be useful to her. What she had done could not be undone, all the long, complex plans she had put into motion, and everything was spiraling toward an end. It wouldn't be long before this last chance had passed beyond her reach.

The bell rang. *The next scene in the last act.* She closed her eyes and gathered her thoughts for a moment. She would have to give a command performance now, and she needed every ounce of energy she had left.

Evan Wasserman forced his way through the door before she had swung it fully open. He looked like a madman, tie pulled down and to the side, hair flying wild about his egg-shaped skull, eye twitching uncontrollably. "They want to introduce this into the general population," he said in a rush. "They want to sell it like some kind of treatment for . . . for . . . high cholesterol levels or something. They don't know what they're getting into, Jean. It's gone too far, do you understand? Too far!"

He clutched at her like a drowning man would cling to driftwood, his face close to hers so that she could smell the sour stink of his breath. "Oh God, Jean, what are we going to do? We've got to shut it down somehow. But your treatment—look at you, you're so pale, God, I'm so sorry . . ."

"Hush, now," she said. She forced a smile, reached up to touch his face with gentle fingers. "It's all right. We've done what we could do, and it's gotten away from us. But I'll be okay."

"Oh no," he moaned. He buried his slick, sweaty face in her neck, and she managed to remain still, putting her hand around the back of his head and holding him to her. His voice was muffled by her blouse. "No, you won't, not if we can't get her to cooperate. We were so close to a break-through, I, I can't lose you."

"Don't worry."

"I *love* you, I'm sorry, but it's true, I always have. I know you don't want to hear it."

"I know you do, Evan," Shelley said. "I love you too."

And then he was trying to kiss her with his slimy, worm-like lips, wet with the salt of his tears, and it took every ounce of her self-control not to pull away from the horrible smell and taste of him.

Finally she got him to the couch, and poured a shot glass of brandy. His hands were shaking too much to hold it. "Here," she said, holding it up for him to drink. "That's better. Now, tell me it again, from the beginning."

She listened as he described his conversation with Cruz and Berger. Then he told her about Jess Chambers's visit.

"We should never have let her become involved," he said. "Now she's sniffing around and she's got her wind up. It's only a matter of time until she puts it all together. She'll go to the state, the papers, she'll expose us both."

"Jess served her purpose," Shelley said. "Sarah opened up again, didn't she? Just as we'd hoped."

"But now Helix is taking over. They're going to cut me out completely, I can feel it coming. They don't know what they're doing with her." Wasserman shook his head. "I just wanted to save the hospital," he said. "And I wanted to save your life. I never thought it would go this far."

"Perhaps they can control it, as they say."

"There's no controlling what she has," Wasserman said. "Now they want to offer the ability to anyone with money enough to buy it. God forbid it gets into the hands of madmen. Dictators? Terrorists? Imagine someone like Hussein with that kind of power!"

Shelley stood up and went to the window, hugging her arms across her chest. *Wait just long enough to add the proper tremor.* She turned to find him staring at her. "What do you think we should do?"

"We have to stop them, and stop her," he whispered. "The way we always talked about. Wipe this obscenity off the face of the earth. Destroy every sample, every record. It has to end right here."

Shelley soothed him, agreed to all he said, let him caress and touch her. Then, after he'd gone, she went back out on the patio.

The air had turned cooler in the late afternoon, and a breeze picked up stray leaves and whirled them across the lawn. She watched the orange and red colors dancing through the deepening shadows, and sensed an air of neglect, as if the grass were just half an inch too long, the shrubs grown out and getting leggy. A dead branch had come down near the edge of the wooded patch on the southeast corner.

The phone was ringing. Shelley stumbled back inside and fumbled for it on the counter, picked up on the fourth chirp.

"Our men lost her," Berger said. "She pulled a stunt at a light, there were witnesses. We didn't have any secondary support, it was only tagged as a shadow. If we knew that she was on to us—"

For the first time that day, real fear washed over Jean Shelley. This was not part of the carefully designed plan. Up to this point, everything had gone perfectly with Jess

Chambers. Shelley had planted the seeds of doubt, challenged her to let it all go, knowing full well she would not. Jess knew just enough to be suitably angry, but not enough to blow things wide open. Wasserman was the last piece of the puzzle, and his undoing would serve as the perfect final distraction for the firestorm that would come.

This would not do. She clutched the phone in a white-knuckled hand, took a deep breath, and let it out. "She wouldn't have suspected a tail. She must have seen you following her and put it together."

"These men are good."

"Not good enough, damn it!"

Berger sighed. "She can't have gone far. We have someone watching her place, the school."

"Then find her. Don't bring her in, just find her and don't lose her again."

"We're working on it. But Philippa and I agree, we can't wait any longer or this is all going to come down on our heads. The director is a liability, he's at the breaking point and I can't predict what he'll do. We've put too much pressure on him, and he didn't like bringing Chambers into this in the first place. I didn't like it either, to be honest."

"It was necessary for personal reasons. Everything we know confirms our decision. She has the family history with her brother, DNA testing was a match, and the results speak for themselves. They've made the connection and it's strong enough to bear weight."

"That's your call. We have what we want."

"Good. There are other endings available to us, if Jess doesn't work out. You understand what I mean?"

"They'll arrive by helicopter shortly."

"Good. When you go in, you've got to be careful. You know what you're up against. The girl is agitated and we don't have her completely contained, whatever you and Cruz say about this new drug. When you move, tell Evan he's done and that we're pulling his funding."

"He won't like that."

"Of *course* he won't like it. That's the point. If he's riled up, it will look worse for him. If you can break him, go ahead. He's got to be the fall guy for this."

Dr. Jean Shelley looked out her window. The hummingbirds were back, hovering just beyond the glass. The sight soothed her. Then why did she feel unsettled, as if there were something she should understand, something she should remember, but could not?

It was probably the sickness at work in her brain. She could feel it coursing through her veins, carrying the killer cells to the farthest points in her body. Microscopic invaders sent to undo her from within. She did not have long now, and she was burning alive.

Where would Jess Chambers go?

When she really thought about it, the answer seemed so obvious she couldn't believe it hadn't occurred to her until now.

"You know what she'll do," Shelley said into the phone. The voice on the other end seemed like a million miles away. "She won't wait. She'll come back for the girl."

"Then we'll spot her."

This was it; one way or another, this was the end of a very long road.

"That's what we want. It's time now. Everyone has to be on alert. Put the wheels in motion."

And please, don't let me down.

STAGE THREE

—33—

The Sikorsky S-76 helicopter lifted off from the private air-field at 3:45 p.m. central time. On board were eight men in full attack gear: STRIKE DOAV Vests, black UnderArmour moisture-wicking T-shirts, goggles, radio, combat boots, Hell-storm Python Light Rappel gloves, and M9 pistols. Four car-ried specially modified M4 assault rifles with dart rounds. One of them held something considerably more dangerous.

The Special Operations team was led by Bertie McDwyer. McDwyer had served ten years with the army, in Europe and then in the Middle East during Desert Storm. He had been assigned to various bases within the United States be-fore joining the army's school for snipers at Ft. Benning.

After graduating he had carried out several clandestine operations, neutralizing high-level targets on five separate occasions without a single complication. Now he was a killer for hire. He was known for striking fast and hard and with-out hesitation. He was young, strong, and experienced.

And at the moment he was scared shitless, for several rea-sons. McDwyer knew exactly what they were up against in this mission, even if the rest of his team did not. He didn't like the way this one was playing out.

This bothered him a great deal. Snipers were supposed to be immune from human emotions such as remorse and fear.

It was a basic tenet of their training, and there was good reason for it. He had seen more than one man killed because of a split-second hesitation on the battlefield.

The helicopter banked left and slipped low under an orange sun. The glint off the chop of a small lake hit McDwyer in the eyes. He winced and glanced away. Like the reflection off the scope of a rifle. It had happened to him only once, but that was enough. A sniper, looking into the lens of another. Predator to predator, like two lions crouched in the brush. He had been first to pull, and he sometimes thought about that split-second difference. Who lived, who died, playing God in the blink of an eye.

"Listen up. Everson and Keene, put that shit away." The two men yanked iPod earbuds from their ears and shoved them into pockets. "We deploy at 1730. I will only say this once. We are to contain and provide cover for ground forces moving in on the facility. Their mission is to locate and subdue the target peaceably. We are on reserve team duty."

Boots tapped, knees bounced. Like purebred horses straining at the bit, McDwyer thought. They were some of the best available. He'd trained most of them himself. They had been told very little about this particular mission, and that was dangerous. McDwyer knew that the most mistakes were made when the team did not have all the facts. But Berger had insisted upon the highest levels of security, and could not be convinced otherwise.

"I know you want to be first in line, but you will obey my orders. A highly sensitive and dangerous subject is housed in this facility. We have strict orders to disable if necessary, but do not shoot to kill. I repeat—anyone attempting a kill shot will be terminated themselves. Permanently."

"Who's the target?"

McDwyer hesitated just long enough for them to see it in his eyes. "A juvenile female."

"Excuse me, sir?"

"Never you mind, Everson. We are a safety net only. I do

not want weapons drawn unless I give the command to move in."

"Sir—"

"I anticipate zero complications on the ground, and I sure as fuck don't expect them up here. Anyone have any problems with that? Good. We have one hour and forty minutes to deployment."

McDwyer distributed a photo and description of the target, and moved back to the front to let them sort it all out. He plopped himself down next to the pilot, a twenty-year veteran who had flown thirty missions in Desert Storm. A family man, and himself a killer of over fifteen people. Jesus, McDwyer thought. He massaged his temples with both pointer fingers. He didn't know why he was thinking about this right now.

"How's the daughter? Any news?"

McDwyer found Keene crouched near his seat. He covered his headset mike. "Keep it off-line, will you?"

"Sorry. You just looked like you could use some company."

"I shouldn't have told you a fucking thing about it."

"Nothing to be ashamed of, sir. We all make mistakes."

"It's not a mistake, Keene. It's a human being."

"Sorry. You know what I meant." Keene scratched his underarm with a gloved finger. "How old is she?"

"She'll be nine next May." McDwyer shook his head. Nine years old, and they'd never even met. The mother was a woman he'd slept with two or three times while on leave from the army, when he was only twenty-three. Barely old enough to have hair on his dick. She'd called to tell him just last week. Why now, he had no idea; maybe she was after money.

In his line of work, family meant weakness. He couldn't afford to let this get in the way. It was bad enough he'd let it slip to Keene. One too many tequila shots last night. It wasn't like him, and he wondered for just a split second whether he was having some sort of breakdown.

"I just figured I'd ask, after seeing the photo you gave out back there," Keene said. "A little girl, about the same age, I thought maybe you were having trouble getting your head around this one. I wouldn't blame you."

"That's enough." McDwyer kept his voice low and hard. "You don't know the first thing about it. Get back there and buckle in."

Keene looked at him for a moment longer, then nodded and returned to his seat. McDwyer glanced at the pilot, but the man stared straight out the windshield and made no sign that he had heard the exchange. It wasn't likely. The sound of the rotor would drown out everything but a shout.

Does Keene have a point? McDwyer didn't know what scared him worse, knowing what this little girl could do if she got away from them, or the possibility of having to line her head up in his sights and squeeze the trigger.

McDwyer had been the kill switch on this project for over a year now, but it wasn't until last week that he'd started questioning why.

The helicopter banked across a field, low enough to cause a ripple in the brush. They were less than an hour and a half away now.

McDwyer wondered, for the hundredth time, what exactly would be waiting for him when they arrived.

—34—

"Didn't think I'd see you again so soon. Your class get can-celed? You forget something, maybe?" The guard's greedy eyes lingered, staring at Jess Chambers's nose, mouth, breasts, and she let him do it, let him hope that she had come back for him.

She flashed him the pass from her bag and smiled, a big, toothy grin. "Has Dr. Wasserman left yet?"

"Don't know, but he might have, I had to use the facili-ties. You want me to radio up?"

"No, that's all right. I'll only be a minute. I just wanted to look for an earring."

"You women are always losing stuff. Maybe when you get done, we can go get that drink. . . ."

Now comes the hard part, Jess thought, and she parked be-hind the hospital again and hurried to the front doors, keep-ing her face down and turned away from the windows. She hadn't wanted to wait for Patrick's help. A lot of this de-pended on luck, but she didn't want to waste another second, now that her mind was made up. God only knew what Wasserman might do to Sarah while they all sat around like career politicians trying to decide the best way to get her out.

She hoped Andre was busy elsewhere. She could only

pray that her photograph hadn't been handed out to everyone who worked in the building.

She clipped her pass to her jacket and walked fast down
the empty hall, listening for voices. She heard them in the
playroom; it was the right time, she had timed it perfectly.

She opened the doors and studied each corner of the
room. There were six or seven children in here now, and
two white-shirted women who might have been counselors.
It did not take her long to find Dennis, in his baseball cap
and sneakers. He was standing by the bookshelves, counting
the books.

She waited just a moment to harden herself for what had
to be done.

The two counselors looked up when she came in but
didn't say a word, and she didn't see anything but mild interest in their eyes. That would change. She crossed the
room quickly. Dennis saw her coming. He smiled. "Onet-
wothreefourfivesixseven. Seven books."

"Yes, Dennis, that's right. Seven books." She leaned into
him and whispered, "I'm sorry about this," and then she put
her hand on his forearm, let her hand rest firmly so he could
feel it.

The reaction was immediate. Dennis jerked away from
her like he had been burned. He shook his head. She steeled
herself and reached for him again.

"Don't touch Dennis, no touching, that's the rules, Dennis
doesn't like to be touched . . ." His voice wound up like a
siren. He backed into the bookcase, eyes rolling, and turned,
not looking at anything now. He flailed out with both arms.
Books fell to the floor with a loud double thump. He pushed
at more books and they teetered and fell like dominoes, pages
fluttering. "No touching, Nononono-*nonono* . . ."

The two counselors got up and came over fast. "You're
not supposed to do that," one of them said over the shouting. "God. Nicki, get someone in here." The other woman

scurried out of the room. "Now, Dennis, calm down—oh, hell."

Dennis had backed himself into the corner and looked like he wanted to go right on through. He was big, clumsy; it wouldn't be easy to get him back in line. He had reached a fever pitch now, his head whipping back and forth, and his voice had begun to stir up the other children, one of them laughing, another starting to throw toys at the screen on the window. *Bang-bang*. The female counselor was trying to get him to stop flailing his arms without touching him again.

I'll make this up to you, Dennis, Jess thought. *I promise.* She ducked out of the room and back down the hall. Wasserman's office door was ajar, she could hear voices. Nobody came out after her. She hoped she had bought herself enough time.

The elevator was damnably slow, and she wished she had taken the fire stairs. Finally the doors opened onto the smell of disinfectant and stale air. *It's cold down here, too cold,* and she resisted the urge to hug her arms to her chest.

The man behind the desk (not Andre, thank God) looked like he had left high school about a week ago. She didn't recognize him. "There's a problem in the play area," she said, as he came around to meet her in his white hospital suit. "It's Dennis. They need help calming him down."

"I'm not supposed to leave—"

"Listen to me. Andre's out for coffee and Evan asked me to come get you. We're short staffed and Dennis is going to give them trouble. Go on now. I'll watch the desk here until you get back."

He swallowed hard. "I'll be just a minute."

She waited until the elevator doors closed. There was not much time. It wouldn't be long before Wasserman and the others figured out what she had done, and why. She had to get Sarah out now.

But the keys proved impossible to find. Behind the desk was an intercom speaker, a series of cubbyholes labeled with patients' names and doses of medication, heavy canvas gloves, and a can of mace. A little three-inch television flickered from the corner, the sound turned low.

The orderly would have the keys on him, she thought, of course he would. If they came back down before she got Sarah to the stairs, she would be trapped. *Damn. How the hell are you going to get through that door?*

Despair settled over her like dusty cobwebs. She had been driven by emotion, by need, not stopping long enough to think more than a few minutes ahead. Whatever she was searching for was close now, she could taste it like blood on her teeth. But she had backed herself into a corner, and now the walls were closing in on all sides as she imagined what might happen to her when she got caught down here.

It's too late. Just get out while you still can.

That was the voice of a quitter, and she refused to listen.

It wasn't until she turned away in frustration that she felt the answer, an unseen presence so vivid she brushed instinctively at her face and hair as if to push it away. Only then did she wonder how she had failed to notice it before. It was as if the air itself were alive.

Jess Chambers felt an odd transient moment of doubling, as if she were looking through two pair of eyes, one outside, one within. The hair on her neck and arms rose as if in warning. For another long moment she stood silent, immobile, and then pushed through into the corridor with a sense that she had stepped into a darker place.

—35—

The corridor was in shadows, and any other residents who might remain behind the padded walls were still. An eerie calm had settled over the basement. Jess Chambers passed each door with ghost images burned into her mind, the feeling that she had been here before, that she existed both on the outside and the inside of these prison cells.

As a psychologist you have to listen to other people's private thoughts, thoughts nobody else ever has to know about. But a child doesn't hide things the way adults do; with children, you don't have the same barriers. So why, in the time they had spent together, did Jess still feel Sarah had been hiding from her?

She knew the answer, in this cold place, inside the buzzing of electric air; Sarah did not trust anyone, not even herself. Things had happened within these walls, accidents that were not entirely blameless.

Mental illness is a matter of mistrust, Jess thought, as she walked. *Never knowing when your own mind might betray you.* Jess had private thoughts, of course. She was sometimes unable to keep her mind from things that might be considered inappropriate. She knew that it gave her distance. But what must it be like to a little girl who had felt responsible for others' lives ever since she had been able to form such thoughts? Who knew with certainty that her every emotion could end up with such dire consequences?

They played into that here, didn't they, Sarah? Made you feel guilty? Made you feel responsible when accidents happened, when you could not control yourself?

The air seemed to pulse, as if in answer. Hands tickled the inside of her skull.

Jess crouched at Sarah's door, the last along the line. She considered the lock. This was not one that could be sprung with a bobby pin. She stood and peered through the little window. Touched the glass and found it ice-cold. Traced a fingernail along the surface; it was translucent, lightly covered by frost. She rubbed it away.

Sarah Voorsanger stood against the far wall. The jacket that had contained her was lying torn and discarded on the floor. Jess was awed by the changes in the girl, how tall and straight she stood now, the power that she held in the depths of her dark eyes, pulsing from her like waves. *Oh, we only saw the barest glimpse of it, didn't we? We only knew the edges of the truth.* Sarah had been afraid before, and her faith and hope of an eventual release had faded long ago; perhaps her urge to fight had faded with them. But now she was stronger, and older, and she had a reason to fight for her life. She had been introduced to a world of possibilities outside this place.

Sarah looked up into the glass, and they found each other. Jess could see her breath, puffing like silver clouds before her face. She could feel something inside her mind, probing.

In spite of her best efforts to subdue it, fear trickled through, cut deep into her gut. Sarah crossed the little room and put her hand up against the glass. Their fingers touched with the window between them. Something groaned, and the glass cracked and buckled. The hand twitched inside her skull.

Jess felt it just in time, fell away from the door as it shrieked and split at its hinges, as it tipped with a shuddering crash to the floor.

Concrete dust swirled and spun like tiny tornadoes in the

following silence. *Jesus Lord.* Jess got to her feet, choking on the thickened air. The door was a twisted chunk of discarded metal lying against the opposite wall. She reached down and touched a ragged edge, yanked her hand away from the scalding heat. She could hardly believe what she had just seen. But the evidence was lying smoking and battered at her feet.

You ain't seen nothing yet.

Back in the outer room, she heard the elevator whir to life.

"Sarah?" Jess said. "We have to go. Now." No response. She peered into the wound where the door had been. Sarah stood just inside the opening. Her lips were blue and she was trembling.

"I was bad," she said softly. "And I liked it. I almost couldn't stop."

No seizures now, she's learning how to control it better. Or was that just a side effect of whatever they were feeding her?

Words rushed and stumbled over themselves in an attempt to get out. "They've been telling you this is bad all your life, Sarah. I know they have. But they're wrong. We can work all this out later, but right now you can't think about all that, not if we're going to have a chance to get out of here. Do you understand? You have to trust yourself. This power is a part of you, just like anything else. It's nothing to be ashamed of—"

"Leave me alone!" Sarah shouted. "Please." She backed away again, into the corner of the padded room. "I'll hurt you, I'll hurt everyone, I won't be able to keep it down anymore."

The elevator stopped and the doors slid open. A moment later Evan Wasserman stepped into the hall. He was flanked by two big men wearing riot gear and protective goggles and carrying police batons in ugly, thick-fisted hands. She saw guns clipped to their belts. *Not cops,* Jess thought. *But they sure as hell know what they're getting into down here.*

She stepped forward, planted both feet, and gave her best bluff. "Hey. Where the hell have you been? She's already gone, I couldn't stop her."

"Shut the fuck up and step away from the door," one of the men said. She heard the fear in his voice, though he was trying hard to keep it down.

A syringe glistened in Wasserman's hand. "You'll never get close enough to her," Jess said.

"That's why you're going to do it."

"The fuck I am."

"She trusts you. You're the only one." Wasserman took a few steps closer. "You can help us, or not. But these walls are reinforced steel and concrete. They're specially made for this sort of thing. Nobody can hear you down here, and there's no way out. Why don't you make it easy on yourself?"

Wasserman's eyes were wild and his tie was missing. There was an air about him of absent neglect, like a home where all the lights were blazing and the grass grew tangled in the yard. *He's lost it*, she thought. *He'll kill us both now.*

And then, with the strength of a fist in the guts, it hit her; why he had agreed to let her into all this, why he had encouraged her to win Sarah's trust, but never given her any real freedom or power in the attempt. What do you do with a girl who defies everything you have ever believed about the world? A girl who cannot be controlled, locked up, sedated forever? A girl who has the power to destroy you? What do you do with her when you've been beaten?

"You end the game," she said. "On your terms. That's what this is about, isn't it?"

"She fought me," Wasserman said. "For all these years she fought me hard. She's ruined this hospital, ruined my life. I had a life once, you understand? Someone I loved. Do you know she's killed two men? I bet that's something you haven't talked about in your little counseling sessions."

His anger and fear seemed to explode from him as he came forward, closer. Jess could smell it like iron within his clothes, his sweat. "She hasn't taken any sedatives in two days," he said. "She's too strong. They've dosed her with something that multiplies the effect. Don't you see? You don't have any choice. We don't have any choice. From the moment she was born she's destroyed everything. It's gone too far now, too far. There can't be any more tests. Who knows what she could do, if she gets out of here!"

"I won't do it, Wasserman. I won't be your executioner."

"Then you're a liability." Wasserman fumbled in his jacket and came out with the gun from his desk drawer. His hand shook as he pointed it at her. "I'll ask you to get out of the way."

"The police know where I am," Jess said. "They'll be here any minute. You need help. Maybe we can talk to someone—"

"Don't try that juvenile psychoanalysis with me. I was treating patients when you were still riding a school bus. I know what I'm doing."

"Sarah's not your enemy."

"She's not even human!" Wasserman shrieked. Spittle flecked his lips. "She'll be the end of us all, do you hear me? You don't know the truth of it! She could rip the world apart by its seams—"

Jess sensed movement from the corner of her eye. Sarah stepped like a ghost from her padded cell. Wasserman paled. His mouth moved but no sound came out. They stood staring at each other in the silent hall.

Wasserman's hand shook holding the gun. Neither of them spoke. Jess was reminded for a fleeting moment of an old western, where the gunslingers met in the middle of the dusty road and faced each other down. Except in this version one of the gunslingers was a little girl, and her only weapon was her mind.

Do it, Jess urged silently. *The hell with all of them. Push. Push hard.*

She felt an answering squeeze, and the blood in her veins turned to ice. The temperature plummeted.

Sarah smiled.

The two men moved up to Wasserman's side and held

their batons in both hands like clubs. "Take it easy," one of them said. "We don't want to hurt anyone. . . ."

Sarah looked from one man to the other. It happened as simply as a breath of wind; a sudden surge of air, a tickle in the back of her mind, and they were thrown backward as if a giant hand had reached out and punched them squarely in the chest.

They landed on their backs with a double thud, skidding across the smooth floor in a tangle of arms and legs, and came to rest still and silent at the threshold of the outer room.

The report of the gun was like a thunderclap in the narrow hall. Jess registered the bucking of Wasserman's hand, the sudden ringing in her ears, and then Sarah shrieked and stumbled backward. A voice answered inside her head, and the mental fist clenched with vicious force. Jess felt herself driven to her knees. Dimly she felt the blood inside her temples surge and throb. Something had been turned loose inside her skull, and now it scampered through fat gray coils and dug its talons into soft flesh. She struggled for consciousness, felt herself slipping, the past and present mingling like ghosts.

Michael, there's a car, get out of the road . . .

Jess bit down hard. The world spun and righted itself.

She looked up through splayed fingers. The frigid air cut like glass in her lungs. Mist swirled along the concrete floor, slipped in tendrils up the gray walls and boiled above their heads like little thunderclouds.

Sarah stood upright. A bloody stain spread over her left shoulder. Her eyes were wide and glittering, her fists clenched. Sweat dripped from her forehead.

The gun barked again, and again; Jess watched in wonder as the bullets slowed in midair, trembled, hung like tiny planets in a thickening wind. Finally they dropped harmlessly to the floor.

Wasserman shook the gun in his hand as if it had suddenly grown teeth and bitten him. It would not come loose.

His flesh began to smoke as metal twisted and melted into his skin. He screamed. Then the look on his face changed. His free hand went to his neck. He coughed, made a sound like a dog with a bone caught in its throat. He shook his head, tried to back away, and stumbled.

A storm was building inside the hall. Jess could sense it coming, a feeling like going deeper underwater.

Wasserman's hand had left his throat and now clutched at his bulging eyes. Blood trickled between his fingers.

"No," Jess said. "Sarah, stop it. You're going to kill him."

Wasserman's feet left the floor. He rose as if lifted by a wind. His head was thrown back now and his limbs were quivering. Blood dripped from his face and was sucked away by the quickening air. His head snapped once to the right, then back again, and then he was tossed lightly to the side and discarded.

A low cracking sound came from under the floor. The tiles shuddered, groaned in protest. Every window in every door blew outward in a rain of flying glass. Jess touched moisture on her face, drew her bloody fingers back. The pounding in her head was fast and furious. Her vision faded, came back again in yellows and reds.

Sarah headed for the stairs at the end of the hall. The door slammed open, twisted on its hinges. She climbed the steps and disappeared out of sight. Tendrils of gray fog slithered after her.

She's not going to be able to stop.

Jess struggled to her feet. Every step was an agony of thudding pain. Moans and squeals of protest rose up all around her as the building took on weight, felt the squeeze of unseen hands.

A shot rang out. Someone screamed from the upper levels. Two more shots in quick succession. The world crashing down around her, Jess ran for the stairs. Her brother's face came as clear to her as if he had been standing at her feet. *You will not get away from me this time. Not again.* She repeated it to herself as she took the steps two at a time, as she emerged into a hailstorm of destruction on the upper floor. Great cracks ran along the walls, Wasserman's door gone, his office turned upside down; three more bodies on the floor, a lot of blood, more guns lying useless against the wall. Papers, wood, and bits of concrete still settling in the wake of Sarah's passage.

Something was wrong. The air had lost its energy all at once, as if a charge had been released. Jess spotted two men in attack gear and rifles peering out from behind doors at the other end of the hall, at the smaller body lying face-down a few steps away.

Then she heard a puff and felt a fist hit her in the right shoulder, and darkness welled up and slipped over her head, taking her down deep with it.

—36—

She awoke to silence, blackness arching overhead into seemingly limitless distance. Her head felt stuffed with cotton, her tongue swollen thick as a sock in her mouth. For a moment she thought she was back in her childhood bed once again, waiting for the sound of the key in the lock at the front door. Then something changed, but in her muddled state she didn't realize immediately what it was.

Finally she was able to focus enough to find meaning in the face peering down at her.

Ronald Gee smiled, his eyes glittering in the light cast from a distant portion of the room. "There you are," he said. His voice seemed to cup and then release her. "Better take it easy. You were hit with a pretty heavy tranquilizer. We were starting to wonder if you were coming back."

"Let me up," Jess said. Her voice sounded different in her ears. A stranger's voice. She tried to lift her arms and could not. Something was very wrong. Gee was not doing anything to help.

"We don't have long," he said. "She'll know you're awake in a moment. I just wanted to say I'm sorry."

"Why on earth—you? You're in on this?"

"It's all part of the overall scheme of things," Gee said. "I don't expect you to understand right away. Dr. Shelley can explain things better than I can. But I want you to know that nothing bad has to happen to you. We can all get what we want out of this. I know it sounds crazy, but it's the truth."

"Where's Sarah?"

"She's safe. You should know that, if you really consider it."

She did. Sarah was there with her, somehow; she didn't know quite how or why she knew, but it was true.

"What about Shelley?"

"She's got loads of money, all that money from her family steel business, billions, she's bankrolled Helix, the entire operation. And she found you. You're a special case, you know. People like you are almost impossible to find. We searched for years."

"People like me?"

"You're a carrier, Jess. We've done a lot of research on this. Autism can be a symptom, you see, it can be traced through generations, through families. Your brother, he was a carrier, and probably your mother too."

"What the fuck are you talking about?"

Gee smiled. "See, I told you I wouldn't be very good at this. What I mean is, you've got the psi gene. It's just been dormant. Oh, it's nothing like Sarah's, I don't mean that. You're not at that level. But you've been in a deep sleep, and we're waking you up. Dr. Shelley's been dosing you with the dimerizer we developed. Slipping them into your drinks, your food. We've gotten the little factory dusted off and chugging away. Can't you feel it, Jess? I know you can."

For a moment he seemed to loom over her in his excitement, and she clenched her eyes shut tight, and then blinked three times. His face with its horrible goatee was still there, but it had retreated a bit, and his grin looked a little less like the Cheshire Cat in *Alice in Wonderland*.

"I don't believe you," she said, but she did, even at this very moment she believed every word. *That coffee in the Cave, the oily rings floating across the surface . . . my God. What have they done to me?*

"I'm sorry I had to pull the wool over your eyes. I really am. But you were supposed to be brought in gently. Look, I'm just a cog in the wheel here. If it had been up to me, I might have done things differently, but it doesn't matter what I think."

A terrible thought occurred to her. "Not Patrick too? Or Charlie?"

He shook his head. "Patrick's oblivious of anything more than two inches beyond his own nose. So wrapped up in that silly group. Shelley knew about your friendship with Charlie, she knew about Charlie's connection with Patrick. It was all set up to happen the way it did. Patrick and I talked about women once or twice, I suggested he make a couple of recent phone calls to put himself back into Charlie's thoughts, you know, old flame and all, and she steered you our way. Neither one of them knew the full truth."

"Why, Gee?" she whispered. "I don't understand."

"Because we needed you," another voice said. "*I* need you."

Dr. Jean Shelley stepped forward into the light. She walked with difficulty, seeming to favor her right leg. All the elegance and gentle grace was gone, and left in its place was this pale, haggard shell.

"I don't have much time," she said. "I have to do whatever I can now, or it will be too late for me. But everything I've told you is true. We needed someone fresh, someone special. Someone who could connect to her like her mother could have, if she were well. We checked into your medical background, school records, intelligence tests. You had some blood taken during a physical, we got our hands on that too. It became clear, with your family history and the test results, that you are a psi carrier. We needed you to make a bond with Sarah, so that when the time came . . ." She shrugged. "You could help us. Help me."

"Help you do what?"

"Convince her to do the right thing. Do you understand? She needs a friend, a mentor to guide her. This ability she has, it's too big for one little girl to hold. We've pushed and tweaked and encouraged it to the point of ignition. The brain is a muscle like any other, and she's been building it up without any sort of regulator. But the company's gotten what they need from her, the scientists have done their thing, and now it's my turn. And you're my safety valve."

"You want her to perform some sort of miracle?"

"I want her to fix her mistake!" Shelley shouted. A vein throbbed in her temple. She shook her head, closed her eyes, and took a deep breath, let it out in a hiss. "I'm sorry, I lost control. That was wrong of me. But this is . . . emotional. I have days left, if that. She can do it. She's done enough to hold it off before, and now that she's stronger I think she can erase it completely. There are plenty of examples of psychic healing, from Jesus Christ himself right on down the line. Why not Sarah? I want her to kill each and every diseased cell, hunt them down and destroy them. She can do that much for me."

"And if that's not possible?"

Shelley didn't answer, just looked at her as if she'd sprouted a second head. Jess knew then, if she hadn't before: Dr. Jean Shelley had lost her mind.

She chose her next words carefully. "What about Wasserman?"

"Evan was a cog in the wheel," Shelley said. "He helped us do the work, consulted with me on medical opinions, but he never even knew I was behind Helix, behind the grant money that kept the facility afloat. When this whole place comes crashing down, he'll take the fall in public for it. I know you think I'm cruel. He had feelings for me, yes, and I manipulated that. But you can't know what it's like. You don't know what you'd do, until you're in my shoes."

"He's dead," Jess said. "I saw Sarah kill him."

"And I will be too, if we can't get her to help." Shelley nodded at someone. Two men stepped forward, into her line of sight. Heavy and large through the shoulders. The muscle. *What are they going to do, threaten to break my legs?* But they only unhooked the straps from her wrists and ankles and then helped her to a sitting position. Gee watched with arms folded across his chest.

She looked around. They were in a huge, empty room. The walls and ceiling were covered with some sort of black material, and there were no windows. The only light came from the open door at their backs. With such little light the room seemed to expand, to stretch into infinity.

"You want to know where you are," Gee said. "Sensory deprivation tanks can expand the mind exponentially. Studies have shown that psi is enhanced when external stimuli are limited. We tested her in here. You think that random number generator trick was cool? You should have seen some of the things she showed us. But we've been able to keep pretty tight controls on her, limiting her with drugs. As she's grown, her abilities have expanded. It would be amazing to see what she's capable of now."

"If you'll think things through, you'll see that this is the only way," Shelley said. "By helping us you're helping Sarah. You're keeping her alive too. Because if she doesn't learn how to control this gift that she has, she won't survive it. Reach out to her and bring her back. Isn't that what you've wanted to do all along?"

"We all win," Gee said. "Just like I told you." He stepped closer to her. "I want to see Sarah do well, just like you. I think she's one of the most incredible miracles ever to walk this earth. We can all learn from her."

Damn it. Think. Her mind felt sluggish from the drugs they had given her. Her hands and feet tingled and she shook them lightly, as if freeing them from sleep. She looked around the little group. They were all watching her, waiting for her to make a move.

"I guess I don't have a choice."

Shelley smiled. A range of emotions washed across her

features, softening them in the gentle light from the open door. "Good girl. I knew you'd understand. I always knew it, from the first moment I saw you." She stepped up to the gurney and put her hand on Jess's shoulder, then leaned in more closely as if revealing a secret. Her face burned with a feverish intensity. Jess resisted the urge to shrug away her touch. "I know I've handled this badly, in many ways. I know you feel betrayed. But try to see things from the right perspective. I've spent the last few years trying to help Sarah, keep her from harming herself. Evan took things a bit too far at the end, but he's gone now. There are a lot of people who want a piece of her, but I can make them go away. I can keep her hidden."

"I have your word on that?"

"Of course. Now, she's safe, in an adjoining room. She's sedated, enough to keep her contained, but we can bring her out of it anytime. What I need for you to do is go in there and talk to her, tell her what you want. I'll leave the details up to you."

Sarah fought her way up through the layers of cloud and fog, clawed her way through with renewed determination until she felt the final gossamer wing slip and part and she opened her eyes. For a very long moment, she did not understand where she was, or what had happened; only that her shoulder hurt terribly under the bandage, and her head felt as if it had been emptied and then filled back up with shards of glass.

I want to go home, she thought, for no reason at all.

You don't even know where home is.

Around this little room were angles and corners of no particular significance; she did not recognize anything. There was equipment nearby, enough that it brought to mind the Room, and then she knew where she was and her little heart broke.

No. I won't do it again.

Memories flooded her mind. The door ripping off its hinges, the two men being flung aside, the doctor being lifted off his feet and choking with blood, and she *liked* it, yes, she did, she had felt the power flowing out of her in a long, smooth wave and it felt good.

She moaned softly. She could control it better now, but somehow that made things even worse.

You are committing a mortal sin, one that cannot be undone.

She had killed him.

He deserved it.

That small voice in her mind was cruel and cut deep. But the thought of it thrilled her all the same, the idea of the ultimate revenge against so many injustices that had been heaped upon her for so long. She could do it to any of them. She could crush them like a bug beneath her heel, make them bleed or burn or slowly suffocate. . . .

No!

The sound of the door brought her back. She shivered at the sudden cold, at the puff of her breath and the realization that she had almost let it go again. It was so strong now, she had to clamp down so hard that it hurt. This thing inside her was like a coiled snake waiting to strike.

For a moment she caught a glimpse of the Room through the door, beyond the familiar figure that filled the space.

Jess Chambers closed the door behind her. Sarah leapt up and off the little bed and flung herself into Jess's arms, ignoring the stabbing pain in her shoulder and the blood oozing through the bandage, sobbing, burying her little face against her chest.

"There, now," Jess said. She held her and stroked Sarah's hair. "Hush. It's all right. We're going to get through this, you hear me? We're going to make our way through."

"They're watching," Sarah said. Her voice was muffled against Jess's shirt, and she pulled away and swiped at her eyes and nose.

"I know it. There's a camera mounted near the ceiling. Don't worry about that. Is your arm okay?"

"It hurts."

"I bet it does. You did well down there, kiddo. You didn't have a choice, with what happened. You know that, don't you?"

"I . . ."

"You kept us both from getting killed. Dr. Wasserman wasn't going to listen to us, there was nothing you could do to change what happened."

"I want to get out of here."

"We can work on that. It's almost time now. You know what they want you to do?"

Sarah nodded, sniffled. "Dr. Shelley, she's sick. She's going to die. And I don't care."

"I don't blame you. But could you help her, if you wanted?"

"I don't know."

"They want me to convince you to try. They think I can get into your head somehow, with this drug they've given me, and there's something to that, isn't there? I mean I can feel it working on me, and I can feel you there. There's this pain in my shoulder, just where you were shot."

"I feel it," Sarah whispered.

"Well, I don't care what they want. I'm not going to convince you to do anything, Sarah. This is your decision. You have to figure it out on your own."

Jess held her out at arm's length, studied her face. Then she pulled her in close as if to hug her and put her lips to Sarah's ear. "Don't make a sound," she said softly. "I know you're scared. I don't think they're going to just let us walk away. But there is another way out. It's not going to be pretty, and people are going to get hurt. Do you understand what I'm saying? Remember what I said before. You have to trust yourself."

Sarah gave a little nod. Fear ripped through her belly and prickled her neck. But at the same time she felt a terrible eagerness to begin, to let it out, to see where it would all lead.

"Whatever happens, it's not your fault. It's time to let it loose, don't hold back."

You are committing a mortal sin.

They deserve it. Each and every single one of them.

"I think you better get away from me now," Sarah said.

Jean Shelley waited just outside the door to the prepping room. The others were watching from inside the control booth. The huge, empty space yawned behind her like something coming to gobble her up, but she kept her gaze focused on the door, waiting for it to open. Willing it to open. *Please.* Her breathing came in shallow little gasps; it was difficult to get air now with the fluid pressing in on her lungs.

As she waited she tried to remember to calm her thoughts, slow her heartbeat, retreat to a meditative state. But she had gone too far now down another path, and her mind would no longer cooperate. She found herself thinking back to the night so many years ago and the strange woman who had arrived at the hospital. Annie Voorsanger had changed her life forever, and she probably didn't even know it. How little Shelley had understood then, and how far she had come.

When the door opened, she knew instantly that it was over. Warmth spread through her body. The girl was beautiful, framed in the light from behind, her face in shadow. Angelic. Here was her savior; here was her life, ready to be returned to her.

They had dosed her with the dimerizer, dialed her up to full power. It was now or never. Dr. Jean Shelley stretched out her arms and closed her eyes. A great peace washed over her as she felt the room temperature begin to drop and her skin prickle.

She envisioned each and every diseased cell withering under the attack. They were in full retreat now as the girl worked her psychic fingers in among the folds of tissue. Playing them like a concert pianist would caress the ivory keys. Shelley smiled a little as her mind brought her back to those days when she could sit at the piano for hours as a child, her father, still alive then and retired from the company, pausing every once in a while to listen from the kitchen as he washed his hands before supper; *go on now, Jean, play the Beethoven.* God, how she missed that. The light through the sitting room window was red at sunset and lit the room up like fire. . . .

"Stop," a hoarse voice said. "What in God's name are you doing?"

Shelley opened her eyes. She frowned. A bloody apparition had appeared at the main door to the observation room.

Evan Wasserman shuffled in on broken, bloody feet. His eyes were nearly swollen shut. Gore streaked his face and caked his hair. One arm hung at an odd angle. The other held a gun. It looked like half his hand had melted into the grip.

He peered at her through puffy lids, a puzzled expression on his face. "Jean, I—I don't understand. We agreed to end this ourselves. Why are there men downstairs?"

"Evan," she said, pleading. "Don't."

"It was supposed to be done quietly," he muttered, almost to himself. "Nobody would have to know. This place would be safe, the children . . ." He looked up at her. "The children!" he screamed, bloody saliva spraying from his mouth. "Look what you've done, bringing her up here. The building is falling apart. My grandfather—"

"*You don't know a goddamned thing,*" she hissed at him, baring her teeth. "You sick, disgusting man. I have everything under control. Get out of here!"

Wasserman shook his head. His features clenched, tears wetting the blood at the corner of his eyes. He raised the gun. "I won't let it happen again," he said. "I—"

Shelley sensed movement more than she saw it, and suddenly Jeffrey was barreling into Wasserman from the shadows, hitting him low and in the side like a linebacker into a running back. The blow carried Wasserman up and into the air as the gun barked and something whined off into the darkness, and then they both hit the floor, slid, and rolled over into the wall.

Shelley turned back to the girl. Something was wrong. The room temperature had plummeted, and yet she felt uncomfortably warm. She felt as if someone had doused her with kerosene and was about to light a match.

The girl had come several steps into the room now. Her eyes were glassy in the faint light, reflecting something red that grew brighter by the second.

The air seemed to shimmer. Shelley looked around her at the black walls, the waveproof walls that were now glowing orange red, that were *rippling* like water running down rock, and at the same time she could hardly see through the cloud of steam from her breath. Ice crystals formed in midair and dropped like tiny diamonds at her feet, only to hiss and boil away into mist.

It was all wrong, she shouldn't be this strong, even with the drugs they had given her. . . .

Shelley's skin was burning, melting off her bones.

She shrieked, but the sound was lost in the unforming of her lips and the slow slide of flesh from her jaw.

To study the self is to forget the self, and to forget the self is to be enlightened by the ten thousand things.

In her moment of despair, she clung to this elusive goal, even as her brain boiled inside its bone shell. She still had not found the ten thousand things. Or perhaps she had; perhaps losing yourself meant finding infinity, everything and nothing at once, and the ten thousand things were a metaphor for that boundless stretch of space where time meant nothing, life did not exist, and the world had dissolved into a great, black emptiness.

Her last thoughts were meant for a Christian God, whom

she had denounced years ago, and her prayers were reduced to childhood rhymes. Everything was wrong, the world was coming to an end.

Jesus, save me.

Then there was only pain.

—37—

Jess Chambers, crouched just inside the open door, looked up in time to see the final release of Dr. Jean Shelley.

She had seen Evan Wasserman come in, hardly believing her eyes; she thought she had watched him die. Then, even more unbelievingly, Jeffrey had done his heroic part. Even now they were still struggling with each other, but Jeffrey had gotten his arms under the doctor's armpits and locked his hands behind Wasserman's head.

The floor had become slick as she gained her feet again and held herself upright against the door frame. It was difficult to see now through the odd mix of heat and cold, as the two met like miniature weather fronts and turned the moisture in the air to steam and then instantly to ice.

Shelley stood a few feet beyond Sarah's tiny form. Her arms were still outstretched, as if in prayer, but her flesh hung off them like uncooked bread dough. Her shoes had dissolved into the floor, and she stood like a rooted human tree as the walls gave off waves of glittering heat. Jess could feel it burning her skin like the sun.

Within the dripping oval of her face, Shelley's lips moved. Something popped, and her skin began to smolder. Smoke poured from her hair, her nose and mouth, rose off her body like early-morning steam from a lake.

Then she burst into flame.

Another door flew open and shouts came from the other end of the room. Sarah turned her head, and Jess felt the electrical charge push past her like a breath of wind. The two guards who had begun to draw their weapons now danced in place like two puppets on a string, their limbs jerking and their hair standing on end. Ronald Gee stood just behind them in the doorway, sparks running from his fingers. His clothes had already begun to burn.

The heat and smoke were swiftly overwhelming everything else. Jess found it hard to breathe, and she pulled her shirt up over her nose and mouth.

Sarah was moving. Jess's eyes watered as she tried to watch the girl cross the room, but she had to turn away to catch her breath, and when she turned back, Sarah was gone.

Jess stumbled out into the crackling, open space. Now that Sarah had left, the air had returned to its normal state, and only the fire was left to burn. Somehow it had gotten underneath and in the walls, and up into the roof. In another few minutes this part of the building would be a raging inferno.

The heat was almost unbearable. It was like standing on melting asphalt at twelve noon in the middle of a desert, waves of sickly heat washing over her from all directions.

She shielded her face and ran past the two guards and Gee, who were now sprawled motionless and smoldering across the floor, and out into the hallway. A little easier to breathe out here. Something cracked and shook the floor beneath her feet. She took a gulp of cooler air, coughed up deep hacking mouthfuls of soot and phlegm, and saw the open elevator shaft yawning like a great black mouth. She headed for the stairs.

One floor down, Jess ran past the playroom. Empty, thank God, they had gotten the children out. She continued to the front entrance.

The doors were gone. A ragged hole of concrete and steel took their place. She looked through, out along the path of destruction.

The man in the blue suit was doing a dance on the front steps, his white hair standing on end, his eyes bulging. Smoke curled from within the sleeves of his jacket. His skin crackled. He held a rigid, frozen pose, and then dropped as if suddenly released, rolled limply down the last two steps, and lay still.

Sarah turned on the lawn and faced the street. There were black cars out there, and vans too. The van doors slid open and men in military attack gear jumped out.

Somewhere overhead, Jess heard the chattering thump of a helicopter. She started to move down the steps, hesitated. This was going to get nasty. If Sarah was distracted, they were both dead. She knew that with absolute certainty. It had all gone too far for anything else.

I don't think they're going to just let us walk away. But there is another way out.

Her own words, spoken just minutes ago. More true right now than ever before.

It's time to let it all loose, don't hold back.

McDwyer looked out over the scene as they came in low over the brush. A few moments ago they had swooped past a series of abandoned buildings, and he thought about landing there and planning a better approach through the ground cover, but decided it would take too long.

Now he was glad he did. He swore as the Sikorsky swooped toward the street. A smoking hole where the doors of the facility should be, windows blown out, and where was the girl? There. On the lawn. This was far worse than he'd feared. She was loose, and nobody had been able to get close enough to her for a clean shot with the drug to dial her down. So much for the ground troops. He spotted several of them, crouched behind cars parked sideways outside the gate. What the fuck were they waiting for anyway?

Then he saw the man jittering on the steps as if he'd caught hold of a live wire, smoke pouring from his head of white hair. *Oh, Jesus.* What was Berger doing this close? He should have known better . . .

The situation had just gone from very bad to full-scale disaster. They would not be able to hold off the authorities for long now, even with all the pull they had on the inside. They had to move fast to control the damage, and Berger was way beyond giving orders. It was his turn. Operation Kill-Switch was under way.

McDwyer checked his weapon, shouted at his men to be ready for touchdown.

More black cars squealed to a stop outside the gates, followed by black vans. Men in full combat gear poured out of them.

Then the impossible happened. One of the black cars suddenly flung itself upward, as if ripped from the ground and tossed by a giant hand.

The helicopter swerved in a violent, adrenaline-pumping sideways dive. McDwyer felt a frozen moment of terror as he watched the car's rear tire slip just inches past the windshield. The pilot shouted and fought with the controls, and for a moment McDwyer thought they were all done. *Punch your time cards, gentlemen.* But then the chopper righted itself, the skids hit asphalt, and he felt his teeth click together as the car landed somewhere nearby with a bone-rattling crash.

He had the door already open before the pilot cut the engine, and he had grabbed his weapon case and was out and moving just before the world exploded.

Sarah stood on the front walk as the sky over her head turned black. Blood soaked through the bandage on her shoulder. But the pain was nothing now; she let it go with the rest, with the glorious, burning energy searing through her body. The air rippled as she seemed to swell in size, as she spread her arms out to the wind. Blue streaks leapt from her fingers to meet the clouds, touched her face, her hair, formed a halo around her head. She gasped, threw her hands higher, eyes rolling backward into her skull.

Out by the gates a car went flipping end over end through the air, narrowly missing the helicopter, which landed hard in the street.

One of the remaining cars exploded. A ball of yellow flame shot skyward. A van went next, the fireball erupting from the rear gas tank. And then the helicopter, with its rotors still turning lazily in the wind, seemed to puff once and stutter before the tanks went up and it disappeared into a blinding flash of white-yellow heat.

Debris tinkled across pavement, chunks of steaming metal thudding and tumbling across the grass. A piece of someone's hand, two fingers attached and twitching, landed next to Sarah's left foot. Across the street, half of a rotor blade buried itself three feet deep into the side of an abandoned row house, the metal end that protruded still smoking.

A man ran screaming across the lawn, his hair on fire. Others within the attack squad who had survived the blasts had gathered their wits about them enough to organize themselves, and the chatter of weapons joined the dull whoosh and crackle of the burning vehicles.

Sarah turned in the direction of the gunfire. The air rippled like a colorless wave passing through, and a crack zigzagged its way across the front lawn toward the guardhouse. The ground opened up and swallowed it with a shriek and a tearing of wood and metal, buckling the gates and melting the asphalt and concrete curb into a gooey mess that looked like a giant stripe of warm chocolate.

The crack continued to snake across the sidewalk, and the front axle of the remaining van fell with a thunk into the gap. The van teetered for a moment on the edge of the wide, black mouth, back end swinging up toward the sky, and then it tipped over the edge and fell with the crunch of shattered glass.

Three men with guns were exposed, still crouching behind

where the van used to be. With a grunt of satisfaction she picked them up and hurled them thirty feet backward, right past the quivering rotor blade, through a clapboard wall, and into the room behind it.

The blast from the exploding helicopter felt like a giant hand pressed firmly into McDwyer's back. The air whooshed from his lungs as the hand gave a violent shove. He was airborne for perhaps ten feet, but kept his wits about him long enough to tuck and roll into the impact with the ground.

Still, stars exploded across his vision with the collision and he lay sprawled for a moment, stunned. The explosions had done something to his hearing. Everything sounded as if it were underwater.

When he got to his feet he was bleeding from badly scraped palms and a gash on his forehead.

He licked his lips and tasted blood. *Nothing broken.* He glanced over at the front steps of the Wasserman Facility. The girl stood there among the smoking ruins. A mini cyclone swirled about her head, blue lightning flashes rippling through black clouds.

The air temperature had plummeted to something approaching midwinter. And yet the fires still burned, and the heat coming off anything the girl's mind had touched was like the blast from a furnace.

He thought back to his years of training, clamped down hard, prayed to God for strength. He had never been so scared of anything in his life. All the reports he had read about her were nothing compared to this. *She's some kind of demon.*

When he felt the ground shake under his feet and the earth cracked open across the lawn, swallowing everything in its path, he turned and scrabbled across the road to the large, black suitcase that had come to rest near the curb.

He had to get to higher ground, get himself under cover, and find a place to take the shot. A small commercial building was located about a hundred yards down the street. He ducked and ran, moving behind parked cars and darting between open spaces. He heard men screaming, another explosion, things shattering.

The first floor of the building was a pizza parlor, or it had been at one time. Now it looked like a crack den. Two black women and a man with piercings through his nose and the tattoo of a dragon wrapped around his neck huddled against the back wall as he kicked through the door. "You stay away!" the man shouted. He was shivering and he held out a gun. "I called the fucking cops. It's World War Three out there. Who are they? Arabs? Are they gonna kill us? Why's it so goddamned cold?"

"Tell me where the stairs are, right now," McDwyer said, ignoring the gun. "And get the fuck out of sight."

The man hesitated a moment; then he must have seen something in McDwyer's eyes and lowered the gun. He led him to a door in the back room. McDwyer slipped quickly up the steps, past three landings and more closed doors, until he reached the roof.

Outside he quickly surveyed the scene: tar and crushed stone flat surface, three-foot-high walls all around. He had no time for testing, had to put things together fast and clean, take the shot, and get out. It was a good spot, plenty of room and the right distance. He could set up on the flat top of a steel vent cover and kneel on the surface of the roof to get her in his sights, all the while keeping himself almost completely concealed.

He set down his case, flipped the latches, and lifted the lid, then set out assembling the unit in thirty seconds flat. The "Light Fifty," or M82A1A, was a .50-caliber, semiautomatic, air-cooled rifle with a Unertl 10-power scope. He would use M2 Browning Machine Gun cartridges in this case.

This was too far away to risk a dart shot, and it was too late for that anyway. They had done extensive research into the type of weapon that would be necessary to take the girl down. These rounds were large enough to kill an elephant. They should do the job nicely.

Jess Chambers watched the man from the helicopter as he ran down the street. At first she thought he was running away from them, but then she saw him kick open the door of what looked like some kind of restaurant.

He's carrying something nasty in that case. The noise had grown deafening all around her now, shrieks both human and inhuman, and particles of ice and dirt whipped at her face. But she did not take her eyes away from that building.

When she saw the wink of something peeking over the rooftop a couple of minutes later, she knew.

She screamed a warning into the wind.

The scope picked up everything, made it just as nice and clean and sharp as a fine sunny day at the beach. The air around her was thick with swirling dust and smoke, but McDwyer was used to conditions of blowing sand in 120-degree heat, and it didn't shake him now.

One shot, one kill. The sniper's motto. With the Light Fifty, he could punch a hole through a person's head from a thousand meters away. *How far is her range?* he wondered. Could she reach him here?

Enough of this nonsense. He was babbling inside his own mind. He settled her face in his sights, took a deep breath, and let it out in a slow hiss.

His hands were shaking. Why wouldn't they be still? He blinked and saw a little girl he'd never met. But this was no ordinary girl he was looking at. He had a job to do. *Come on, you son of a bitch.*

A woman was shouting and gesturing from the front steps, pointing. Inside the eye of that flat, cold scope, Sarah turned to look his way.

Predator to predator, like two lions crouched in the brush.

This time, that split-second difference went the other way.

Jess shouted Sarah's name again. *There, over there. He's got a gun.* At first the girl didn't seem to hear her, and then her eyes rolled and tried to focus. She glanced at the rooftop where Jess was pointing, and instantly a huge ripple of pure energy went tearing away from her, flattening everything in its path like the blast wave from a bomb, vaporizing the last remaining men where they crouched and hid, parked cars and light posts tossed into the air and tumbling like windblown leaves, as if something immense and invisible had gone lumbering down the street.

A bullet screamed past Sarah's face and her head snapped back; the bullet ricocheted off the wall of the Wasserman Facility, leaving a six-inch-deep crater in the brick. She moaned. Blood began to ooze from a furrow on the left side of her scalp. The thing that had wormed its way into Jess's mind clenched violently.

Jess caught another flash of muzzle fire from the roof, and a chunk of steps disintegrated at her feet.

And then the invisible lumbering beast reached the building.

Windows exploded inward as immense pressure came to bear against the walls. For a moment, the structure held, and then with a screech and horrible grinding roar, the lower floors gave way.

It was like a wrecking ball hitting a house of matchsticks. Bits of brick and wood exploded out the back, peppering the surrounding areas with white-hot shrapnel. The top two floors collapsed down into themselves, and a cloud of brick and concrete dust billowed outward and swirled in the wind.

Sarah screamed. She screamed again, as the strange blue fire licked up and down her body and the storm reached a fever pitch.

Jess felt the gathering pressure in her lungs, inside her

head, as if she had been grabbed in a vise grip. She took a step forward, then two. Had she been wrong all this time? Was it too late, had they pushed it too far?

You're hurting me. Please. When we first met you asked for my help. Let me give it to you now. Let me make it better.

At first she didn't even realize she hadn't spoken aloud. But Sarah seemed to hear her. When she looked back on it later it was one of the many things she would puzzle over in wonder, but now she didn't think about any of that. She managed to get down the steps without falling and stood a few feet away.

Sarah was trembling. Blood ran freely down her face. Her eyes glittered blue fire in the deepening dusk. *I can't stop. It's too hard.*

That's the easy way out. It's all over now, they're all gone. You did it. Sarah, did I ever lie to you? Can't you trust me now?

It hurts! Sarah opened her mouth and let out a soundless scream. She threw her head back and the blue fire swarmed over her. *Oh, it hurts. . . .*

And Jess Chambers, who had come awake many nights sweating and full of blood and the screech of tires, did not hesitate now. She knew that many of the wounded did not get this chance.

She reached out with both hands and grasped Sarah's arms just above the elbows.

The strength of it hit her like a train coming down a long straight track. Every muscle in her body lit up and clenched at once, and she found herself unable to move, unable to breathe, as the blue fire ran down and through her like a lightning rod, as sparks jumped from her toes into the ground. A million frozen images flashed through her mind, her life passing in one constant stream of light and dark, neurons firing like a billion stars in the great deep darkness of space.

She tried to cry out, tried to give life to the mindless scream; but nothing came, she saw nothing finally but blackness, and the only sound she heard at the end was the thunderous, throbbing beat of a heart.

—38—

She did not know exactly how long she lay there, but it couldn't have been as long as it might have seemed, because she woke to the sound of sirens.

She found herself lying stretched full-length on the ground. The spot where she had been standing before was bare and scorched.

The sirens were growing rapidly louder. She sat up, spat out the taste of iron and stale sweat. Her body ached, trembled like a newborn's. She smelled earth and burned flesh, and smoke from the swiftly growing fire that licked around the edges of the Wasserman Facility and spread through the dry brush in back.

How she had survived it she didn't know; how could she possibly have survived the sort of jolt she had taken? But the black clouds above her head had broken up and the sky was lighter now. The wind that had come out of nowhere was slackening.

It had ended, far more swiftly than it began.

Sarah lay ten feet away in the grass. Unable to find the strength to stand, Jess crawled to her side. The girl lay on her back, her eyes open and glassy. There was a lot of blood, too much blood. Sudden panic filled Jess's lungs and made her feel as if she were drowning. *No. Not now, not after all that. I won't let you die.* The scalp wound looked ugly, but it wasn't deep. She ripped open Sarah's top, found the dark, puckered bullet hole high in her shoulder. The bandage had slid off entirely.

Blood oozed up through the hole, more slowly now. She tore a piece of bloody cloth and pressed her palm to it to stop the bleeding.

"You're all right," she said. Her throat felt burned and raw as a wound. She gathered the girl's head into her lap, stroked Sarah's hair. A tiny spark like static electricity jumped under her hand, while she kept her other palm hard against the gunshot hole. "I told you, I'm going to keep you safe. You hear? You're going to be *just fine.*"

Sarah gave a great, shuddering sigh. She blinked. "It— hurts," she said.

"I know. We'll make it better soon."

"I'm sorry. I didn't mean to . . . I didn't mean it."

"Don't you worry about that. Don't you worry. What they've done to you, they deserve it."

Tears blurred her vision, turned light into rainbows of color. The hospital had begun to burn faster now. Thicker, black smoke lifted from the roof and drifted lazily in the suddenly calm air.

A few other children emerged from their hiding places. They gathered silently to stare down at the strange couple in the grass like respectful mourners. For a moment this all felt like a dream, and then Jess looked and saw what was left of the man lying at the foot of the steps, hair smoking and skin black and cracked, saw the door blown from its hinges and the darkness inside, and she felt like screaming. She looked down the street at the bodies and the twisted wreckage of cars, and most of all the huge, gaping hole where the sniper's building had been.

It was desolation, destruction. It was Armageddon. She blinked, seeing everything through a broken prism of light. She could not make it all go away. It was too late for that.

The sirens were very close now. Any moment they would be here.

Sarah coughed and her lips stopped moving. For a moment the air crackled and spat; then the feeling dispersed like smoke from a dying fire, and everything was calm. Jess closed her eyes against the stink of the burn, the shattered remains of what had been left behind.

She waited for somebody to come.

EPILOGUE

Here are the smoking ruins, the scars, and the drift and the silence of what used to be. The Wasserman Facility left deserted among the scrub brush and the wilds of greater Boston. Fingers of burnt wooden limbs point jaggedly to the sky, as overhead a triangle of geese flap southward for winter. Soon the remains will be lightly coated with a fine snow, the first of the season sprinkled like a handful of dirt on the lid of a coffin before it is tucked away and forgotten.

The land lies abandoned as all around it life goes on. The Wasserman Facility has joined the ghosts of its kin, and memories of the laughter and screams of the children are all that remain, until even those drift away, carried by the stiff breeze.

The burial was held on Wednesday morning, in a graveyard in Wellesley adjacent to a white clapboard church. About fifty people gathered under a drizzling rain, their faces matching the color of the sky. Black umbrellas clutched in white-knuckled fists held off the worst of it. The expressions of those in the first row were blank, or tired, or bored.

They probably barely knew her.

But as Jess Chambers looked more closely she began to see familiar faces. A few of the mourners were colleagues;

she recognized Professor Thomas with a younger woman, who clung to his arm with one hand and clutched a handkerchief in the other. Some of those gathered along the right were students, red-eyed and blowing their noses into white tissue as Jean Shelley's casket swung and scraped against dirt on its way down.

The casket was a symbolic gesture. They had been unable to recover anything at all from the wreckage of the fire. The inferno in the observation room had blazed so hot and strong that even Shelley's bones had been reduced to dust, every trace of her existence erased and blown away.

Evan Wasserman, or what they thought was left of him, would be laid to rest tomorrow in the plot adjacent to Jean Shelley, as his will had requested.

She searched the faces again, looking for those who might appear to be a bit more out of place. She recognized two of the investigators who had already spoken to her at length at the hospital, and another younger man who might be a plainclothes cop. But nobody else stood out. Anyone left from Helix or the Wasserman Facility would be too smart to come here, she thought. Their business with Sarah was done, and Shelley's and Berger's deaths had probably thrown everything into chaos. They would wash their hands publicly of the entire mess. If there was anyone left at all who knew the full truth.

The whole story was still coming together in bits and pieces, very few of which the investigators had shared with her. But they clearly didn't know everything either. What *was* clear was that Jean Shelley, with a large portion of the significant holdings she had inherited from her father's steel business, had founded Helix Pharmaceuticals nearly eight years before with at least two other players. It was a privately held company specializing in gene therapy and small-molecule drug discovery, and had remained fiercely independent and guarded until recently, when rumors had begun to float about an investment opportunity. It was said that the company was offering a significant stake in a particularly exciting preclinical program, before an IND had even been filed. They would need a large cash infusion to move into clinical testing. None of this had been confirmed yet, but it was likely only a matter of time before more details came to light.

Why someone with a fortune as large as Shelley's would have taken a job on the faculty of a small graduate school wasn't immediately clear. The most obvious explanation, that Shelley had planned the whole thing even as far as five years back, raised other unsettling questions that Jess would rather not explore. It was more likely that she had done it simply because she could, and because it left her closer to where Sarah was being held.

For the past two days, Jess had been struggling to come to terms with a new image of herself, and it wasn't pretty. She had let Jean Shelley play her like a fine baby grand. The professor had manipulated and controlled her nearly every step of the way.

The fact that Shelley was an authority figure should not matter in the slightest, Jess told herself. She was being trained to notice just this sort of deceit in other people. She should have been more aware of what was happening.

She felt unbalanced, unsure of herself or her own motivations.

But this wasn't the only thing she was struggling to understand. Another part of her mind had yet to face something even more unsettling. Shelley and Gee had told her she was a psi carrier. What's more, she had been dosed with some sort of drug. Were they telling the truth, and if so, what exactly had it done to her? What did it all mean, if anything?

The minister said his last few words and closed his Bible with a snap, hunched against the wind and drizzle. When the ceremony was finished and the mourners had begun to file away, Charlie gave her a gentle hug, careful to avoid the painful spots. Then she held her at arm's length and looked her over. Jess knew she was pale and rumpled, out of sorts. "You're the walking wounded, girl. Should have stayed in that hospital bed."

"I had to come, Charlie." *I had to see her into the ground. Even if she's not really in there.*

"Don't I know it. But that doesn't mean a whit to your poor old body."

"I'm fine, really. Just some scrapes and bruises. I'm like one of those dumb lucky miracles, people who get hit by lightning and walk away with barely a scratch."

"Are you done with the talking?"

"I've got interviews later today. They let me off the hook to come here, but they're itching to get back to it."

"What are you telling them?"

"Nothing really. They don't know a thing about Sarah. Children's Services had her as deceased for years. As far as the government's concerned, she doesn't exist, and I'm not going to do anything to change that."

The official theory so far of the destruction of the Wasserman Facility was a rupture in the ancient gas line that ran all the way from Blue Hills to the old Boston State Hospital complex. Pockets of trapped gas had gathered in various locations underground, and when one of them was sparked by an electrical short the explosion caused a chain reaction, taking Wasserman's building down along with the surrounding brush and half the street.

How that explained the rest of it, Jess had no idea. There were too many dead men at the scene, along with the pieces of the destroyed helicopter scattered among the debris. Someone would have to be held accountable.

"You done good," Charlie said. "I know it might not seem like it right now, but what happened is the way it had to be. Someday you'll see it the same."

"Maybe, Charlie. Maybe you're right. But it doesn't keep me from feeling pretty damn guilty. A lot of people died. I could have done something differently, gotten her out somehow without causing her to tear the whole place to shreds. You know?"

"They would have killed you, to keep her," Charlie said. "You know it as well as I do. There was nothing that could have changed that. It was fate. That and the almighty dollar."

Jess looked out across the cemetery to the street. For some reason, she thought about Maria's face. *Embrujado. Haunted.* Something shiny winked in her eyes, and then was gone. "I don't know what to think anymore," she said.

"What you need is a hot bath, lots of bubbles, and someone to scrub you raw."

"I'm going to disappear for a while, Charlie," she said. "I'm leaving Thomas Ward. I just can't bring myself to care about the degree anymore. This whole experience has changed my perspective. I don't know if psychology is the field for me."

"Take your time, sweetheart. Don't make any rash decisions. The mental health field will be a colder, darker place without you in it. Can I see you back to the hospital?"

"I've got an errand to run first, a couple of them actually."

"I'll go with you, then. You blew up my car, I can't go anywhere else right now anyway."

Jess looked at Charlie and saw that there would be no changing her mind. She smiled, insanely glad at that moment to have such a friend, and wondering how on earth she had earned the honor. "We'll take a taxi," she said.

Over one hundred yards away, Philippa Cruz lowered the binoculars and handed them to the driver standing to her right, and he switched the umbrella he was holding to his other hand to take them.

Droplets of water spattered the shoulders of her suit jacket. She rubbed at her eyes to get the grit out. She'd forgotten the last time she had slept. Her hair was lying limply across her face and the fine lines around her mouth and brow had become more pronounced. It had been a very long couple of days.

They were parked among a row of other cars and far enough down the street to remain unnoticed, but she had a clear line of sight to the graveyard and the small group of people gathered there. With the high-powered binoculars, it was almost as if she stood shoulder to shoulder with Jess Chambers.

"No sign of her," Cruz said. Not that she had expected the girl to be there anyway. They would be keeping her out of sight for a while, maybe forever. That is, if she was still alive.

Cruz had been on the premises when the disaster had taken place. Unlike Steven Berger, she had decided early on not to stick around and see what happened. Cruz was not interested in saving any lives except her own, and she supposed that saving lives had not been Berger's motivation either. He had remained out of pure greed. They had not had the time to remove their most sensitive and important research, and he was simply trying to protect his valuable assets.

What Berger didn't know was that Cruz had been keeping separate records on all of her own findings since the beginning. She was far too smart to lose them in something as silly as a fire.

She watched as the mourners slowly filed out of the cemetery. The big black woman hugged Chambers and they talked for a few minutes. Then a taxi pulled up to the curb, and the two women got in.

Cruz was dying to know what exactly Chambers could do now, if anything. She had received four separate doses of the dimerizer drug, which should have been enough to induce psi gene expression for some time. But it was impossible to tell for sure without a blood test.

Through careful research, they had identified her as one out of a possible three carriers in the area. Shelley had been instrumental in making all that happen, using her many contacts in the medical community to identify those with a family history of the particular type of autism that served as a marker for psi, then working up detailed psych profiles based on any significant events or trauma in the subject's past. The final step, DNA testing, was a relatively simple process that could be accomplished by acquiring hair, blood, or skin samples.

Their extensive research had shown that psi carriers often formed some sort of mental link to each other. Shelley had hoped that Jess would be able to draw Sarah out and influence her to perform for them. The evidence was still foggy on that, as far as Cruz was concerned. She strongly suspected that it was her new formulation of the dimerizer drug that had caused the girl to come out of her fugue, but now they might never know for sure.

The ultimate plan had been to make Jess Chambers the second subject in the later phases of their testing model, in order to verify the effectiveness of the drug candidate. Psi carriers would be the first target, and she was a perfect choice since she hadn't shown any obvious signs of ability before. The gene was natural to the carriers and simply had to be activated and then controlled, which was a much easier thing than cloning and implanting the gene on an adenovirus, then injecting it into the muscle tissue of a noncarrier.

One step at a time, Cruz thought. It was difficult for her to hold back, to let the science develop. She was so eager to try new things.

Now they would have to come up with an alternate plan. Another carrier, perhaps. Or she could just go ahead and clone the gene, multiple samples of which were still sitting in storage in a safe location. Either way, she would have to let the girl go for a while. The shiny new facility in Alabama was empty and waiting for them, but everything was too hot at the moment. She needed to sit out the storm.

Moving everything overseas for a year would serve the purpose nicely.

She opened the back door to the car and slid inside, welcoming the warm, dry puff of air against her skin. The

Asian man in the back offered her a small white towel. She dabbed at her face and neck. The towel had been heated against the vent. That was the most pleasing part of Asian culture, their thoughtfulness.

That and the money this man could offer her. Enough to fund the project for two more years in relative quiet and seclusion.

The Asian man asked her if she was comfortable. She smiled, nodded. "Thank you," she said. "Shall we go? I believe the plane is waiting."

He gave the nod to the driver and they pulled out into traffic, the long black car blending in among the others as they wound their way toward a new future.

Jess and Charlie stopped briefly at a Hallmark gift shop, and then climbed back into the taxi for the ride to the group home in Cambridge.

The general feeling about public housing for the mentally ill in Massachusetts has seen a dramatic change in recent years. State-run permanent residence programs are few and far between. The Massachusetts Department of Mental Health, or DMH, provides mostly rehabilitative residential programs; group homes and shared apartments are the rule, and patients may remain in them until they learn how to live on their own.

The Young Adult Shared Apartment Program is part of DMH's Specialized Rehabilitative Residential Programs, and it is exclusively for clients between the ages of eighteen and twenty-seven. Residents share an apartment with other roommates, and receive twenty-four-hour counseling and support, including educational and community activities.

Charlie remained in the car. Jess was directed by a very cheerful woman to the third level of rooms, where Dennis Brigham was being introduced to his new surroundings.

The young man was sitting on his bed and a counselor was working with him on tactile impressions, letting him touch and examine the comforter, the pillow, the small study desk that would remain his property through the duration of his stay.

Jess stood in the doorway and studied him. He still had the same red baseball cap yanked down tightly over his head, and his socks were pulled up over his calves. He had been cleanly shaved this morning.

"Hello, Dennis," she said. "How are you feeling today? I've brought you something."

He cocked his head at her and offered a very wide smile, but she could not tell if he recognized her or not. She kept some respectful distance between them, and held out the fluffy white teddy bear with the red ribbon around its neck. It was the best the Hallmark store had to offer, and though it looked nothing like the one she had given to Sarah, the one Dennis had tried to take from her that day in the playroom, it would have to do.

The counselor, a pleasantly round man in his thirties with glasses and a receding hairline, took the bear from her and put it on the bed. "He'll need to get used to it," the man said. "There are a lot of new things in his world these days. We're working on touch. He's got a bit of an issue with personal contact."

"I know," she said. "I was with him, before. I helped out a little bit at the Wasserman Facility."

"Ah, okay. So you do know, then. Would you like a moment with him?"

She nodded. Dennis had picked up the bear and was clutching it to his chest, rocking with it, slowly rocking back and forth.

"Do you love me? Then say it. Saaaayyyy it."

"I love you, Dennis," she said. "I'm very sorry about what happened."

The counselor had been taken by surprise when Dennis picked up the bear so quickly. Clearly there was some connection between the two of them. He watched the worn-looking young woman with concern as tears rolled down her face, made as if to touch her arm, then thought better of it. This one did not look like she liked to be touched either.

He left them alone, closing the door quietly behind him.

A day later, Jess was well enough to be released from the hospital. Otto howled at her when she returned to her apartment, wrapping himself around her legs and purring loudly. Charlie had been good enough to feed him, but he was clearly starving for attention. She gave him enough tight squeezes that he eventually wriggled out of her arms and went stalking off across the floor with his tail held high, as if suddenly offended by such a shameless show of need.

She spent the next two days answering a few more questions from investigators, painting in the eaves by her window, and watching the leaves fall. She was intent upon appearing to the outside world as though she were resuming her routine, and so she went shopping, saw Charlie for lunch, and played at the life of a normal twenty-something in the city.

But inside, she was itching to go.

A week after the fire that destroyed the Wasserman Facility, she made a few calls, notifying the school and landlord of her intentions, then packed Otto into the car and delivered him to Charlie, who accepted the burden without a second thought and gave her the information she needed. Jess saw her chance and took it.

The address she had been given was a single-family home in a residential pocket on the outskirts of Framingham, small but carefully kept on a corner lot. Traffic was light in this neighborhood.

Jess noticed the children's slide and swing set, partially obscured by the hedge and gate on the side of the house. She rang the bell, and a young woman opened the door. She was pretty and lithe, with hair that tumbled across her shoulders in thick, dark curls. A little boy of about four peeked out from behind her legs. "Welcome," she said. "Come on in. Jay-jay, go find a toy to play with, please."

Patrick was waiting for her in the living room. "You've met my sister and nephew, then," he said, when she entered. "Isn't he a little devil? Kate, we'll be a few minutes."

"I'll take him outside to play," she said. "Just let me know if you need anything."

When the woman had left them alone, Patrick crossed the room quickly and drew Jess into his chest without a word. She remained stiff at first, and then felt herself relax and return the embrace. She was surprised to realize that it felt good.

"You're all right," he said. It wasn't a question, but a statement of relief. She nodded anyway. "I wasn't sure of the details," he said. "Charlie feeds me pieces of information when she can."

"Thank you," Jess whispered.

"For what?"

"For being there. For what you did for her. For both of us."

Patrick had arrived at the Wasserman Facility before the first rescue vehicle, and quickly surveyed the scene. They had made a fast decision. Sarah needed immediate medical attention, but it could not be through normal channels. They still didn't know who else was involved, who might want to get their hands on her, and they didn't know what she might do to a stranger who tried to touch her. Patrick knew a general practitioner who would treat her carefully and with no questions asked. After that, she had to effectively disappear.

He loaded her into his car, while Jess remained behind to look after the other children. It was one of the hardest decisions she ever had to make. She still did not know if she could trust him completely, but his connection to Charlie was very much in his favor.

"Nobody followed you, then?" he asked, releasing her from the embrace. She was caught up in his eyes again, the unsettling nature of them, the duality. He could not hide his true feelings, even if that was what he wanted to do. Like two sides of one personality, laid bare for all to see.

"I asked the cabbie to be careful," she said. "I watched too. There was no one."

"Good." He smiled down at her, touched her cheek. "Thank God you're okay." Then he drew away. "You'll want to see her. She's this way."

He led her through a narrow, darkened hallway to the rear bedroom. Sarah lay among the soft sheets, tethered to an IV and a bandage taped to the wound on her head, her eyes closed and little brow slightly furrowed. As Jess entered, she seemed to relax, the tension easing in her face. She opened her eyes.

Jess Chambers felt a prickle in her skin. She looked down; her hands had come up and forward as if by their own accord. She took two steps to the bed, reached out, and touched the girl's fingertips. An electrical charge jumped between them like static electricity.

She reached up to caress Sarah's brow. Sarah smiled at her through the bandages and the shadows, and the pain and sadness was gone, her eyes were lighter now, and free.

A week later, the girl was well enough to get out of bed and move around. They waited another three days, and then packed everything up and said good-bye to the little house in the quiet family neighborhood.

The trip to Jacob's Field took no more than twenty minutes. The Beechcraft was waiting for them near the gate, fueled up and ready to fly. Sarah sat with Patrick in the back, her eyes growing large and round as they taxied and then lifted off into the air, soaring upward through the low layer of clouds that had settled around the airport in the lazy, blue cold of a November day.

Gilbertsville was the same as she had left it, but something had changed at the Voorsanger household. Jess could sense the difference as soon as they pulled into the dirt drive. Sarah sat forward in the rear seat, her excitement and fear a nearly physical presence in the rental car with them.

Cristina Voorsanger came out of the screen door as Patrick cut the engine. She wore a faded flower-print dress and a knitted cotton shawl, and she looked years older, the lines in her chapped face as deep and raw as if they had been etched with acid.

They all got out of the car. Cristina stopped dead in her tracks as Sarah came out from behind Jess, and her face went white.

"We're here to see Annie," Jess said. "Her little girl wants some time with her."

Cristina did not say a word for over a minute, and they all stood and watched her, waiting. Her breath puffed white before her face as she studied the girl, her eyes devouring her features, searching for something.

Finally she looked up at Jess and Patrick. "Knew you'd be coming," she said. "I could feel it. Then I read about the fire back in Boston, at a children's facility? I could guess the rest." She turned back to Sarah. "You like cookies? Bunch of people dropped them off this week." She glanced back at Jess. "Ed passed. Heart gave out. Doctors said it just up and ruptured in his chest, just like that. Never given him a whit of trouble before."

"I'm sorry to hear that, Mrs. Voorsanger."

"Please, I told you. It's Cristina. Who's this handsome man?"

Jess introduced Patrick, who came forward and shook her hand. "Pleasure to meet you," she said. "Excuse my outfit, I'm not myself today—"

The bang of the screen door made them all turn. Annie Voorsanger had come out onto the front steps. Her black hair was loose now and fell to the base of her neck. She wore a sheer cotton nightgown the color of cream, lace gathered about the wrists and along the hemline. The out-line of her naked body showed through the fabric. She was barefoot.

"Annie," Cristina said sharply, "what on earth—"

Jess could feel the energy gathering, the familiar buzz lighting up every nerve in her body and overwhelming everything else. This time it seemed to be coming from two directions at once, or three. Annie stumbled down to the cracked front walk, took two shambling steps forward, then fell to her knees. A high, keening noise wrenched itself from her throat.

Sarah tore past them all, into her mother's arms. They clutched at each other. The keening noise grew louder as the electrical charge crackled and released itself all at once, as a sharp breeze lifted the dust from the ground around them and swirled a tornado of debris, the mother and her daughter cocooned as they sat among the broken flagstones.

Cristina told them they could stay as long as they wanted, and Jess had the feeling she was pleased about the arrange-ment, if still apprehensive at what the future might bring. But Annie was clearly different now, her eyes showing more life in them, though she still did not speak. She and Sarah formed an immediate and permanent bond, or perhaps one had been there all along; they sat for hours together, neither one of them saying a word, all conversation going on at some other level where voices were no longer necessary.

When Sarah was not with Annie, she and Jess spent the time together, their own bond permanently forged as well. Jess read aloud to her, or played board games like Parcheesi and Candyland, which Cristina had dug up from the shelves in the cellar, or they took walks down the long dirt drive and admired the crunch of brown leaves underfoot.

Jess knew this life could not last forever, but right now it was a good one. She felt herself healing inside, regaining the confidence in herself she had lost. Soon she would have a better idea of where she wanted to go from here, but for now, this was enough. Patrick remained the perfect gentleman, though she knew he wanted more from her.

Perhaps in time, she would be able to give it.

One crisp fall afternoon, less than two weeks after they had arrived at the Voorsanger farm, Sarah took Jess by the hand and led her outside. Patrick was in the kitchen helping Cristina clean up after lunch, and Annie was napping in the bedroom upstairs.

Sarah pulled her eagerly down the path and to the rear of the barn. "I want to show you something," she said, her eyes shining. "You know how I've been feeling better lately? My chest is almost healed. The scab came off today, and it's only a little pink and puckered there now. Before, I couldn't do . . . you know. Maybe a little, but not much. But now . . ."

She turned and faced a small drift of leaves that had piled up against the side of the barn. Her little face screwed itself up into a look of deep concentration.

It was a particularly calm day, not a cloud in the sky. But suddenly a touch of wind wafted over them, the temperature plunged, and the pile of leaves swirled and lifted up, bits and pieces drifting and darting around their faces.

"You see?" Sarah said, turning back to her as the debris settled around their feet. Her little face was shining with pride. "I can control it just fine, nothing happens now. I can do whatever I want, and nothing bad happens!"

Jess touched the girl's face. "Good for you," she said. "Good for you, Sarah."

But the girl had something else in mind today. "Now you do it," she said.

"I can't, honey. I'm not like you."

"Sure you can," she said, insistent. "You just close your eyes, and reach out, and you . . . push. Just push. Try it. Please?"

Jess felt a fluttering in her chest, and frowned. In the weeks since the accident she had sensed something different about herself, something foreign that had settled down to live deep inside her breast. But it had been so long since she had taken any of the drug, surely whatever effect it might have had on her was long gone now.

She turned back to the remains of the leaf pile. The wind had died down, and the sun felt warm on the back of her neck. "Go on," Sarah said eagerly. "Try it."

Jess closed her eyes. She imagined herself reaching out with long fingers like wind, pictured the leaves lifting themselves up and scattering before her touch.

Inside her mind, something twitched; she opened her eyes to see the slightest breath go whispering through the pile. A single cracked and brown leaf trembled at the edge of the ground, whirled and lifted up as if suspended in the air, and then drifted down again and was still.

"There," Sarah said, into the silence, into the cold and still loneliness of the bright fall afternoon. "I told you, didn't I? I told you so."

Jess nodded. She wrapped her arms around her chest and shivered.

On the long walk back to the house, Sarah reached out and took her hand. Her grip was warm, and Jess's hand remained so long after she had let go.

Turn the page for an advance look at Nate Kenyon's next
terrifying novel...

THE BONE FACTORY

Coming in July 2009

And thus I clothe my naked villainy
With old odd ends, stol'n forth of holy writ;
And seem a saint, when most I play the devil.

—William Shakespeare, *King Richard the Third*

PROLOGUE: BLOOD

Winter's frozen fingers caressed Joe Thibideau's face, his breath twisting in great clouds of steam to ice his eyelashes. The moon was bright as he moved as quickly as possible across the three inches of fresh snow that softened the ground. Little eight-year-old Melissa had been reported missing yesterday afternoon, and that was a long time in this weather. The night was brutally cold, and she was almost surely frozen stiff by now, a ghostly statue in the blue-white moonlight.

He immediately tried to wipe the image from his mind, but it kept coming back again, and chilled him more than the cold ever could. As the deputy sheriff in the small town of St. Boudin, Thibideau had never had to search for death until yesterday. Anyone dead was right out in plain sight, in the middle of a nasty car wreck, or perhaps a logging accident.

But this was different than anything he had faced before. This time, they had a killer in their midst.

The first victim, a local farmer named Eddie Brosseau, had been discovered yesterday morning about three miles away, stuffed inside the front end of an abandoned truck out in his field. He was missing his head, his right arm and part of a shoulder. The reason for this gruesome dismemberment was anybody's guess; Thibideau personally figured that whoever killed the old man had trouble fitting the whole body into that little import's engine cavity. Maybe there were other reasons, but he preferred not to think about it any more than was absolutely necessary.

Then the girl had disappeared from her home while gathering some wood from the shed. He remembered the desperate voice of the mother on the phone: *We usually fill the wood box together. I never let her go out alone, especially on a cold day like that.*

Joe Thibideau had a daughter of his own. If Melissa had fallen victim to the same brutal bastard who killed Eddie, he only hoped he'd have the chance to nail the son of a bitch. Never in all his forty-seven years had he wanted anything so badly.

Of course, the girl could be a simple runaway, or she might have gotten lost. And yet he couldn't shake the feeling that they were linked together by a single savage thread.

He moved through a thicker patch of alders, and paused with his back against the rough bark of a tree. He had lost the others about twenty minutes ago. He should keep close by, he knew, but they had been searching in the cold for nearly two days. It was time to take a chance. He had a hunch. Just another hour or two couldn't hurt, right?

And maybe, just maybe, if the girl was still alive, he could do something to keep her that way.

A branch snapped and sent its burden of heavy snow thudding to the ground. He jumped, almost dropping his flashlight and hitting his head against the tree trunk, which only caused a fresh shower of snow to fall on top of him. Shaking snow from his collar, he pulled a compass and then the map from the left pocket of his parka and smoothed it out over his knees, holding the flashlight in his mouth. The areas already searched were circled in bright fluorescent green on the map. They had been over about four square miles directly behind the house. She could have been picked up by a car, could be fifty miles away from here by now. So far they had been betting against that, since the house was a good half mile off any provincially plowed road, and the driveway hadn't shown any fresh tracks.

But they couldn't rule it out.

The map didn't have it, but the hydroelectric plant was less than a mile farther south. It was supposed to make use of the old mine shafts in the area to produce enough power to light up most of Quebec City and parts of northern Maine into the twenty-first century and beyond. Construction on the new plant had been halted a couple of months back, but he was sure the old Jackson mine building was still there, and it might be just the place for a lost little girl to seek shelter. Or for a killer to hide a body.

The moonlight dimmed and a few fresh snowflakes began to filter their way down as Thibideau made his way through the bare patches and drifts. The trees here were spaced a good distance apart, their lower branches gray and stunted, and a snapped twig under his foot sounded as loud as a gunshot. He knew his way around well enough to keep from getting lost; in any case, the road down to the hydro compound was probably still impossible to get through by car. They'd stopped construction late that fall when the first heavy storm blew in. He never could understand the idiot who organized that whole project. Winters in this remote area of Canada were a bitch, and nobody but that special contractor (who was, incidentally, originally from California) thought they could get the place finished without building a quality road to it first. Now there was no doubt that contractor was out of a job, but it was too late for the road. The ground was rutted, frozen hard as a rock, and covered with a foot of snow. So the plant just sat like some huge, hibernating beast, waiting for the scientists and construction workers to wake it up in the spring.

A few more minutes of walking and he came to a break in the trees and the entire vast, unfinished compound spread out below him, a huge and gaping hole in the earth with several small buildings scattered around it, including the old mining building beside the frozen river. The river itself cut through the woods directly below, at the foot of a steep bank scattered with small saplings and naked shrubs. It sat as a silent warning, like a line drawn in the dirt by a childhood bully. *Cross it and you're gonna get yours.*

The scope of the thing was remarkable. Until now he had never seen the place, and standing here at the edge, he found it lived up to the stories he had heard in town. Hell, it blew the stories out of the *water*. Trees had been cut down for what seemed like miles in every direction; the place looked like the center of an atomic bomb blast, the half-completed buildings dotting its edge like props for a toy train set.

Standing there gaping, it took him several minutes to realize that something seemed out of place, something more than just this alien blast site in the middle of dense woods. In another second he knew what that thing was, and crouched behind the trunk of the biggest tree he could find on the upper slope, trying to calm his thudding heart. Partially hidden behind the old wooden mine building just across the river was a snowmobile, cleaned of snow and with what looked like fresh tracks behind it.

He killed the beam of the flashlight and slipped it into his coat pocket. The flakes had stopped falling again, and the light of the moon was enough out here. He felt the sweat inside his mittens and the shake in his legs, and the fiery rush of adrenaline lit up his body like an electric shock. *There's nobody else around, you could be dealing with the fucker right here, right now, just you and him, one-on-one.*

He scanned the entire complex slowly, watching for any movement, or light, or bit of smoke. Nothing.

Come on now, she could still be alive. He unzipped his jacket, and pulled his .38 out of its holster, trying desperately to keep his hand steady. There was no time to get help; he might have been seen.

Slipping out from the protection of the tree trunk, he made his way down the steep bank, stumbling and sliding until he reached the ice at the bottom. Nothing stirred, and he hurried across the frozen river toward the closest structure, a half-completed building along the right edge of the pit. Out in the open, he was painfully aware of how vulnerable he was under the moonlight, with the snow crunching under his heavy boots. He would have to move fast.

He made it to the corner of the building without incident, and leaned carefully around the other side. The complex looked like a ghost town. The entire side of this structure was open, and great drifts of snow filled the inner section, its surface completely smooth. Moving out and around it, he kept the gun held out at arm's length, like he'd seen cops do in movies. He'd never pointed the gun at anything other than the targets at the range, and it felt uncomfortably heavy and awkward now.

He walked quickly along the edge of the pit to the left, making for the old mine building. At the wall he crouched and crawled under a window, then slowly raised his head and peered into the darkness. It was lighter outside with the moonlight, and he had to cup his hands to the dusty glass and squint. Even then he could see only shadows. His hand shook and rattled the gun barrel against the glass. Once again peering in, something caught his attention. One of those shadows, over in the far right corner, slumped over in some impossible position, looked like a body.

A little body.

Sweat began to roll in little beads down Thibideau's forehead, stinging his eyes. *What if it's her? Christ, what if the killer's standing right there just out of sight, in one of the deeper shadows?*

But she could be hurt, unconscious...

He crouched and ran along the wall until he reached its edge. Blood pulsing impossibly loud in his ears, he stuck his head around the corner. He found himself looking at the door of the building, shut tight against the cold. Cutting off his fear as best he could, he tried the handle. It swung open with a dull scraping sound.

It was the smell that hit him first—an overpowering, rotten stench that clogged the nostrils and made him gag, staggering backward until he could get his parka zipped up to cover his face. Even then it was there, the unmistakable smell of death.

Right then he almost turned and ran. But the thought of that little girl, maybe still alive and scared at least as bad as he was, made him take a step into the darkness.

The blackness surrounded him, swallowed him and welcomed him with the utter equality of the blind. He blinked stupidly, eyes adjusting to the deep black shadows around him, and stood frozen with his gun held out as things began to take shape. A dim patch of light from the window shone onto the floor, and he shuffled towards it, closer to the wall until his hands met with something hard.

Jesus the flashlight, I forgot the fucking flashlight in my pocket.

How could he be so stupid? Holding the gun in his left hand, he pulled the flashlight out of his jacket and aimed it at the wall, switching it on.

The thing he had touched was an animal, or at least it might have been at one time. It looked to be the size of a raccoon, and it was covered in dried blood and frozen stiff.

There was no head.

Joe stumbled backwards, and the beam of the flashlight lit up the entire wall. It was covered with the carcasses of animals and bare bones, a grotesque and sadistic trophy case. Blood ran in drips and blotches down the wood, staining it a dull coppery brown.

He turned and saw the girl. She had been thrown into a corner, her body broken and battered and her clothes ripped to shreds. Her head was twisted at an impossible angle and her dull, dead eyes stared at him vacantly.

The doorknob was slick in his gloved hand, old and slippery metal, and then the door opened and he stumbled into the cold. The smell would not leave him, it followed him as he struggled across the snow, and then he saw his tracks and there were *another pair, oh Christ, another pair*, and he spun around wildly, losing his balance and dropping his gun.

Joe Thibideau never had a chance to get up. A shadow fell across his path, followed by a searing pain in his shoulder, moonlight flashing on a silver blade that rose up and plunged down again and again, speckling the pure white snow with his blood.

PART ONE:
PAST TRANSGRESSIONS

—1—

David Pierce walked into the office expecting the worst. A loud, balding man in an expensive suit, or an old bastard with nothing on his mind other than to keep a young guy like him from getting a job. The past few months he'd run into both; one he couldn't stand enough to work with, the other wouldn't give him the chance.

Third time's the charm. I wonder if they give out awards for this stuff? World's greatest ass kisser, professional job searcher. As long as they paid him, he'd be willing to get called just about anything.

But the guy was all right.

"Welcome to Hydro Development, David. Michael Olmstead. Call me Mike." He stuck out his hand, and David took it. The hand was smooth and dry, but the grip was firm. "Glad you could make it."

Olmstead released his grip and flipped through a file folder on a neatly organized desk. "Please, sit down."

David smiled and nodded, keeping his expression as neutral as possible. Showtime. *Ass kisser. Not as flattering, but more accurate.*

He sat in the wide, comfortable chair offered to him, and

waited until Mike settled down in the leather seat behind the massive oak desk. He took a quick glance around, admiring the dark wood of the walls, the soft lighting and thick carpeting. Lots of money here.

"Let's get right down to it. We want to know what you can do for Hydro." Mike leaned forward and put his elbows on his desk, hands steepled in front of his sharply defined nose. *Every little detail of this man is sharp.*

"Well, I've worked on two other hydropower plants, one right out of school, and one for six years that ended last July."

"EPC?"

"That's right. I was involved in development with them, primarily doing research on the possibilities of pumped storage and overseeing the reservoir construction plans."

"Well, this job will be overseeing exactly that kind of thing. We've been a little old-fashioned in the past, but now it's time to take the big plunge, so to speak." Olmstead smiled.

"You're going to harness a portion of the St. John River through an underground storage facility."

"Done some research? That's good, we appreciate the initiative." Olmstead tossed a folder across the desktop in front of him. "There's a lot of hydro activity up in Quebec and New Brunswick, make no mistake about that. Most of the rivers coming off the North coast of the St. Lawrence have a big dam or two. But a lot of that power goes to the pulp mills. With the Jackson project, we want to supply New Brunswick with all the power it's going to need for years. Down into Maine too. And pumped storage is a safe and effective way to get that power. It involves quite a bit of man power, but if we can pull it off, this will be one of the largest successful underground pumped storage hydro facilities ever. If you do work with us, you'll be getting all you can handle."

David flipped through the folder's pages, past engineer's notes, schematics and technical summaries. "Selling to Canadian Power and Light. Big company."

"That's right. You'd be involved directly with the planning and development of the lower reservoir and tunnel, and getting us back on track."

They discussed the plan details for a while before Olmstead took the folder back and stuck it in a desk drawer. "There are plenty of men working on this thing already, but most of them are at our branch offices in Quebec City at the moment. This is a major project, and we want to make sure everything's done right. After that, there would be an opportunity to stay on in the area and work with maintenance and the lease agreement, that and figuring out how to keep the damn tunnels from icing up. That is, if you're not bored to death by that time."

"My wife and I are easily entertained. We both read a lot, watch movies. And Jessica—she's our little girl—she's got three or four make-believe friends by now, I think. Maybe this would give me some more time to spend with her. I don't do that enough."

That seemed to make an impression. "I know how it is. I was going to ask you about your family. It does get lonely up there, or so I hear. A close family unit is really important to us. We need to know you're intending to stay around for a while. Anyway, this place is pretty isolated. Bitch of a winter, too."

"Yeah, I read about the problems you guys had keeping it going." This seemed for an instant a little too critical, and David winced.

Olmstead just smiled, running a hand through his patch of well-groomed hair and sitting back in the relaxed pose of the successful businessman. "You got that right. What we really need is someone to be smart and work with people, not against them. We'll have a big crew on site eventually, and they all have to use each other to get things done. Know your stuff, and take advantage of it. Frankly, I think you can do it, looking at your job experience and schooling. You've been in and out of the business for what, ten years? You know what makes a plant tick by now. You've worked with pumped storage development. And your references are good, with the exception of the EPC job."

There was a sudden, uncomfortable silence. David cursed silently. Of course he knew it would come up, had to, but still he hadn't been prepared to face it so soon.

"I'm not going to lie to you. Your boss at EPC had some pretty loud ideas about how you handled yourself there."

"Look, I can explain all that." David paused, and found Olmstead had leaned forward again, studying him closely, waiting. He didn't look away. "The guy was a prick."

Olmstead raised one eyebrow in an almost comical expression of surprise, then laughed. "I admire your courage. I spoke with your supervisor myself, and frankly, I'd agree with you. Now I hope I'm reading this right. You had a difference of opinion, got tired of waiting around for real opportunity and decided to go out and get it."

David nodded. "That's about right."

"Again, I admire your courage. Not exactly what I would have done, not with the economy the way it is, but I understand. I think that shows some initiative that could be put to use. Of course, I'm not the only one that makes that decision."

David forced a smile. "I hope you'll put in a good word for me. I really want this job. I know what it takes. I worked in Alaska on my first project, so I've had experience with the cold. As far as Hydro goes, this has always been the place I've wanted to be." *I just got three million interviews in other places for kicks.* "And working in Canada might be just the thing for my family life."

"Could be. And the scenery's beautiful, believe me. I went up there to check the spot out before we started construction last summer. Thick pine forests and lots of wildlife. There's a hell of a lot of logging going on too, but you'd never know it in most places. And the water coming off the peaks is just about the most pure thing you've ever tasted."

"Sounds great." Of course, he would be spending the winters there too. *Not saying much about those, are you?*

"Listen—" Olmstead stood up and stuck out his hand. David took it. "I have a couple other interviews, but I can say that you are the most impressive so far. If this works out, we'll need you to start right away. The place has been completely shut down for months, but we need someone to evaluate the current situation and advise on next steps. We'd take care of getting you a place to live, as soon as something opens up, and of course we'll pay for it. Salary's more than fair, but the benefits are fantastic—full health, dental, the works. Not that there are any dentists within a hundred miles of that place."

Olmstead grinned, and David felt a momentary touch of revulsion; just a touch, but nonetheless it was there. That grin had reminded him of the Cheshire cat in Lewis Carroll's *Alice's Adventures in Wonderland*.

"I'm ready. Thanks for everything, and give me a call if there's anything else you need to know."

David thanked him and left. The interview had gone pretty well, he thought. He had liked Olmstead, not counting that quick moment of distaste; nerves really, that was all. He had already dismissed it. His history with EPC was bound to come up, and with all the problems he had run into before, this time was a pleasant surprise. Olmstead didn't seem to care much about what McDougal had to say, which was lucky. McDougal could be a real son of a bitch.

As he walked out the doors and into the bright sun he considered Olmstead's last comment. A hundred miles—a little exaggerated, maybe, but it got the point across. A skilled doctor could be fifty miles away for all he knew. What if someone caught the flu, or worse, broke a leg? Thinking about the possibilities made him nervous. If he got this job, he'd have to make sure Jessie understood the rules. *Have fun, kid, but don't play in the woods.*

JOHN SKIPP
AND CODY
GOODFELLOW

Pastor Jake promised his followers everlasting life…he just didn't say what kind. So when the small-town televangelist and con man climbs out of his coffin at his own wake, it becomes Judgment Day for everyone gathered to mourn—or celebrate—his death. Jake is back, in the rotting flesh, filled with anger and vengeance. And accompanied by demons even more frightening than himself. What follows is a long night of endless terror, a blood-drenched rampage by the man not even death could stop.

JAKE'S WAKE

ISBN 13: 978-0-8439-6076-1

To order a book or to request a catalog call:
1-800-481-9191
This book is also available at your local bookstore, or you can check out our Web site **www.dorchesterpub.com** where you can look up your favorite authors, read excerpts, or glance at our discussion forum to see what people have to say about your favorite books.

WRATH JAMES WHITE

Could serial killers be victims of a communicable disease? Fifteen years ago, Joseph Miles was attacked by a serial child murderer. He was the only one of the madman's victims to survive. Now he himself is slowly turning into a killer. He can feel the urges, the burning needs, getting harder and harder to resist. Can anything stop him—or cure him—before he kills the only woman he's ever loved? Or before he infects someone else?

SUCCULENT PREY

ISBN 13: 978-0-8439-6164-5

To order a book or to request a catalog call:
1-800-481-9191
This book is also available at your local bookstore, or you can check out our Web site **www.dorchesterpub.com** where you can look up your favorite authors, read excerpts, or glance at our discussion forum to see what people have to say about your favorite books.